Dr Wells and Detective Superintendent Walsh crossed the room to inspect the corpse. For some reason, the doctor looked slightly irritated. Forensics assistant Anna Ferreira showed them how the barely visible bruises on the back of the skull of the deceased formed the same pattern as her hand. As she watched, Wells placed his big, masculine hand where hers had been, the four fingers and thumb overlapping the bruises almost exactly. She saw the two men exchange looks and she felt a surge of excitement. This time there was no doubting her observation.

A MOMENT OF MADNESS
A TANGLED WEB
Fairfax and Vallance mysteries

DEADLY AFFAIRS
INTIMATE ENEMIES
A WAITING GAME
TO DIE FOR
John Anderson mysteries

TO DIE FOR

by
Peter Birch
A John Anderson mystery

CRIME & PASSION

First published in Great Britain in 1997 by
Crime & Passion
an imprint of Virgin Publishing Ltd
332 Ladbroke Grove
London W10 5AH

Crime & Passion series editor: Pan Pantziarka

ISBN 0 7535 0034 5

Typeset by Avon Dataset Ltd, Bidford on Avon, B50 4JH
Printed and bound in Great Britain by
Mackays of Chatham PLC, Chatham, Kent

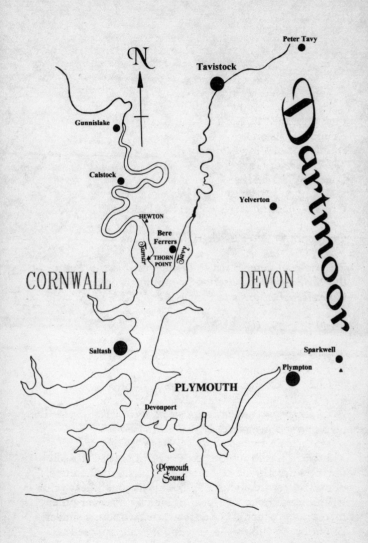

ONE
Tuesday

To Detective Inspector Violet Krebs the corpse appeared to be staring blankly at the leaden sky. It lay on a bed of vraic and muddy shale beneath a low slate ledge, arms flung wide in a grotesque parody of friendly greeting. Failing light and the dull grey of the Tamar mud flats did nothing for the scene, with moist air and a sharp wind blowing from the direction of Plymouth adding the final touch of misery. Police tape fluttered in the wind. The little group of police officers stood glumly by, none speaking.

Krebs looked up to stare out across the mud flats. On another day the scene might have had a lonely beauty, but now it was merely depressing. On the opposite shore a cluster of whitewashed houses with grey slate roofs gathered behind a quay. Yachts and fishing boats scattered across the flat between the river channel and the shore. To the south a headland pushed out, hiding the Tamar bridges and the skyline of the city. To the north the river ran straight for a mile or so and then curved away to the west between steep, wood-shrouded hills. At her feet the band of shale formed a little promontory between expanses of slick mud that reflected the drabness of the sky. The body must have washed down river and been caught on the promontory as the tide fell.

She turned her attention back to the dead man. He had been in his fifties, fairly tall, comfortably fleshy and dressed in a manner that suggested a good income and simple tastes. Nobody would have given him more than a glance in the street. He must have looked safe; fatherly, she thought.

'Poor bastard,' she heard Sergeant Mallows mutter. 'Where the hell are forensic?'

Krebs half-turned to the sergeant, intending to rebuke him for his tone but catching herself before she spoke. She had few enough friends in Plymouth division without antagonising Mallows, an old-fashioned career officer who had been a sergeant when she was still at school. Since her promotion to DI over the heads of two older male colleagues she had been the object of resentment among CID. 'Pet poodle' was among the nicer of the remarks that had been passed at her expense, a reference to the support from senior officers for her fast-track promotion. While she could understand their attitude, it still seemed unreasonable. After all, it was hardly her fault if they had failed their promotional exams.

'Ahoy there, Violet!' a cheery voice called out, breaking Krebs's depressing chain of thought. She turned to see two figures at the top of the low slate cliff that bordered the tidal flats. One, a large bony man with an unkempt mop of mid-brown hair, came down in two well-coordinated jumps, the tails of his tatty, brown tweed jacket flapping behind him. Krebs smiled as she saw that it was Dr Morgan Wells, the senior forensic pathologist for the area. Wells at least always treated her with hearty courtesy. Of course he had no reason to consider her a threat, but she suspected that his attitude would have been the same in any case.

Dr Wells's companion took an easier route down to the mud, only jumping the last foot to land with a soft crunch on the shale at the top of the flat. Krebs realised that this must be Dr Wells's new junior, a girl whose name she didn't know. She was small and compact with a face so fresh as to be almost childlike, her look of innocence only given the lie by the expression of intense interest on her face as she followed Dr Wells over to stand beside the corpse.

'Afternoon all. Well?' Dr Wells asked with an air of cheerful bonhomie completely out of keeping with the sombre setting.

'Drowned, I'd say, Dr Wells,' Sergeant Mallows replied.

'I'll be the judge of that, shall I?' Wells replied firmly but without rancour. 'Cheery looking fellow, ain't he? Who found him?'

'A couple of kids. They're up at the cars with PC Fields,' Mallows continued.

'Have they touched anything?'

'You've got to be joking!'

'Just checking. Right, OK. We'd better get on with it. Oh, by the way, Anna, the tall redhead is Detective Inspector Krebs, Violet to her friends and the brightest thing to pop up in the Devon and Cornwall constabulary in many a long year. The others are Mallows and Trevane, beat-pounders of the old school. You lot, this is Anna Ferreira, who for reasons best known to herself has decided to follow a career contemplating the dead at close quarters.'

Krebs nodded to the young woman who returned a shy smile. Forensic science might seem an odd choice for a girl who could only just be out of university, yet a refusal to conform to an expected stereotype was something the detective could understand. Her own career had been a long series of confrontations with people who thought they knew what was best for her. First her parents and teachers trying to steer her into design or fashion because of what they saw as an artistic temperament. Then there had been the collapse of her engagement to Patrick because of her refusal to give up her career. Finally the transfer to CID, after which things had been going relatively smoothly.

Dr Wells had peeled on long rubber gloves and was now opening a squat, brown leather case. Krebs watched as the two police scientists bent over the corpse, the elder working with quick, experienced motions, pausing occasionally to make a point to his trainee. At length they got to their feet.

'Drowned it is,' Dr Wells spoke casually, 'I suppose you smart-alec detectives will want to play around for a while and then we'd better get Charlie Boy here over to the lab.'

Anna looked on as Dr Wells snapped his gloves into place and wriggled his fingers to fill the tight latex. Between them lay the white, flaccid body that had once been a human being. Several years studying zoology and then medicine had inured her to such sights, although she still lacked Dr Wells's total imperturbability. A wallet in the man's suit pocket had identified him as one Charles Draper, apparently the unlucky victim of a fall into the murky waters of the Tamar. What, she wondered, had happened to him? Possibly he'd been out walking and had slipped, one instant of lost balance, probably a sharp pain as his head struck something, and then nothing, nothing ever again. One moment he'd have been carefree and relaxed, maybe admiring the Devon scenery. The next moment he was dead.

'This is purely routine, of course,' Dr Wells was saying, breaking into Anna's gloomy reverie. 'Accidental drownings of this sort are by no means uncommon around here. Yachtsmen mainly, though we've had a canoeist and a couple of fishermen. The Tamar's more dangerous than it looks, deep mud all along the estuary and odd holes in the slate further up which a fisherman can just step into and vanish. Weighed down by his thigh-waders, you see. We get fewer deaths in these parts from fire than we do from incautious tourists

4

getting drowned, falling down mine shafts, dying of exposure on Dartmoor, you name it.

'Note, I am now opening the left lung, the contents of which may tell us quite a lot about the cause and manner of death. Ah ha, what have we here? Plant matter, particles of shell, an entire shell. Clearly he drowned in shallow water to have taken in so much solid matter. Note, though, that the fingernails are clean, which suggests that he didn't have much idea of what was going on. You see, a drowning victim who is conscious grasps at anything they can reach, so in a shallow water drowning such as this you usually find mud and silt particles under the fingernails. I suspect we may find a high level of alcohol in his bloodstream. I've known of drunks drowning in puddles no more than a couple of inches deep, you know.'

Anna watched as Dr Wells carefully extracted the water and detritus from the dead man's lung. The weed was simply pieces of indeterminate plant material, the shell apparently from a small Ramshorn snail. The clarity of the fluid and intact state of the tissues seemed to indicate that a hypotonic solution had entered the lungs. Both the type of shell and the lung damage suggested that Draper had swallowed fresh water.

'So he drowned up river then? In fresh water?' she ventured, hoping to impress Dr Wells with her observations.

'Eh?' he replied. 'No, no, I don't think so, although of course we'll have to test. Why do you ask?'

Anna immediately felt a flush of embarrassment, stammering slightly as she gave her reply. 'I – I thought that if he had drowned in salt water the fluid would have been less clear,' she answered. 'Wouldn't hypertonic salt water have caused blood plasma to be drawn out osmotically, with burst papillae as a result?'

'Clever girl!' Wells replied. 'But no gold star for you this time, my dear. Sea water would indeed have caused the effect you describe so neatly, but brackish, estuarine water would be less concentrated and so might not. Still, I must analyse the salts in our sample to be sure. Would you care, perhaps, to place a small bet on the outcome?'

'No, I'm sure you're right,' Anna replied hastily. The shell, after all, could well have been washed down from further up river. It seemed foolish even to mention it. In fact, she reflected, it was foolish of her even to have thought she would notice something that he had not. He was, after all, over twenty years her senior and had a wealth of experience in the field of forensic science. Indeed, it was largely his air of maturity and utter confidence in himself that had led her to make the mistake of going to bed with him when she first took up her place as his junior. They had proved incompatible, both in terms of their expectations of sex and of emotional commitment, and it was she who had declined the opportunity to build the encounter into a proper relationship. Since then, she had found working with him carried an undercurrent of embarrassment, although he had basically taken her decision well, never doing more than passing the occasional half-joking, half-sarcastic comment.

The door swung open and the detective in charge of the Draper case, Detective Superintendent Walsh came in. Anna knew him only as a distant, older figure, attractive in the way that she found such men attractive but very remote and professional. Dr Wells walked across to speak to him. Left to her own devices, Anna studied the corpse. Charles Draper had clearly been very average, fairly tall, fairly big, a plain face, straight, short, thinning grey hair. As she bent to look at his head, something caught her eye, a discoloration of the skin, barely visible among the sparse hairs at the nape of his neck. She moved closer and examined the area, finding an oval bruise. Was it the shape of a thumb? Perhaps, or was she just letting her imagination run away with her? If it was the mark of a thumb and indicated that Draper's head had been

6

held in a grip, then there would be equivalent marks where the fingers had bitten into his scalp. Anna lifted Draper's head carefully and placed her hand as if to grip the skull. Each fingertip lay below a faint bruise similar to the first, with another larger bruise directly above her middle finger, where specks of greyish material had caught between the hairs.

'Dr Wells,' she called, 'I think there's something you should see.'

Wells and Walsh crossed the room, the doctor looking slightly irritated. Anna showed them how the faint, barely visible bruises formed the same pattern as her hand, the regularity undeniable. Anna stood back as Dr Wells motioned her aside. As she watched, he placed his big, masculine hand where hers had been, the four fingers and thumb overlapping the bruises almost exactly. She saw the two men exchange looks and felt a surge of excitement. This time there was no doubting her observation.

Detective Chief Inspector John Anderson walked briskly along the corridor, his face an impassive mask that concealed his thoughts. A summons to the office of Detective Superintendent Parrish was the last thing he needed. Parrish had never approved of his style, considering him unorthodox, a maverick. 'Team players' were what Parrish liked, a phrase used all too often and one that definitely did not describe John Anderson.

Over two months had passed since the disastrous Hamilton kidnapping case and the area had been remarkably calm. Nevertheless, Anderson had been unable to shake the feeling that Parrish was waiting for an excuse to ensure that on his retirement the last person considered as a replacement would be John Anderson.

Anderson gave the superintendent's door a perfunctory knock and stepped in. Parrish was sifting through some papers and didn't look up immediately. Anderson took a chair and sat down, determined that if Parrish wished to indulge himself in assertive gestures then he would not rise to the bait.

'Ah, John,' Parrish began, 'thank you for coming up.'

Anderson waited as Parrish paused and shuffled his papers into a neat pile.

'Look, John,' Parrish continued, 'I know things haven't been running too smoothly recently, but I'd like to give you a chance to redeem yourself.'

Redeem himself! Anderson thought, his irritation at Parrish's attitude tempered by amusement. What was Parrish going to ask him to do, become the community liaison officer?

'We need to send a man down to Devon, and I'd like you to go,' Parrish was saying.

'Devon, sir?' Anderson asked, surprised at the unexpected tack of Parrish's remarks.

'Yes, there's been a murder, someone by the name of Draper. He lived in our area so we're bound to be involved in the investigation. Normally, of course, they wouldn't need anyone from here to actually go down, but as it happens, Draper knew a fair number of influential people, including the Chief Constable. To cut a long story short, there's pressure from above to send someone down, more for show than anything, I imagine. It needs to be someone quite senior, of course, and, not to beat about the bush, John, I think you could do with a break.'

Anderson leant back in his chair. Was Parrish trying to shuffle him out of the way into what was likely to be an essentially passive job? If so, why? Anderson thought for a moment and decided that Parrish's motives were actually of little consequence. In any case, a break from Guildford would indeed be welcome, very welcome. However, with Pat Fielding still recuperating and Bill McKie dead, they were short of senior officers in CID. He pointed this out to Parrish.

'That's not really a problem at present, John,' Parrish replied.

'With Jo Blackheath here from Reigate and a new DI being drafted in soon we can manage without you.'

'Very well,' Anderson responded, 'I imagine that I am the most suitable person. Who will I be working with and who will be running the investigation at this end?'

To Anderson's amusement, Parrish's expression changed from wary stubbornness to relief. Evidently the Superintendent had been expecting a higher degree of resistance.

'Hmm, ah, right,' Parrish responded after a moment. 'Yes, you're to meet a Detective Superintendent Walsh in Plymouth. An efficient man I understand, fairly newly promoted. He has a reputation as a good team leader.'

'And at this end?' Anderson queried, ignoring Parrish's dig at his abilities.

'The new girl, Blackheath, I thought, unless things get complicated,' Parrish replied evenly. 'It'll give her a chance to settle in here, make her feel she's appreciated.'

Anderson merely nodded. Detective Sergeant Joanna Blackheath seemed a basically competent officer.

TWO
Wednesday

Detective Superintendent Walsh tapped a white-board which showed a neatly drawn map of the Tamar estuary. At the bottom was the sea and a shaded area that indicated the extent of Plymouth. Above that the Tamar snaked away to the north, twisting through a series of bends that made its length more than double the straight line distance from Plymouth up to Gunnislake, which Walsh had marked at the top of the board. Various tributaries opened from it, both from Cornwall to the west and Devon to the east. Neat red triangles marked the location at which the body had been found and other significant points. Next to the map a series of photos depicted the dead man from a variety of angles, others adding detail to the macabre display.

'This is what we know, then,' Walsh said briskly. 'The victim was Charles Draper. Fifty-two, a bachelor, lived alone in the Guildford area. According to Dr Wells, he drowned at some time around 3 p.m. yesterday but had only been in the water a comparatively short time before being found washed up on the tide. Water in his lungs was found to be brackish, indicating that he drowned in the estuary rather than up river. Where in

10

the estuary we don't know. In all probability it happened between Thorn Point, where he was found, and Gunnislake, here, above which the water is fresh, but we could be looking at anywhere from Plymouth up to the top of the tidal zones of any one of half-a-dozen tributaries. Particles of concrete in his hair indicate a blow to the top of the head, probably a fall. His last meal was fish and chips, skate to be exact, not too long before he died.

'The reason I'm on this one, and the reason there are five of us here, is that this is no accidental drowning. It's murder. For this information we may thank Dr Wells's astute junior, Anna Ferreira, who noticed the bruising on the back of Draper's head. I was there at the time, as it happens, and without her sharp eyes we might well have missed it.'

Walsh paused and indicated one of the photographs before recommencing.

'His blood contained a high level of alcohol and traces of morphine. It appears that he was rendered incapable and then drowned by being held in a grip to the back of his skull and having his face pushed into shallow water while barely conscious. He wouldn't have had a chance. Even so, the killer would need to be strong and is certainly large. The bruising indicates a hand larger than mine. So, our murderer is almost certainly male, probably over six feet and between say fifteen and sixty, which is at least a start.'

'Motive?' DC Heath, the youngest member of the team, asked.

'At present,' Walsh replied, 'we have no idea. Draper had no record and we don't know what he was doing in this neck of the woods. Guildford are sending a man down and are also extending the investigation in their area. I know it's unusual, but a specific request was made. He's a DCI John Anderson.'

John Anderson smiled to himself as he eased the BMW off the A38. A break from Guildford and all that was associated

11

with it was what he sorely needed. With Pat Fielding still recuperating and far from ready to return to work, and the new DS, Joanna Blackheath, still learning the ropes, he had had more than his normal workload. Perhaps Parrish was right for once: the strain had been getting to him. A breath of Devon air should do him good, both physically and mentally, and besides, the case sounded intriguing and would hopefully provide scope for his talents even if he were not leading the team. He had spoken to Walsh on the telephone and the man sounded competent. Also, the long drive down had given him time to think and his mind felt fresher than it had for a long time.

The drive through Plymouth to the police station proved longer than he had expected, with a thick band of suburbs surrounding the centre. Ranks of terraces, their architecture typical of both the West Country and turn of the century urban expansion, took up most of the space, interspersed with a surprising amount of undeveloped green space and areas of modern concrete estate housing. The centre itself proved to be a confusing tangle of roads, among which he eventually found the station. As soon as he arrived Anderson was shown up to the office of Detective Superintendent Walsh.

'John Anderson,' he introduced himself. 'We spoke on the phone.'

'Robert Walsh,' the other man replied, rising from his seat and offering his hand.

Anderson gauged Walsh automatically, noting the man's erect bearing and brisk, economical movements. Walsh stood perhaps an inch taller than himself at about six foot one, his hair an iron grey. The plain charcoal suit and silver-grey tie matched the keen, no-nonsense expression of the man's face. Efficient, systematic, a good man to work with on a day-to-day basis, Anderson decided.

Anderson took the offered seat and sat back, watching Walsh steeple his fingers and frown while he composed his thoughts.

12

'Right,' Walsh began, 'we have achieved a fair bit since yesterday. Primarily, Draper's car has been found. It was in a lane near a hamlet called Hewton, only a couple of miles from where his body was washed up at Thorn Point, which is six or seven miles up the Tamar estuary from here. The area in general is the Bere Peninsula, a strip of land between the estuaries of the Tamar and Tavy rivers. It's pretty well cut off, despite being so close to Plymouth. The best access to it is actually from the north, towards Tavistock.

'Had we thought it was accidental death, it would have been a typical place from which to take a walk in nearby National Trust land. Out of the way, true, but then so are most unspoilt places. As it is, it means that the murderer was almost certainly with Draper and that they walked down to the river together. It's a good quarter-mile down a rough, steep track. Draper weighed over fifteen stone. To drag or carry him that far would be quite a feat.'

'Coercion?' Anderson put in. 'It seems a remote place for someone from as far away as Guildford to be just by chance.'

'It might have been coercion,' Walsh continued, 'but frankly I doubt it. No, the theory we're working on is that Draper knew his killer and had arranged to meet him there for purposes of his own. Forensic are going over the car but as yet haven't come up with anything useful. We've also appealed for witnesses in the area but so far drawn a blank. The car's a mid-blue Sierra Sapphire, less than distinctive. There's a small farm about three hundred yards from the spot the car was found in, otherwise no house for the best part of a mile. Most of the area is thick woodland or small fields with high hedges, pretty well concealed. Actually, it's beginning to look very carefully planned. In fact, if young Ferreira, a new girl in forensic, hadn't noticed the bruising in among the hair on the back of his neck we'd have said accidental death and left it at that. Draper wouldn't have been the first day tripper to drown in the Tamar. Of course we can't be one hundred per

13

cent certain that Draper was there at all. The car could have been left there as a decoy, but that seems less likely.'

'I agree,' Anderson replied. 'So we're looking for someone the victim knew. Someone he knew well enough to take an afternoon stroll in the woods with, and someone who had a strong reason to want him dead. That should narrow the field. We've put a DS on the case at Guildford, Joanna Blackheath. She should have a report some time tomorrow. Meanwhile, I'd like to go over to the forensic lab and take a first-hand look at the evidence.'

'Help yourself,' Walsh spoke easily. 'I'll get someone to show you the way. First, though, let me give you an idea of the role I want you to play in the investigation. If things go fast, I'll have plenty of jobs for you. Otherwise, take a fairly free rein, following any leads you see as significant.'

'Fine,' Anderson answered, pleased by Walsh's flexibility, an attitude that he knew Graham Parrish would never take in a similar situation.

As he left the office, Anderson felt buoyed by the meeting. To have worked under an officer who he found hard to respect would have been galling to say the least. Walsh, on the other hand, seemed both astute and keen to allow Anderson to make the best of his own abilities.

Anderson was shown to the lab. Dr Wells proved to be out and he was greeted by a young woman who he took to be Anna Ferreira. Petite, intense, somewhat shy but clearly highly intelligent, her quick, bright manner spoke of life and energy. Also, her white lab coat was open and Anderson couldn't help but notice the swell of her breasts under her thick canary yellow sweater and the gentle curve of her hips below her tightly belted waist. When he had introduced himself she was eager to show him the evidence that had been collected, but was adamant that Dr Wells would have to be there before anything could be looked at in detail.

She talked him through the details of the autopsy, her light, girlish manner belied by the precision of her description. Anderson was impressed. Always drawn to intelligence in women, he found Anna's combination of a shy, sweet manner and a pin-sharp mind more than slightly appealing. He watched her as she talked, noting the big, deep-brown eyes and the thick, dark hair caught up in a functional bun, her faintly olive complexion and pretty, vivacious features.

'This is the solid material found in his airways,' she was saying, holding up a sample bag in which he could make out green and brown matter but see no details. 'Bits of weed and shell. The water he drowned in was pretty shallow, maybe no more than a few inches. He was held face down, his face against mud, poor man. If he'd been fully conscious, we'd have expected mud under the fingernails. Apparently similar accidents are quite common: there was a drowning a couple of years ago, when a yachtsman slipped, caught his head on an anchor and drowned when the tide came in.'

'Yes, Robert Conway, I actually knew him,' a deep voice broke in.

Anderson turned to greet the newcomer, evidently Dr Wells. They clasped hands and Anderson at once noticed the extra, and unnecessary, touch of strength the big scientist put into his grip. Clearly a man who felt the need to assert himself. Unnecessarily, Anderson considered. At perhaps six foot three and with a rangy, powerful build, Wells was not a man to be overlooked in a crowd.

'Anna was just going over the evidence for me,' Anderson explained. 'A clever set-up. It looks as if whoever the murderer is nearly got away with it.'

'You're not wrong,' Wells answered. 'It would be the fourth, no, fifth, similar death since I've been working here, so it seemed pretty straightforward. Of course we'd have picked up the alcohol and morphine levels in Charlie Boy's blood, pure routine, but then that wouldn't necessarily imply murder now, would it? As it is, I should imagine we've a good chance of catching up with the fellow. Having said that, he's done a fine job of covering his tracks.'

'Oh?' Anderson questioned.

'Yes, I've been over the car with a fine-tooth comb. One or two mud samples, soil from the lane and also greensand and chalk, nothing else. Hard not to get greensand and chalk traces on your boots in your part of the world. A few fibres which all match Draper's clothes so far, a chocolate wrapper and that's really it. Possibly he may have met the murderer where he parked or while he was walking. Of course we've picked up all sorts of stuff from the area, but it'll be a while before we know if any of it is relevant. Actually, with the rain and the way the wind's been blowing anything useful's likely to be halfway across the Channel by now.'

'I see,' Anderson replied. 'Everything was clearly well planned, and in my experience such plans tend to leave traces of their own. The best angle would seem to be to look for a motive.'

Wells shrugged carelessly, his manner indicating that he had done his part, a gesture that Anderson found a touch annoying.

'Better get back to the car then,' Wells said. 'Come along Anna, we can't be flirting with detectives when we should be working, can we now?'

Anderson left the lab with mixed feelings. Anna Ferreira delighted him, both in terms of her appearance and her personality. Working with her was bound to be a pleasure, at a professional level at the least. Wells, by contrast, he found distasteful. The big man's attitude to him had bordered on condescension, while he was paternalistic towards Anna Ferreira. Working with Wells was not a task he looked forward to.

In Guildford, Detective Sergeant Jo Blackheath was in a much brighter frame of mind. She saw being chosen to handle the

Guildford interviewing in the Draper case as a deliberately given chance to prove her competence. In the few weeks she had been at Guildford there had been little opportunity for her to do more than day-to-day work. Also, recent events at the station had strengthened the air of camaraderie among the junior CID officers. John Anderson was professional and remote, highly competent but not a man who engendered friendship from his colleagues. Gerry Hart was friendly, although she suspected his interest in her lay more in getting her into bed than any more noble concern. The others hadn't really let her into their ranks yet, not in the full sense. Hopefully a neat, cleanly solved case would improve her position in their eyes.

Charles Draper proved to have lived in an isolated cottage in the maze of little roads to the south-west of Guildford. Small fields, numerous woods and a tangle of little valleys at every possible angle made the area hard to orientate in and exaggerated its remoteness. The cottage was halfway along a lane that was little more than a track, and set back fifty yards from the road. A ring of gravel centred on an ornamental pond fronted the cottage, the stones worked into little channels and furrows by Monday night's heavy rain. The pond itself was a shallow concrete basin, the plinth hidden in a tangle of variegated ivy. A small statue acted as the centrepiece, a naked boy urinating, his chubby buttocks presented to the cottage door. The vulgarity of the piece surprised Blackheath. Still, she reflected, it could have been worse – it could have been a fountain. The rest of the garden consisted of a neatly trimmed lawn surrounded by hedges and a half-wild area, long, lush grass set with patches of daffodils shaded by a full-grown oak. In the very centre was a cast iron frame supporting an old-fashioned swing, the ironwork now rusty and the wooden seat grey and encrusted with lichen.

The interior of the cottage was neat and showed no signs of disturbance. Draper's tastes had been good, but simple.

17

Modern appliances were notable only by their absence and even the television was a small black-and-white model. The furniture, on the other hand, was antique and evidently valuable even to an untrained eye. His sole indulgence appeared to be clocks, numerous beautiful examples of which decorated every room. She felt a twinge of envy for his comfortable wealth. He had clearly been a man to whom concepts such as promotion and economy would have been quite alien.

With no evidence of a struggle, or anything to suggest that Draper had left his house other than of his own free will, Blackheath left DCs Gerry Hart and Nick Parker to finish going over the cottage and went out into the garden. Standing in front of the cottage the view was entirely shielded by thick hedges. From the back, however, in clear view of the cottage's big patio doors, she could see another house, a larger, two-storied structure of red brick across a field and partially screened by a loose hedge of oak and hawthorn.

She walked briskly across the field, feeling somehow out of place in her sensible combination of trousers and blouse. The house was typical of the area, comfortable, cultivated and hinting at old money, although in practice it was a rare person indeed who had more than two generations of wealth behind them. Blackheath knocked at the front door, waited and then knocked again, annoyed at the thought that there was probably nobody there on a Wednesday morning. As she was about to turn away the door opened, revealing an elderly lady wearing a slightly puzzled expression.

'Good morning,' Blackheath began, producing her warrant card at the same instant. 'I'm Detective Sergeant Blackheath. There's no reason to be alarmed, I'd just like to ask you a few questions.'

'Questions?' the woman replied. 'Oh dear, well, I suppose you had better come in. Would you like a cup of tea?'

Blackheath accepted the tea, though more in an effort to

set the woman at ease than from any desire to drink it. The house was spacious and old-fashioned with a faint musty smell, as if from apples stored for too long. From the kitchen window there was a good view across the field. The windows of Draper's main room were clearly visible. Indeed, anyone with a pair of binoculars would have been able to see directly into the room.

'May I ask your name?' Blackheath addressed the elderly woman as she accepted tea in a china cup.

'Edith, dear,' the woman replied.

'Your full name?' Blackheath asked patiently.

'Oh, Mrs Herrick, Mrs Edith Herrick. Oh dear, I'm afraid I'm not really much good at this sort of thing. Do sit down, won't you. Would you like a biscuit?'

Blackheath declined the biscuit and took a chair at the heavy wooden kitchen table.

'Do you know Mr Draper from the cottage across the field?' she asked.

'Oh, it's him, is it? I might have known. Frightful nuisance he is, and I can't say I'm surprised if he's in trouble. Do you know, he even put a horrid little statue in his pond, I expect you've seen it. Facing our house if you please.'

'He's a difficult man, then?'

'Certainly he is. I own the land, you know, and I'd really like the cottage so that my granddaughter can have it, but Mr Draper has a lease and he won't move. He really is most unreasonable. I have offered him quite a sum, but I believe he is quite wealthy anyway.'

Blackheath smiled to herself. For all Mrs Herrick's vague manner, it made a refreshing change to interview someone so ready with information. 'And when did you last see Mr Draper?' she continued.

'Oh, let me see. Yes, he was doing some gardening on Sunday, yes, that was it. It was raining on Monday, you know.'

'So Sunday was the last time you know he was in the cottage?'

'Oh no, he was in on Monday night. I remember because his light was still on when I went to bed. He normally retires very early, and I happened to be making myself some cocoa. I do believe he had a visitor.'

'A visitor?'

'Yes, the light was on in his living room, and I could see their shadows on the curtains. Mr Draper doesn't often have visitors, you know, it's really quite unusual.'

'Do you have any idea what time the visitor arrived?'

'No, I'm afraid not, but it must have been quite late, because Melanie went over to try and persuade him to move out. At tea time that was, and he was on his own then. We did have tea early, though.'

'Melanie?'

'My granddaughter, poor thing. I told her she shouldn't have married that dreadful man — '

'And do you have the second man's description?'

'In the cottage? Oh no. I really couldn't be sure at all. My eyesight is not what it was, you know.'

'Then it could have been a woman with Draper?'

'Well, perhaps. I suppose it might have been, although he doesn't have any lady friends that I know of, you know. I don't believe he ever married.'

'Might your granddaughter have seen this man?'

'Oh no, Melanie went home after tea. I suppose she might have passed him in the lane, though. I don't think he had a car, or at least I didn't hear one. I always hear the cars in the lane. Now you come to mention it, there was a car, but much later. It woke me up. I'm a very light sleeper, you know.'

'Do you have any idea as to what time this was?'

'Oh, in the middle of the night. I suppose it was someone who had become lost. The lanes are quite a little maze, you know.'

'I would like to talk to your granddaughter, Mrs Herrick. Does she live locally?'

'Oh yes, in a little flat in Guildford, since her divorce. Terribly poky it is, that's why we wanted the cottage. The divorce was terrible, you know. Why, Melanie even changed her name back to be rid of that awful man's memory – '

'Thank you, Mrs Herrick,' Blackheath broke in, 'you've been most helpful.'

Blackheath left Mrs Herrick's house after taking Melanie Herrick's address. Feeling distinctly happy with herself she crossed back to Draper's cottage. The case was going well so far, or at least as well as could be expected. How, she wondered, would DCI John Anderson get on in Devon? Her impression of him was of a man determined to keep things running his way, intelligent, flexible with himself, yet a poor team worker and not someone to give a junior an easy chance to prove herself. To solve the case without his input would be very satisfying.

'Anything?' she asked Gerry Hart, who was on his knees in the doorway of Draper's cottage.

'Nothing to speak of for forensic,' he replied, 'but the wall calendar in the kitchen more or less covers Draper's movements throughout this year. Most recently, he had made an appointment with a Mr Cutts for Monday but no time was specified.'

'Good, we're getting somewhere.'

'Another thing which might be relevant,' Hart continued. 'Draper had a nephew, a James Draper, who lives in Plymouth. Judging by the wall calendar, James Draper seems to have visited at the end of last month and stayed a week.'

Jo Blackheath smiled. That would keep John Anderson busy while she followed up her leads. She glanced at her watch. He would now be in Devon, but it would be best to interview Melanie Herrick before giving her report.

Blackheath drove back into Guildford pondering the case.

It seemed safe to rule out Mrs Herrick as the actual murderess. Melanie Herrick remained an unknown quantity. Also, their motive was weak, although she had known weaker. Cutts seemed a more likely suspect, but there was insufficient data to go on as yet. James Draper also could not be ruled out. Was the car in the middle of the night relevant? Almost certainly not if Charles Draper had been killed in Devon in the early evening.

She drove back to the station and lunched in the canteen before walking over to Guildford Park Road, where Melanie Herrick had her flat. Somewhat to her frustration, Melanie Herrick proved to be out and she spent the rest of the day ensuring that the paperwork was precisely in order. Despite an innate dislike of paperwork, Blackheath recognised its importance, knowing that avoiding technical errors could make all the difference when a case came to court.

When she finished she ran a check on the name Cutts. She recognised this as a rather over-optimistic move and, as she suspected, nothing helpful came up. That seemed sufficient for the day and for a moment her hand hesitated over the phone before she decided against it. Thursday would do for the report to Anderson, and besides, that had been the arrangement.

THREE
Thursday

Detective Superintendent Walsh pushed briskly into the room, the door swinging to behind him and smacking loudly into the frame.

'Right,' he began without preamble. 'Nothing in the woods, nothing in the car, and nobody saw a thing, but there was enough alcohol and morphine in Draper's body to put a horse under. So today we go through the wood again, very, very slowly. Pick up every sweet wrapper, every cigarette butt, every used condom. If our man left so much as a hair I want it found, labelled and tested. Whether it'll do us any good, God alone knows, but at present it's all we've got. Wells is out there already. DCs Heath and Pentyre, you come with me, we'll go over the main body of the wood and the track. DS Dunning, DI Krebs, take the car park and the lane. John, go and pick up Anna Ferreira from the lab and go over the foreshore. There will be some people from uniform to help. Any questions?'

Walsh looked out at the assembled group. Nobody responded. Used to his quick, efficient manner, the team knew better than to speak up unless there was an important point to make. John Anderson alone chose to speak to him, falling into step beside him as they left the room.

'I'm surprised the car failed to yield anything,' Anderson confided. 'Presumably it has been thoroughly checked?'

'Dr Wells has been with us for over twenty years,' Walsh replied. 'By and large I've been pretty impressed with his work and his evidence has been the turning point in more cases than I care to remember. No, if Wells says he drew a blank then it's safe to assume there's nothing more to find. The wood, though, that's worth going over again. A large area, thick undergrowth, even a couple of mine shafts. They'll be explored today as well. Do you have anything back from your DS in Guildford?'

'Not as yet. She's scheduled to call this morning. If anything crucial comes up they can radio it through to us.'

'Right, I'll be in touch later then,' Walsh answered as their paths diverged. He watched Anderson's retreating back for a moment. The DCI seemed sharp and efficient although somewhat over-civilised for a police officer, his tailor-made suit of fine wool appearing more appropriate to a barrister than to a detective.

Anna Ferreira stood looking out across the tidal flats at the area in which Draper must have met his end. It was certainly a lonely place. She stood on a long abandoned quay, the relic of the time when the Bere Peninsula had been a major mining centre. To either side of her thick woods curved backwards around the bend of the river. Opposite her, the Cornish side was a patchwork of woods and fields, a pair of houses on the crest of the hill the only human habitation visible.

She glanced at her watch. 9.20 a.m. and the tide had been steadily falling since they had arrived. Given that it was Thursday and that the high tide marks indicated a movement towards neaps, on Monday when Draper died there would have been a high spring tide at around 7.00 p.m., perhaps a

24

little later allowing for how far up the estuary they were. At 3.00 p.m., when he had been killed, the tide would have been below half, forcing the murderer to cross a hundred yards of glutinous grey mud to reach the water. That seemed to be asking a bit much, even of a strong man. Disliking the urban confines of Plymouth, she was a frequent visitor to the area and had quickly learnt that the mud banks of the estuaries were best avoided.

'Sir,' she called to Anderson who was zigzagging slowly along the quay, fastidiously avoiding any contact between his suit and the wet reeds that bordered the wood.

He looked up at her call and came over. She noted his firm, authoritative step, a manner that she found highly attractive. In him she sensed the controlled, self-aware character that appealed to her. His age was right too. His steady eyes and the subtle patina of grey in his hair spoke of maturity and confidence. He seemed a bit formal, but had been polite, even charming to her as they had driven up from Plymouth police station in his car. Also, she had twice thought she detected a streak of subtle, ironic humour in him that suggested a greater depth of personality that was immediately obvious. True, he made her a little nervous, but that was nice in a way. For a moment she let herself toy with the idea of indicating to him that she was available, then dismissed the thought. After all, he was only likely to be around for a few days and starting an affair with a man who promptly vanished didn't seem a wise move. On the other hand, it wouldn't hurt to flirt a little and see how he responded.

'Have you found anything?' he asked as he joined her.

'Nothing solid,' she responded, 'just something odd. When Draper was killed — and Dr Wells is certain it was between 2.00 p.m. and 4.00 p.m. — there would have been no water under the quay. Draper might have been drowned in one of those little pools, but then it wouldn't have looked like an accident. Besides, the body would have been lying out for everyone to see for two or three hours.'

'Are you sure?' Anderson queried.

Anna explained the details of the tide, watching Anderson's face as he rapidly ingested the information and considered the implications.

'That raises a lot of questions,' the detective said after a moment. 'The murderer has been scrupulously careful in covering his tracks but still might not have realised about the tide. Possibly he was content to leave the body to be found here and it's only chance that it wasn't discovered before the tide came in. After all, I'm told it was raining for most of the time on Monday. That would have weakened the accident theory, though. Let me see, what would I have done in the murderer's place?'

Anderson considered the problem for a moment more. Assuming that they were in the right place, the decision would have been difficult. Standing here with a partially conscious man on a wet Monday afternoon, having found that the tide was out, what choice would he have made? It would be too late to back out, and he would have to act quickly, rain or no rain. After all, most of the far bank was open land and any farm worker in the fields could have seen him.

Draper could be suffocated in the mud but that would look suspicious. He could be drowned in a pool and left on the mud flat. That too would look suspicious. Draper could be dragged out to the water's edge and drowned there, but then the body would be taken down river instead of sticking in the reed beds near the quay. It would have increased the risk, but on a wet Monday afternoon, under pressure and with no better option it would have seemed the best choice. The theory fitted all the observed facts but relied on the murderer crossing a broad stretch of mud with fifteen stone of dead weight to support. Was it possible? They knew the murderer was strong, but how deep was the mud?

'I wonder how deep that mud is?' Anna asked. Anderson looked at her with a new respect. She had clearly followed the same line of reasoning as he had.

She laughed and turned a bright, somehow impudent smile to him. 'I suppose we'd better find out.'

'I'd really rather not,' Anderson said, making no attempt to mask his distaste for the task and brushing pointedly at the leg of his suit. 'This is pure wool, after all. I think it's more a job for a constable.'

'Well I don't mind,' she replied. 'It's quite warm for March and this makes a change from hours spent poring over a microscope or a line of petri dishes.'

Anderson had been looking out across the river and was slightly shocked to find that Anna had kicked her shoes off and was tugging at her belt. Uncertain precisely what she intended, he watched from the corner of his eye as she wriggled her jeans down over her hips and stepped out of them. Her legs looked good, firm, muscular thighs rising to a well rounded bottom encased in white cotton pants that were mostly lace. He wondered at her casual exposure of what most women would keep hidden except in the most intimate of situations. What could her motive be? An attempt to flirt without seeming brash? Perhaps so, in which case she was certainly having the desired effect on him. More likely she was simply indifferent to showing her knickers and legs off in front of a man just about old enough to be her father.

Bare from her thighs down, she climbed down the stone steps that led to the mud, disappearing from view. He walked to the very lip of the old quay and peered down. She was standing immediately beneath the quay, the mud oozing up between her bare toes. She looked up and smiled.

'It's shallow enough here,' she called up. 'There's a little mud on the surface, then rough stones, mine waste I suppose. This quay used to be for loading barges with ore from the mines up in the wood.'

Anderson watched as she walked out, each careful step taking her a fraction deeper until she was almost up to her knees in mud. Her jumper only half covered her bottom, leaving the full swell of her cheeks showing with only a scrap of white lace to cover them. As she was obviously indifferent to the display she was making, he watched in silent appreciation, wondering if in different circumstances she would be more self-conscious.

'It's not getting any deeper,' she shouted, now around a hundred yards away and near the edge of the water. 'There's firm mine waste under my feet.'

She started back, Anderson now turning his attention to the tight V of her crotch and the shape of her breasts under her jumper. If she slipped, he reflected, she'd probably strip her jumper off with the same casual aplomb with which she had removed her jeans, which would be interesting. Then again she'd probably want to borrow his jacket, which was a much less enticing prospect as it would undoubtedly get covered in mud. As she was nearing the quay she stopped and stooped down, a moment later pulling a mud-smeared object up to examine it.

'What is it?' Anderson asked.

'A pen,' she replied. 'A big fountain pen.'

She scrambled back up to the quay. Anderson took the pen to be bagged, holding it carefully between finger and thumb to minimise his contact with it.

'I'll be able to knock most of the mud off when it dries,' she remarked casually. 'How much more should we do?'

Anderson looked to either side before replying. 'We should do another sweep of the quay. The mud will have to be gone over properly as well, but I intend to pull rank on that one. In fact as soon as you're dressed I'll ask Robert Walsh if he can spare us. I'd like you to show me the place where Draper's body was found.'

They continued to search. Anna's plastering of mud dried

quickly in the warm spring sunlight. Anderson tried not to let her state of undress distract his attention. Before too long she was able to flake the mud off and dress, after which they climbed back up the steep path in search of the Super-intendent.

Anderson's request was accepted by Walsh after a moment's reluctance. Ten minutes later he was parking the BMW at Bere Ferrers station, having heeded Anna's warning that going further by car would end in scratches to the pristine silver paint. As it was there proved to be a mile of muddy fields separating the nearest piece of road from Thorn Point and he was soon cursing his lack of forethought in not using boots as his suit trousers became increasingly soiled. Anna, he noted, had no such qualms, her trainers and jeans rapidly becoming smeared with mud of which she took no notice whatever. Indeed, she seemed completely at ease, relaxed, as carefree as if she had nothing more to concern her than enjoying the warm spring day.

Despite his mounting irritation with the conditions, he found himself becoming increasingly aware of Anna as a woman rather than as a colleague. For a start her tiny waist, well formed bust and rounded hips combined to give a sexual overtone to even the most innocent of movements. Secondly she was definitely flirting with him, a situation that surprised him slightly, but to which he had no objection at all. Indeed, her admiration delighted him, especially with her being perhaps as much as twenty years his junior. Would she want that admiration to build to become a physical relationship, he wondered. The answer could well be yes, yet he felt that he would need to judge his behaviour towards her carefully if things were to develop along the lines he hoped they might. Her status as a trainee medic quietened his qualms about not getting involved with colleagues. She was not, after all, under his direct line of command.

He breasted the last rise of ground to find the Tamar

estuary spread out beneath him. Anna came up beside him, standing so close that he could feel the soft, full swell of one breast against his arm. He caught a faint scent, floral but understated, clean, very feminine and a sharp contrast with the prevailing odour of mud and cows. Anderson felt himself shiver. To put his arm around her supple waist would have been so easy, but it was too soon, he need to be fully certain of her response.

'That's Thorn Point, ahead and to the left of the big salt marsh,' she was saying, her arm indicating a low promontory where the hill on which they were standing jutted out into the river. Anderson studied the scene. To the right and beneath them a maze of curving channels broke up an area of pale grey-green reeds and grasses, a salt marsh filling what would otherwise have been a small bay. Beyond that the foreshore continued in a more or less straight line, the beginning of the wood in which they had been earlier clearly visible before the river swung away in a grand curve to the north-west. Projecting from Thorn Point itself was a low barrier of shale, now visible but clearly covered at high tide. He estimated that this barrier must block nearly a third of the channel when the tide was low and it was easy to see how the body would have caught on the bank if it was drifting down river on a falling tide. Did that make sense? Anderson cursed himself for his lack of the relevant knowledge. He was about to ask Anna but thought better of it, hesitating to reveal his ignorance.

'Shall we go down?' Anna asked.

'No,' Anderson replied, 'this is really what I wanted to see.'

There did indeed seem little point in visiting the actual site, especially as the process clearly involved walking through a copious amount of mud. The matter of Anna's presence was also becoming increasingly urgent. A gloomy mud flat, and murder site to boot, was no place for intimacy.

'Actually,' he continued, 'I could do with lunch and I'd

like to buy a local tide table. Do you know this area at all?'

'A bit,' Anna replied. 'I sometimes come out here on the train from Plymouth. There's a shop in Bere Ferrers, and a pub. I think they do food. There are always lots of yachts and things, so they'll probably have a tide table.'

'Good. I could drive you back first, unless you'd prefer to join me for lunch?'

'Yes please. That is, I'd like to have lunch with you, if you don't mind.'

They turned to walk back the way they had come, Anderson considering his companion as they went. His question had been carefully gauged, neutral in meaning but designed to make her response informative. She still seemed at ease but there was an added vibrancy, nervousness even, to her movements. Coupled with her response, her manner suggested that she was fully aware of his intentions and not averse to them. There was no hint of brashness about her, though, more timidity, vulnerability even. Shy yet accepting, a combination that put a lump of desire in Anderson's throat.

The pub proved to be a small building built of the local slate as part of a terrace. Inside, low oak beams forced him to duck as they moved through to the eating area. The decor struck him as cosy without too much of the fake decoration that marred so many such places. He pulled out a chair for Anna at the corner table, ensuring as much privacy as possible, then seated himself and scanned the blackboard that advertised the day's selection in brightly coloured chalk.

The inclusion of local scallops on the menu and of an estate-bottled Fourchaume on the wine list put an end to any doubts and also to his resolve not to drink. By the time the food arrived there was an unspoken agreement that their relationship was more than merely casual. How it would develop was a different matter. Anderson felt both flattered and excited by her. She seemed very aware, yet he was unsure as to whether she had the maturity to interact with him in the way he needed.

They ate slowly. Anderson described his cottage in Scotland and a few details of his life. He admitted frankly that he was divorced but then steered the conversation to her life. The last thing he wanted to discuss was his ex-wife Sarah. He learnt that Anna had studied zoology at Oxford before branching into forensic science and that at present she was employed specifically as Dr Wells's junior.

'He seems somewhat possessive. Do you think he resents my presence?' Anderson remarked.

'He and I were – lovers,' she spoke hesitantly.

'Ah,' Anderson replied, immediately realising the cause of Dr Wells's attitude towards her. 'Look, it's certainly not my intention to cause any difficulties.'

'No, no, don't worry,' Anna continued. 'It was brief and not very successful. He and I aren't – well, right for one another.'

'Too old?' Anderson asked wryly, hoping that his words would draw a disclaimer from her.

'Oh no, it wasn't that. It, well –'

Anna trailed off and raised her glass to her mouth. Anderson watched her sip at the rich Burgundy, her huge brown eyes wide and infinitely appealing. Once more a lump rose in his throat. She was so desirable, intelligent and confident, bold even, yet strangely meek. He imagined how her face would look at the point of orgasm, filled with uninhibited ecstacy in response to him.

'Go on,' he urged, keen to know if whatever fault had caused her relationship with Wells to fail might also be a hindrance to what he knew was a mutual amity. He looked back to his unsuccessful relationship with the accountant, Catherine Marshall. Her pleasure in his control had been all too evident, yet at the end she had been unable to cope with her own feelings. Anna seemed different. Possibly here was a woman with the sexual needs that made Catherine Marshall so attractive to him, yet aware and in control of those feelings in a way that his ex-lover was not. Still, Anna was a great deal younger than Catherine.

'He –' Anna began, 'he wanted to control me.'

'Sexually?' Anderson asked as his heart sank.

'No, no, the opposite really. He just wanted me to be as he pictures me, not how I really am. Sexually, he liked me to be in control, but I wasn't really because he'd make all the decisions. I don't suppose that makes much sense.'

She had begun to trace a pattern on the table cloth with her middle finger. Anderson judged the gesture to indicate tension and a touch of embarrassment. She clearly wanted to explain, but was unsure of herself. Or she wanted him to think she was unsure of herself, he corrected himself with a trace of cynicism.

'I think it makes sense,' he replied when it was clear that she was not going to continue. 'Possibly he needs a woman who will take the lead, but with his appearance and personality that sort of woman is unlikely to be attracted to him in the first place. So he tries to mould the ones he does attract to suit his needs.'

'That's it exactly,' she answered. 'I felt I was being moulded, but that's just not me. I suppose I'm more like him in fact. Everyone says I'm always trying to run things, but –'

As she trailed off again Anderson felt a sudden urge to be alone with her. Suddenly he was sure she'd respond as he wanted her to, it was just a question of time and place.

'I see you've already found the best pub in the area,' a voice interrupted his thoughts.

Anderson looked up to see Robert Walsh approaching them with a half-pint glass of beer in his hand.

'May I join you?' Walsh asked politely.

'Of course,' Anderson replied in kind, biting down a pang of frustrated lust while immediately amused at his own reaction. As Walsh sat down, Anna glanced at Anderson over the top of her glass, her expression hard to judge. Possibly irony, or amusement, perhaps even a similar melange of emotions to those he felt himself.

Walsh sat down by them, describing the results of the morning's work, which already appeared to be of limited value.

'We've rigged up a winch over the big mine shaft by the path,' he explained. 'A specialist will be going down after lunch. It's an obvious place to dispose of things for anyone in the wood with a guilty conscience.'

'Why do you think he didn't simply drop the body down there?' Anderson asked.

'Good question,' Walsh replied. 'I suppose he could have overlooked it. The engine house wall screens it from the path. Come up and watch the operation in any case. Dr Wells says it'll be flooded and a hopeless task, but you never know.'

Anderson nodded and took a sip of his wine. Why more effort hadn't been made to hide the body was certainly a puzzling question. Speculation as to exact reasons was pointless, yet it seemed increasingly likely that the murderer had intended the body to be found. Why, though, was a question that needed more data before being asked, let alone answered.

They waited while Walsh finished his lunch, chatting easily but without the intimacy of their earlier conversation. Anderson's mind gradually regained its equilibrium, the idea of seducing Anna being shelved for a more opportune moment. The excellent bottle of Fourchaume was a more permanent loss, Anna finishing it off with gusto while he sipped ascetically at his single glass. Unfortunately his hope of working the wine off with a bout of energetic sex with Anna was now impractical.

When Walsh had finished they left the pub and drove back to the wood. To Anderson's regret instructions had been left for

Anna to return to Plymouth and she left with a Panda taking some of the search team from uniform back. Having extracted a promise from her to meet him after work, he walked down into the wood, following the heavy cables that presumably led to the power winch installed over the head of the mine shaft. When he arrived they were already preparing to lower a member of the search team into the hole.

Anderson stood in the doorway of the derelict engine house, extremely glad that it was not his job to explore the mine. In front of him the ground dropped away steeply, then disappeared over a lip of raw slate into the hole. On the far side he could see the first part of the shaft, bands of glossy slate in shades of grey, blue-grey and an iron-stained brown, dripping with water and hung with moss, liverworts and fern, continuing as far down as he could see. Anyone with vertigo would have had to back away or risk losing their balance and plummeting into the dark. The thought was appalling and it amazed him that such an obvious hazard was left wide open without so much as a fence around it.

The man was lowered down, at first his voice echoing from the depths, then his radio taking over, eerie booming sounds still audible from the shaft whenever he spoke. At just over a hundred feet, which Anderson estimated would be at the level of the surface of the estuary, the man called a halt, having found water. The winch went into reverse, raising the man slowly to the surface.

'Anything?' Walsh called as the man found his footing and released his harness catches.

'Nothing, sir,' the man replied. 'Water at one hundred and twenty feet. A couple of adits join higher up, but I don't think we'll be getting anything out of there.'

'How about under the water?'

'Do you know how many cave divers drown, sir?' the man asked, looking horror-stricken. 'There could be another two, three hundred feet of shaft under the water, sir, black as pitch and full of mud unless it hasn't rained for a month. Aside from that, it'll likely be choked with old mine gear, chains, maybe the old cage lifts. Maybe it'd help you catch your man, maybe not, but there's a goodly chance of losing more if you try it.'

'Fair enough,' Walsh admitted, 'we'll only try further exploration as a last resort. I won't risk my men's lives on an off chance.'

Anderson nodded to himself, agreeing with the Super-intendent's decision. The conditions of the mine added to his previous line of thought, though. A weighted corpse pushed down the shaft would have been gone for good, the chances of it ever being found absolutely negligible. So why, with the mine shaft and plenty of heavy chunks of slate conveniently to hand, had Draper's body been left floating in the estuary where it was certain to be found? The obvious answer was that that had been the murderer's intention, but how would a murderer benefit from the body of his victim being found?

'Ah, Anna,' Dr Wells spoke as his junior enter the lab, 'off flirting with detectives again?'

Anna blushed furiously but fortunately Dr Wells was peering intently through a lens and could only see her from the corner of one eye.

'I don't suppose he's really your type, though,' he continued. 'A bit skinny and not tall enough, eh? I suppose you'd be looking for something a touch more masterful.'

'Who are you talking about?' Anna replied innocently, drawing a booming laugh from Dr Wells.

'DCI Anderson, our friend from Surrey,' Wells laughed. 'Don't tell me you haven't noticed? He looks at you like a cat eyeing a fishmonger's stall.'

'Thanks,' Anna replied sarcastically, determined not to be browbeaten. She compared Wells's manner with that of John Anderson. Where Wells was bluff, hearty and rather coarse,

John was civil and considerate. She supposed Wells had a right to feel somewhat piqued at her for turning him down after their first sexual encounter, and imagined that he would recover his initial friendliness after a while. The two men did have similarities, though. Both of them expected their own way, but giving in to John would be a pleasure and she suspected that what he wanted was pretty close to her own needs. If they'd had time, she would have liked to take him to a special place of hers, an abandoned narcissus field now grown into a tangled wood and hidden behind thick hedges. She wondered if she'd have had the courage to ask him to smack her bottom. How good it would have felt being put across his knee, her panties being pulled down, the delicious shame at her exposure, her bare bottom pink and vulnerable in the open wood, waiting for punishment, and then the smacks, warming, tingling –

'Oh and by the way,' Dr Wells said, breaking the fantasy she had been building up as she walked over to her bench, 'you've lost your chance to have a second crack at me. Tomorrow night I have a date with *la belle Violetta*, a.k.a. DI Krebs. Now there is a real woman.'

'Good,' Anna remarked, 'I hope you get on. Have any of the specimens from this morning come in yet?'

'Indeed they have,' Wells replied, suddenly cheerful. 'This afternoon's menu is, for an *entré,* forty-two assorted condoms. Next, *la grande assiette des fruits de mer* including a rusty penknife, three boots and an entire fishing rod. Then, the *pièce de résistance*, a mouldy old jumper in a garnish of used loo paper. And last, but by no means least, a pair of delicate pink panties, discarded, no doubt, during some sordid liaison between two of the local teenagers. A motley collection, I'll grant, but when our divine leader Detective Lord High Superintendent Walsh says everything, then everything it shall be. Actually the only thing that might conceivably be relevant is the pen you found while wading bottomless in the mud for the amusement of your detective friend.'

'I was not bottomless!' Anna retorted.

'DC Heath tells a different story, my dear!'

'I wasn't. Anyway, why do you think the pen might be useful?'

'Well, it's gold-plated so it wouldn't have rusted anyway, but there was no marine growth on it at all, so it had only been there a few days at most. Also, it has a name engraved on it, Nathan Cutts. Mr Cutts, at the least, needs to be eliminated from enquiries. It's quite a common make, so I doubt it'll lead us to him by a trace, yet it could prove useful.'

John Anderson returned to the station feeling better than he had for a long while. Anna's coy flirtation had touched a chord and he felt rejuvenated and more than ordinarily self-confident. Now it was simply a matter of bringing the morning's encounter to a successful conclusion, and he would be meeting her as soon as he had completed his section of paperwork. As he entered the door the desk Sergeant caught his attention.

'DCI Anderson?' the man asked.

'Yes,' Anderson replied.

'Fax for you, sir, from Guildford.'

Anderson took the fax. It was from Jo Blackheath, he saw, as he scanned her concise summary of her investigation. Firstly, there was a Mrs Herrick and her granddaughter, witnesses and just possibly suspects, though Blackheath thought it unlikely. Secondly, Draper had a nephew living at an address in Plymouth. Thirdly, a visitor, probably a man by the name of Cutts, had been with Draper up until at least 9.00 p.m. on the Monday night.

Anderson immediately recognised the inconsistency. At 9.00 p.m. on Monday Draper's lifeless body had been floating on the dark waters of the Tamar estuary, close to two hundred miles away from his cottage in Guildford. He immediately asked to use a telephone and was quickly put through to Blackheath. Five minutes later he replaced the receiver and walked away, deep in thought.

Mrs Herrick hadn't positively identified either of the men she saw as Draper. Indeed, at her age it was hard to be sure of her statement at all. She might have her evenings mixed up. On the other hand, if she was right, then who were the two men and what had they been doing in Draper's cottage? Alternatively, old Mrs Herrick might be less vague-minded than Joanna Blackheath assumed and the whole thing could be a carefully constructed lie designed to distract them. The situation was complex, but at least there was something to get his teeth into after the frustrating lack of data in Devon.

Anderson went to his office and completed his paperwork with his normal care and deliberation, leaving the report on Walsh's desk before making for the door with the feeling of a full day's work completed.

Anna was already waiting for him, resting against the wing of his car with her bag thrown across her shoulder in an easy, girlish manner. The sight of her immediately rekindled his need. She greeted him cheerfully and within a few minutes he was drawing the BMW up outside the Victorian terrace in which she was renting an upper-story flat.

'This will seem very small to you, and you'll have to excuse the mess,' Anna remarked as they arrived. 'I'd prefer to move further out, but then I'd need a car and I can't really afford it yet.'

'It's better than the accommodation I had at your age,' he replied. 'At least you have a garden.'

'Which I can't even use,' Anna laughed. 'It goes with the ground-floor flat. Anyway, I prefer things wild – hedgerows and woods and secret places lost in the country.'

Anderson clicked on the car alarm and followed her up the steps, catching up with her as she fumbled the key into

39

the lock. She was clearly nervous and excited, anticipating the culmination of the encounter that had begun that morning. His own need echoed the signals she was giving and he decided to take things into his own hands without further preamble. As soon as they were in the hallway he took hold of her arm and pulled her towards him, kissing her full on the lips. Her arms went around him and her mouth opened under his, their tongues meeting, her body trembling against him.

'I'd like to make love to you,' he told her openly as he pulled away, her taste filling his mouth.

'Shhh, my neighbours will hear,' she breathed in response, her voice low and husky. 'I'd like that too. Come up.'

Anderson's pulse quickened, the urgency in her voice changing his desire for her into a very immediate reality. She squirmed away and ran laughing up the stairs. He followed, shutting the flat door behind him and joining her on the sofa in her main room. As he took his seat beside her he saw that her eyes were bright and moist, her lips slightly parted.

She turned to him, shaking her hair out of its restraining bun to fall in a soft, black cloud around her shoulders. Anderson leant forward, took hold of her waist and kissed her heavily on the mouth. She responded, eager and a little clumsy but alive and hungry for him. He felt his penis stiffen and let a hand slide onto one full, round breast, feeling its shape under her jumper as their mouths worked together.

He eased her back far enough to allow him to take hold of her jumper and lift it over her breasts. Her bra followed, Anna helping to pull the cups up, Anderson catching her breasts as they fell free of constraint. He rubbed his thumbs over the swollen nipples, drawing a moan of pleasure from her. Her breasts felt heavy and full in his hands, soft pillows of flesh which he kneaded for a space before burying his face between them. Her arms went around his neck, pulling him into her. He slid his hands gently down her flanks, stroking

40

the smooth skin as his mouth found one of her nipples, drawing a squeak from her as his teeth nipped at the little bud. She lay back on the sofa, sighing again as he kissed her breasts, then her neck, letting his tongue flick softly against the sensitive flesh under her jaw line. Anna began to let out little sobs, her body shivering under his hands. He had been wrong to think her possibly immature sexually. Her response showed an astonishing lack of inhibition.

He pulled back, using his fingertips to stroke her breasts and neck, her body arched in pleasure, eyes closed, chest pushed out for his exploring hands. Her willingness was absolute, almost overwhelming in fact, yet the ache in his groin was too urgent to ignore. He kissed her again, once more finding her response a trifle clumsy but full of need. With one arm around her shoulders, he slid the other hand down over the slight rise of her stomach, moving onto the material of her jeans to cup the soft swell of her sex. She moaned again, even more urgently, and her body twisted in his arms.

Anderson relaxed his arms, allowing Anna to twist underneath him until she was on her knees on the sofa. She looked back over her shoulder, not speaking but with her huge brown eyes wide in silent appeal. Once more the sheer hunger of her need for him took him aback, but it was far too late for misgivings. Her mouth was slightly open, her tongue moistening her lips as she watched him undo his fly and release his penis into his hand.

Anna made to undo her belt but he stopped her with a word, instead reaching under her belly and snipping open the belt and the buttons of her fly. The swell of her bottom felt firm against his penis, the denim rubbing against his shaft and balls as she gave an expectant wiggle. Her position exaggerated her tiny waist, making her hips and bottom seem even fuller, a shape that delighted Anderson as he took hold of her jeans and eased them down over the plump globes, revealing the tight white cotton-lace panties stretched taut over her cheeks. He dropped into a crouch and kissed one full buttock as he began to pull her pants down, going slowly, kissing each bit of flesh as it was exposed. The panties joined her jeans at knee level, leaving her delicious bottom quite bare, with a wisp of dark hair showing between her thighs.

'Put your knees together, pull your back in,' he told her. Anna obeyed, bringing her bottom into full prominence, her cheeks open to show the tight, pink spot of her bottom-hole, the plump lips of her vulva pouted and open, ready for his cock. She sighed as his tongue brushed her vagina, then gasped as the questing tip found her clitoris and flicked against it, bringing her completely on heat.

The muscles of her thighs began to tense as his tongue explored the most sensitive areas of her vulva. Just a little more and she would probably come, but he didn't want that yet. He pulled back, one hand lingering on her bottom, the other nursing his erection.

'Please, John, now,' Anna asked.

Anderson ignored her, instead standing up and stepping back to admire the sight she made, her beautiful, naked bottom open and ready for him to penetrate. With her jumper up her breasts were hanging down, her hair tumbled over her face and falling forward. The sight was enchanting, infinitely desirable yet also vulnerable, a feeling enhanced by the contrast of her shameless exposure and his clothing, disturbed only to allow access to his penis. Something about her position struck a chord in him, making him determined to have her actually reveal her need for him in words.

'Ask me,' he said, keeping his voice low and easy even though his penis felt as if it was about to burst.

'Please!' she begged. 'Put it in me!'

'Properly,' he demanded as he undid his own belt and let his suit trousers fall open.

'You bastard!' she retorted. 'OK, please fuck me, John. Put your prick in my pussy, come in me, please, I beg, use me, fuck me!'

Anna's voice had risen to a shrill and urgent peak, reminding Anderson that there might well be neighbours in downstairs. Still, if she wanted to announce to them that she was begging to be fucked, then that was up to her. He took a condom from his pocket, unrolling it down the length of his penis slowly and deliberately while she watched with an expression of desperation on her face. Resisting the urge to torment her further, he stepped forward and put the head of his penis against her quim, guiding it in with his hand. Anna moaned as her vagina filled with cock, pushing backwards and rubbing her bottom against him in abandoned lust as he took hold of her hips and began to move slowly in and out.

After a moment he felt her hand reach back to find her vulva and rub at her clitoris, masturbating uninhibitedly as he fucked her to a slow, firm rhythm. Her breath began to come faster, the cheeks of her bottom tensing as she neared orgasm. He felt her shudder as she came, the muscles of her vagina contracting fiercely around his cock again and again as her climax tore through her, her muted gasps finally turning to screams as she forgot all about being quiet. Finally she sighed and relaxed, laying her head on her folded arms and lifting her bottom to take his strokes more comfortably.

'Don't rush,' she purred as his pace quickened. 'I'm OK, just take your time.'

Anderson replied with a grunt. The muscles of his legs were burning, distracting him from the ecstasy of having his cock buried in her warm, wet hole. He changed his grip, putting his hands on her buttocks and pulling them open. For a second he caught the scent of her sex, recharging him. At that moment his own pleasure started to climb, his cock beginning to spasm as he reached the point of no return. Her glorious bottom was quivering and bouncing as he rode her, his hands kneading the flesh as he grunted from the strain and ecstasy. A moment later he reached orgasm, draining himself into her and pulling the softness of her buttocks hard against his thighs, his fingers locked into the flesh of her hips.

Anna gasped as the breath was knocked out of her, his final thrusts forcing her to brace herself against the sofa. He slowed, then stopped and a moment later his penis was being withdrawn slowly from her vagina. She turned and smiled at him, a big, happy, sleepy smile of utter satisfaction.

FOUR
Friday

John Anderson folded his arms and let his weight settle against a cast-iron radiator. At the front of the room, Walsh was going over the information that Thursday's work had revealed, information that was already familiar territory to Anderson. Blanking out Walsh's voice, he took the opportunity to look over the other members of the team, officers whom he had met only briefly on the previous day.

Nearest to him, seated and fiercely intent on Walsh, was DC Heath, a tall young man with sandy hair and a long face. A shiny new suit, neat tie and plain haircut completed the image of eager youth. Anderson judged him competent if inexperienced, an officer very much at the learning stage of his trade. Beyond Heath was the other DC, Pentyre, a stocky, heavily muscled man with black hair cut to a rough stubble. His round, bull-like face suggested a coarse good humour. He sat hunched forward, his massive shoulders stretching the back of a worn, brown leather jacket. He seemed old to still be at the rank of Detective Constable. A good man to have behind one, Anderson imagined, but not the type to produce striking insights or any sort of innovation.

DS Dunning was leaning against a table behind the other two men. Like Pentyre he was stocky and dark-haired but less powerfully built and distinguished by a thick moustache and thinning hair. A brown suit and an open collar with the tie knotted loosely beneath it produced a careless image to which Anderson felt an automatic antipathy. Inefficient perhaps, lacking in application, he considered while reserving full judgement until he had a better opportunity to talk to the man.

Anderson had already noted a laddish companionship between the three men, a companionship that clearly excluded the remaining member of the team, DI Krebs. That a degree of tension should exist between Krebs and her male colleagues was not surprising. She was clearly younger than either Dunning or Pentyre – indeed she was remarkably young to have reached the rank she held. Anderson had heard something of her ability from Walsh and could see his logic in promoting her over the heads of her older colleagues.

She sat across the room from him, intent on the details of the briefing. Her most obvious feature was a head of bright red hair, now tied back with a short length of black ribbon. Pale, lightly freckled skin, a small, straight nose and eyes of an exceptionally pale blue-grey complemented high cheekbones and a rather sharp chin to give her a look that was pretty yet somewhat aloof. This was accentuated by her body, which looked lean and muscular rather than slim. Indeed the long muscles of her calves were, if anything, over-defined. Her white blouse and black ribbon tie reminded him of women's formal academic dress, the pale grey skirt suit completing the impression of reserve and seriousness. Her shoes alone suggested an element of vanity in her otherwise strictly practical make-up: patent black leather with thin, high heels.

'Violet,' Walsh was saying as he turned to face the room, 'I want you to go and see James Draper. 108, Gaitskell House on the Leighdon Estate, near Crownhill, you know the area. Some of you may remember Draper. He was pulled in for drugs a couple of years back. Uniform caught him red-handed but unfortunately he was selling icing sugar, not cocaine. Mainly, of course, you're telling him that his uncle's dead, but we do need to verify his whereabouts on Monday, so be subtle. I'm sure I can rely on you, but take someone with you.'

None of the three seated detectives moved to volunteer and Anderson noted a trace of annoyance on Walsh's face. Having already deduced that the alternative to interviewing Draper would be a long day spent going over police records or interviewing barely possible witnesses, he quickly raised a finger to attract Walsh's attention.

'I'd be happy to go,' he said.

Walsh nodded and sent a questioning look to Krebs.

'I'd prefer to be the senior officer on this, sir,' she replied curtly.

Walsh was about to speak when Anderson cut in, 'I'm not suggesting I lead the interview. I'll simply observe.'

Walsh looked back to Krebs, who nodded.

'Right then,' Walsh continued. 'Dunning, Pentyre, continue the house-to-house interviewing, working up river. Heath, get what information you can on people called Cutts in the area. With the name of Cutts turning up at both ends of the investigation, we have a likely name for our man, but unfortunately a name is all we have, except for his pen. Right, any questions?'

Nobody responded and the meeting broke up, Anderson joining Krebs and heading towards the car park. She walked briskly, her heels clicking on the floor as he fell into step beside her. Her manner struck Anderson as professionally detached, icy even, and he determined to make her aware of him as more than simply another male colleague.

'Crownhill is out along the A386,' she informed him. 'It

shouldn't take more than ten minutes to get there.'

'I'll drive us there,' he replied, more as a statement than an offer.

Krebs gave a short laugh. 'Your car is that big silver BMW, isn't it?'

'Yes,' Anderson replied.

'Then we'll take a car from the pool,' she continued. 'You'd be lucky if they only took the wheels.'

'Thank you for the advice,' he answered. 'Is the area rough then? I always think of the West Country as peacefully rural. I suppose Plymouth is a naval town, though.'

She laughed again. 'That's not such a problem, well, not for CID anyway. Uniform might disagree. Our main problem is drugs – couriers coming in on ferries, small boats and through the airport, and dealers and junkies. Also, the unemployment rate is about as high as anywhere. Some of the estates would give London or Manchester a run for their money.'

'The Leighdon Estate is one of them?' Anderson queried, mentally contrasting James Draper's living conditions with the apparent affluence of his dead uncle.

'Not the worst, but hardly genteel. I remember Draper – an arrogant brat, but perfectly cool. He took pleasure in deliberately baiting us. Of course he knew that it was only icing sugar in the bag, so he could afford to be arrogant. At the time I half suspected that he was some sort of decoy, but nothing ever came of it. Apparently he's well known in Devonport, but they've never been able to pin anything big on him.'

Arriving at the car pool, they selected an inconspicuous blue Rover 114 and drove out to the Leighdon Estate. It proved to be an ugly cluster of concrete towers plastered onto an open hillside and open to the full force of the west wind. Anderson looked at the buildings in disgust, wondering what

48

could possess anybody to build such a place. Six grim towers stood up from a maze of access roads and low walkways interspersed with yellowish grass and a handful of forlorn trees. A boarded-up pre-fab in the middle of the largest open space proclaimed itself to be the community centre in letters of faded red paint. The nearest of the towers was marked as Gaitskell House.

'It won a design award in the late sixties,' Krebs was saying. 'You can see Dartmoor from the upper flats. On the other hand, you can see the upper flats from Dartmoor.'

Anderson nodded, glancing up at the balconies of Gaitskell House. Certainly the view from the top would be impressive, and, judging from the size of the blocks, 108 would be quite high – high enough, perhaps, to command a view of the Tamar estuary.

'Do you intend to present this visit simply as a call to inform Draper of his uncle's death?' he asked as they reached the bottom of a graffiti-covered stairwell next to which a lift stood open, the OUT OF ORDER sign fallen to lie flat on the concrete floor. Anderson wrinkled his nose in disgust at the smell of stale urine before continuing. 'It could be worth phrasing our questions carefully to see if Draper already knows anything, for instance that his uncle drowned.'

'I had thought of that,' Krebs replied pointedly, 'and I suppose it's worth a try, but I don't imagine he'll see two senior officers being sent to give him the bad news as a mark of our respect for him.'

'True,' Anderson conceded, 'if he is involved, he'll be on his guard from the start, though, and if he's not, he need not concern himself.'

Krebs didn't answer but quickened her pace on the stairs. Anderson followed, glancing occasionally to the side to watch the panorama of Plymouth spread out beneath them as they ascended. Krebs, he realised, regarded her fellow officers more as rivals than colleagues, an attitude which clearly included

49

him. Despite her impressive physique and smart dress, both now more evident as she climbed in front of him, her long legs accentuated by seamed stockings, he felt she compared poorly with the charming vulnerability of Anna Ferreira. As an officer, on the other hand, she seemed bright and efficient.

They reached the tenth floor and found Draper's flat. Anderson, mindful of his promise to take a back seat, let Krebs knock and stood back as the door swung open. As she introduced them to the slim young man who stood in the doorway, Anderson watched for signs of alarm. None were evident. Indeed, Draper seemed neither surprised nor concerned at a visit from the police. He was dressed only in tatty jeans, his skinny white chest and bony feet bare. His hair was shaved at the sides and short on top, framing a loose-featured face that made for a look of casual insolence.

'Sue, get your knickers on, it's the pigs,' Draper called back into the flat as Anderson and Krebs entered. Anderson remained firmly detached, despite Draper's manner. Automatic antagonism was a common reaction from some members of the public and over the years he had learnt that it bore little relevance to their guilt or innocence. A moment later a slovenly blonde girl emerged from a side door. Her glance was openly hostile, with none of Draper's unconcern. She walked into the middle of the room to stand with her back to a broad window as Draper threw himself down on to a sofa.

'The sugar's in the top cupboard,' Draper joked. 'Help yourself.'

'We're not here to search your flat, Mr Draper,' Krebs replied. 'In fact I'm afraid we have bad news.'

'Oh, yeah?' Draper replied, his facetious manner fading a trifle.

'It's your uncle, Charles Draper,' Krebs continued. 'I'm afraid he died earlier this week.'

'What, old Charlie? You're joking. I only saw him a couple

of weeks ago. He was all right, he was. Dead – fuck – what happened?'

'He died in an accident, I'm afraid, and as you appear to be his closest relative, we'll have to ask you to identify the body. Also, I'm sure you'll understand that we need to ask you a few routine questions.'

'Why?'

'Purely routine, Mr Draper. Essentially we would like to know your whereabouts last Monday afternoon so that we can eliminate you from our enquiries.'

'Well I wasn't in Surrey for starters!' Draper responded, throwing an amused look at his girlfriend.

'He died in Devon, Mr Draper.'

'Devon? Oh well then, it's a fair cop, luv, slip on the cuffs,' Draper laughed, holding out his skinny wrists. ''Cause we all know, if there's a crime in Devon, then it's down to yours truly, James W. Draper!'

As getting sensible responses from Draper was clearly going to be an uphill struggle, Anderson took the opportunity to glance around the flat. Squalid was the first word that came to his mind. The room that they were in was a square living room decorated in a dull grey-blue. A tatty three-piece suite in shades of orange and brown, another shabby armchair in a worn green material and a couple of low tables made up the furniture. Posters advertising various pop bands and a couple of crudely erotic prints made up the decoration. There were no books at all. He normally considered a person's choice of books a good source of information to their character. In this case, their very absence was informative.

Doors lay open to kitchen and bedroom, both of which had the same look of cheap squalor as the main room. Clothes were strewn liberally over the bedroom floor, with a few articles straying into the living room. Most appeared either masculine or unisex, the sole exception being a pale blue bra thrown casually across the bed end. Anderson glanced at

51

Draper's girlfriend, noting that her breasts were clearly bare under her T-shirt. Nothing else within his range of vision could clearly be identified as feminine.

There was a generally stale smell, in which Anderson detected elements of frying oil, unwashed clothes and a floral air-spray. The conditions repulsed him, adding to his feeling of distaste for James Draper.

Three features struck notes of discord with his over-whelming impression of a low-income flat inhabited by a single male who was anything but house-proud. Firstly there was the music system, a stack connected to large speakers, clearly both powerful and expensive and accompanied by a collection of compact discs that Anderson estimated would have cost a thousand pounds or more in total. Secondly there was the bed, a vast, vulgar monstrosity upholstered in crimson satin-effect material. A label showing at the bottom identified it as a water bed. Thirdly, there was a mobile phone on the bedside table.

'Mr Draper, perhaps you could answer my question,' Krebs continued patiently.

'Monday afternoon,' Draper replied, rising to his feet and holding his chin as if in deep thought. 'Let's see now, what was it on Monday? Pick up my stash? No, that was Sunday. Rob the social? No, that was Tuesday. Murder uncle Charlie? Oh yeah, that was Monday. Yeah, I remember now, you're right.'

'Mr Draper, please could you be serious for one moment.'

Anderson pondered Draper's response. His initial shock, which appeared genuine, had very quickly given way to a sort of pantomime act with himself and Krebs as foils for Draper's humour and Draper's girlfriend as the audience. Was this because he was entirely innocent and therefore could afford to play the fool? Alternatively he might be playing an elaborate bluff, but in either case he clearly had a low opinion of the intelligence of the police, an attitude that often led to mistakes. As Krebs's gentle approach was clearly getting nowhere, he decided to exert some authority on the young man.

'Mr Draper,' Anderson put in, 'this is a very serious matter and you are wasting our time. Your uncle is dead. He was drowned in the estuary and was found on the mud flats. Our pathologists have determined the time of death at some point during Monday afternoon. Now, please tell me your whereabouts on that afternoon, preferably providing someone reliable as a witness, or we can continue this conversation at the station.'

Anderson caught a quickly suppressed look of fury from Krebs. Draper laughed and struck a dramatic posture as if under great stress.

'Finally Mutt speaks,' Draper began in an overdone parody of a film commentary, 'his stern voice striking fear into the lowly suspect. The villain, gabbling foolishly, gives an alibi that proves he was nowhere near a particular point on the stated day. Being stupid, he forgets that Mutt hasn't said a name for the place and drops himself right in the shit.'

Anderson drew in his breath, maintaining a cool exterior in the face of Draper's deliberate taunting.

'Your answer, please, Mr Draper,' he said quietly.

Draper laughed again. 'You should've done your homework, you really should, because, Mr Detective, on Monday afternoon I was near the estuary, very near the estuary, because – and here's the punch line – I spent most of Monday in the Devonport nick on account of a being involved in an "incident" with some piss-artist down at the Matelot's Arms. If you don't believe me, you can give them a ring.'

'We will, Mr Draper, thank you for your cooperation,' Krebs answered. 'Did you know your uncle well?'

'That's better,' Draper replied, speaking to Anderson. 'See what a bit of charm can do? Yeah, Charlie was all right for an old boy. I used to visit him when I wanted a bit of peace and quiet, and me and Sue used to stay there when he was off looking for clocks, didn't we, Sue?'

Sue responded with a nod.

'Shame he got done in,' Draper continued, 'but if you're after me for it you're looking at the wrong guy. Tell you what, though, he didn't half have an argument with some bird while I was staying there. Screaming like fuck she was, about how it was her place and he had no right to be there and a load of other stuff. Fuck knows what she was on about. I reckon she would have done him in, given half a chance. Here, are you serious about him being found down here?'

'Yes,' Krebs replied, 'I'm afraid so. Can you describe this woman?'

'Yeah, since I'm "helping you with your enquiries", I reckon I could. Taller than you, bigger knockers too. Dark hair, in a right state. Maybe thirty, maybe a bit less.'

Anderson noticed a trace of a flush on Krebs's cheek at Draper's casually impertinent reference to her breasts but decided not to interfere. Instead he studied Draper's face, looking for tell-tale signs of hidden stress or satisfaction at having evaded them. Nothing was obvious, but Draper's manner seemed too casual, too confident, as if he had had a chance to rehearse what he was saying, changing his tone to suit his convenience and retain control of the situation. Anderson had used similar techniques often enough himself to read the signs. He would have handled the interview differently, yet it had to be admitted that Krebs had managed to gain at least some information.

The woman Draper was describing was probably Melanie Herrick, strengthening that lead, although, of course, were Draper involved it would be in his interest to put her up as a suspect. Possibly that was why he had so suddenly changed style from the deliberately obstructive joker to the helpful citizen. On the other hand, if his alibi held up – and Anderson had no doubt that it would – then he was entirely in the clear as the actual murderer. Besides, Draper's skinny, under-muscled frame hardly fitted the pattern that forensic had built up of the murderer's physical characteristics.

'Thank you, Mr Draper,' Krebs was saying. 'If you could just come down to the station for the identification later this morning.'

Draper agreed, his girlfriend anxious to accompany him. He then let them out, leaving Anderson to face Krebs's icy glare as the door closed behind them. Anderson simply smiled and shrugged, disinclined either to apologise or to discuss his interruption of her interview pattern. After all, at the end of the day, he held a higher rank than her.

'Well, he's not the murderer,' he said after a while. Krebs replied with a reserved nod. 'On the other hand, he didn't act like a surprised man, more like someone who had rehearsed his piece.'

Krebs didn't reply, instead stopping to stare out across Plymouth from the stairwell. Anderson stopped beside her, considered a word of apology and then rejected the idea. Beneath them the city spread out in a panorama of houses on low, rolling hills, dull white paint and the grey tones of slate and concrete being the predominant colours, interspersed with an occasional bit of drab green where a field had become enclosed in the urban sprawl. To their right the hill rose steeply, so that the crest was on a level with them. Beyond the houses was the estuary, a placid expanse of brownish grey studded with the masts of many small boats and in turn giving way to the faded green and greys of the Cornish side of the river. A jut of land blocked their view up river, the same jut that made most of Plymouth invisible from the hill above Thorn Point and the place where Charles Draper's body had lain on the mud flats.

'He was the same with the icing sugar business,' Krebs finally spoke, 'cocksure little shit.'

Anderson turned in surprise at her sudden vehemence,

realising that her calm manner had hidden an annoyance at James Draper stronger than his own.

'I agree,' he responded, 'but unfortunately the people who one would most like to be guilty seldom are.'

Krebs nodded, shook her head as if to rid herself of something unpleasant and turned to the stairs. Anderson waited a moment more, watching the bob of her bright red pony-tail as she descended the steps, then followed her.

Melanie Herrick sat staring glumly out of the window of her flat. Across the road the lines of the main London line ran through a deep cutting. A train clattered past, gathering speed as it left Guildford station. Melanie's eyes followed it with a bored expression, wishing she were elsewhere, anywhere, but preferably in the cottage which she had wanted as hers since childhood. She tossed out her long, dark hair and got to her feet, walking through to the kitchen to make another of the endless cups of tea that she drank with almost ritual regularity.

It had not always been this way, she reflected as the kettle switch clicked into place. At school, Carl had been her knight errant, the tallest, strongest boy around, the one all the girls wanted, and the one who had chosen her, the tall, shy girl who never had much to say. Of course at the time, while he was flattering her with every corny line in the book, she had never considered that it was her early maturity that appealed to him. Also, with her innocence and lack of friends she had never realised that accepting full sex marked her as something of a catch and as something to be held on to.

Really it had gone downhill from her marriage. She had only been nineteen, Carl twenty. Five years later and he had still been a garage mechanic, his life settled comfortably into a round of nights out with his mates, football and snooker. Her romantic illusions had collapsed completely, leaving her life as a routine with nothing to do but play the pretty little wife, cooking his dinner, bringing him and his mates their beer, cleaning up the mess the next day, and so on, and so on.

Then there had been Duncan and the afternoons of frantic, passionate sex at her grandmother's house while the old lady was in the garden, or in one case making tea in the next room while Melanie was taken to a hasty climax on the Chesterfield. It had been good, but inevitably Carl had found out, and then there had been the rows, the accusations. Then he had started to hit her when her affair became common knowledge and his so-called mates began to make jokes at his expense. Finally she had snapped and left him, only to have Duncan run off with that awful Sophie within the week. She had imagined Carl would have come to hate her and be glad to be rid of her, but instead her leaving had only redoubled his fury and he had set out to get her back, one moment whining and bringing her flowers and chocolates, the next threatening her and bawling to the whole street that she was his and had no right to leave. With hindsight she could see that he had always regarded her as a possession from the start. To him she had simply been the girl with the biggest tits and best bum at school, then the wife who treated him as a god, obeying his orders and doing everything he wanted in bed. An object to boast about to his mates and to show off in the street, never a person, just a possession. Duncan hadn't been much better, using her for sex and then leaving the instant she needed support instead.

Finally there had been the divorce, with Carl's solicitor rubbing her infidelity in her face and fighting her every attempt at an even settlement. The flat had been intended to be a stop-gap, with the pretty cottage on her granny's land supposed to be given up for her by a 'gentleman's agreement' between her late grandfather and the tenant. Some gentleman, she thought, Mr bloody Draper –

The doorbell rang, snapping Melanie out of her depressing train of thought. She knew from her grandmother that the police were invesigating Charles Draper in some way,

57

and so it was no surprise when the woman to whom she opened the door introduced herself as a Detective Sergeant Blackheath.

She showed the policewoman up to her flat and sat down, feeling nervous despite herself. She knew from her grandmother that the interview was to be about Charles Draper, but no more than that. The detective's manner seemed formal, aggressive even. Possibly Draper had complained after she had lost her temper and shouted at him. When had it been? Monday? Yes, but several other times as well. Surely they would have sent someone round before now?

'Would you like some tea?' she asked the policewoman as the kettle clicked off. The officer declined and waited patiently while Melanie made herself tea and sat down again.

'How may I help?' she asked.

'We need you to confirm one or two details concerning a Mr Charles Draper,' the policewoman began. 'You do know Mr Draper?'

'Yes,' Melanie replied.

'And you saw him last Monday?'

'Yes.'

'At what time?'

'It was just after we'd had tea, but that was earlier than usual because I had to get back. Perhaps three o'clock or so, I can't be sure exactly.'

'And you definitely saw Draper and spoke to him?'

'Yes, I said I did. Look, I'm sorry if I shouted at him, but –'

'We're not concerned with that, Miss Herrick. When you left your grandmother's, what did you do?'

'The usual, I walked to the station and caught the train back to Guildford.'

'You don't drive?'

'No, Carl didn't want me to learn, and –'

'And did you see anybody on the way, or can you

remember any cars passing you in the lane?'

'No, not really. I mean – maybe, I can't be sure. I was still cross over Draper. There may have been cars but I don't think so. I'm sure I'd have remembered any people though, there's not much reason to come down our lane.'

'So you can confirm to me that Draper was in his cottage at around three o'clock and that you saw nobody else?'

'Yes.'

'Would anybody other than your grandmother be able to confirm your movements?'

'Well, no, there was nobody at the station. The train driver maybe, or someone at Guildford station? No, probably not. Hang on, has something happened to Mr Draper?'

The policewoman paused. Melanie was finding the Detective Sergeant's cold, formal manner intimidating. More-over, the questions implied that she was under suspicion. She sipped her tea, feeling nervous and insecure. Blackheath seemed strong, self-confident and utterly in control, charac-teristics which Melanie could not even pretend were part of her own nature.

'I had better inform you at this stage,' Blackheath began again, 'that Charles Draper died last Monday. His body was found by a river in Devon on Tuesday morning.'

'Oh, how awful!' Melanie gasped. 'To think of all the things I said about him, and now he's dead! Oh no, that's horrid! Hang on, do you mean he was killed? You can't think I had anything to do with it!'

'At present,' Blackheath continued calmly, 'we simply wish to establish the facts of the case. I'm sure you understand that as the last person we know to have seen Charles Draper alive, we will need to eliminate you from our enquiries.'

Melanie sat speechless, unsure of what to say but finally managing a bleak nod of affirmation.

'We will of course make inquiries of the railway staff,' the policewoman continued, 'and I'll be in touch if we need to ask any further questions. Meanwhile, if you think of anything, call me at the station, here's a card with the number.'

Melanie accepted the card with numb fingers and put it down on the tea table. She could feel herself shaking inside as Blackheath rose and made for the door. When the door had closed she sat down, her hand shaking too much to lift the tea cup. She felt small and scared. If that was what an interview was like, what would it be like to be arrested by Blackheath? What had she said her name was? Jo? Yes, presumably short for Joanne, or Joanna, but somehow masculine. Not that there was anything masculine about the detective's appearance. On the contrary, she was quite small, delicate even, with her golden-blonde bob haircut and heart-shaped face. Her eyes had been hard though, strong, uncompromising –

Melanie stopped herself. No, she thought, it was ridiculous, she wasn't thinking straight. How could she project the sort of feeling that tough, self-reliant characters like Carl and Duncan had stirred in her on to the policewoman? For goodness sake, Blackheath was a woman!

Melanie smacked herself on the back of the hand, a mannerism her mother had taught her to deal with moments when her over-zealous imagination was beginning to run away with her. The act brought her down to earth and she managed to take a sip of tea without spilling it. Her mind settled down, suddenly clearer than it had been in months. Now that Draper was out of the way, as soon as all the fuss blew over she would be able to have her cottage.

For the first time in several days Melanie Herrick allowed a smile to cross her face.

Blackheath closed the outside door behind her and turned her steps towards the centre of Guildford. Melanie Herrick seemed genuine, although she could provide no alibi and it seemed unlikely that any would emerge later. She would have to ring Anderson in Devon and check to make sure that the times matched. Intuition pleaded against Melanie Herrick being a murderess. True, she was tall for a woman and had a fair share of natural muscle; she could just possibly have drugged and drowned Draper and it was just possible that her hands were big enough to fit the marks on Draper's head that the people in Devon had described. On the other hand, her character seemed very soft and she didn't drive – or at least she said she didn't drive. Of course there could be an accomplice, an accomplice shielded by carefully contrived statements from both the Herricks. The option seemed too fantastic, yet could not be ruled out altogether. Again the line of deduction foundered on the lack of data from Anderson. She would have to call him when she got back to the station.

The next task, however, was to speak to Draper's solicitor, a Mr Worth. Worth had already been informed of Draper's death and it was simply a matter of trying to shed further light on Draper's life and possible motives for his murder. Worth's practice was located in one of the new glass and brick office buildings towards the centre of the city and an easy walk from Melanie Herrick's flat. Blackheath had frequently seen the distinctive design of smoked glass windows set in brick facing of a deep red and sloped backwards to give a futuristic effect. They were visible from the main road, but she had never been inside. However, she quickly found Worth's offices and was shown into the waiting room by the receptionist.

A moment later one of the office doors opened and a thin woman in a blue suit was ushered out by a large, white-haired man with a genial expression. This proved to be Worth, who introduced himself and offered Blackheath his hand, enfolding her own in his heavy, soft paw. He waved her into the office and ordered coffee without asking for her preference, then ambled over to the massive leather upholstered chair behind his desk, sat down and folded his hands across his ample stomach.

'Make yourself comfortable,' he said cheerfully. 'Poor old Charlie, eh? Nice fellow, we used to have a round on the links together occasionally, not that he was much of a player, but then neither am I. I do think a lot of people take their golf far too seriously nowadays, don't you?'

'I've really no idea,' Blackheath admitted.

'Ah ha! Don't play. Sensible girl, time idly spent and all that. Sadly I have only too much time to spend idly. So did Charles. Have you seen his clocks? Never mind, to business. What would you like to know?'

'As you know,' Blackheath began, 'Charles Draper didn't die naturally, he was murdered, drowned in fact. This happened in the Tamar estuary in Devon on Monday –'

'I assume you mean the Devon side of the Tamar estuary,' Worth broke in.

'Yes,' Blackheath replied, thinking Worth's comment somewhat pedantic.

'Details, details, my dear,' Worth carried on, 'the stuff of which good detective work is made. Anyway, carry on.'

'There's no obvious motive,' Blackheath continued, 'and I imagine that you might be able to add something to the facts that we've collected so far.'

'Ah ha! Facts,' Worth said, beaming jovially and raising an admonitory finger at her. 'Facts, of course, which I am not obliged to produce.'

'No, but –'

'Fear not, I have no intention of making life difficult for you. What, after all, would it gain me? To the best of my ability, and within reason, I will tell you what you want to know.'

'Thank you, Mr Worth,' Blackheath replied. Old Mrs Herrick's vague wanderings and Melanie Herrick's timid shyness suddenly seemed very easy in comparison with Worth, who seemed determined not to be succinct. 'Most importantly, I'd like an idea of the value of Draper's estate and who the beneficiaries are.'

'Simple enough,' Worth answered. 'I am Charles's executor and from his estate I shall receive two fine clocks, items of not inconsiderable value. The rest of the clock collection is to be distributed among his friends, including, if I remember rightly, and I generally do, your own Chief Constable, Colin Farrell. The bulk of the estate, however, goes to his nephew James. James I have never met, and Charles, although always keen to play the indulgent uncle, regarded him as something of a wastrel, a drone if you will. Do you read Wodehouse? No? Ah, but you should. That is why James was not made executor when he reached his majority.'

'And how much will James get?'

'Ah ha! You cut to the point. The sum will be substantial, just short, in fact, of one million pounds. Now there you have a potential motive!'

Blackheath considered. Certainly an inheritance of that size might well provide a motive for murder.

'Did James Draper know that he stood to inherit so much?' she asked. 'And roughly how old is he?'

Worth paused, interlacing his fingers and then steepling them before replying.

'In answer to your first question, probably,' he said thoughtfully. 'Charles was not a secretive man. Obstinate, yes. Irritable at times. Not, however, the sort to use his will as a lever. Maybe, maybe not – after all, he didn't expect to die. As to age, James would be twenty-five or twenty-six by now, I imagine.'

Blackheath ran a quick calculation in her head. If James Draper knew that he would inherit and his uncle might be expected to live twenty, even thirty or more years, then he would have the prospect of becoming rich at around fifty.

'Do you know how James Draper gets by?' she asked.

'Not in detail,' Worth replied. 'However, if I remember rightly, his father, who was Charles's brother and a fair bit older, left James a moderate house and at least some money when he died. He is an only child and if I remember rightly he sold the house. No, you'll have to check that up for yourself, I'm really not at all sure of the facts.'

Once more Blackheath cursed the difficulty of having an investigation in two parts of the country so widely separated. Still, James Draper's motive was undoubtedly stronger than Melanie Herrick's. The facts of the case seemed to be coming together smoothly, although her earlier hope of solving the case from the Guildford end now seemed remote. Efficient, precise work on her part could do her no harm, though, especially with the Chief Constable taking a direct interest in the case.

'Thank you, Mr Worth,' she said evenly. 'That covers what I wanted to know, but is there anything else you can think of that might be of interest?'

Worth paused, again steepling his fingers over his stomach.

'Hmm, let me think,' he began. 'Not really. Do you know about the disagreement over his lease of the cottage?'

'Vaguely,' Blackheath replied. 'I've just been speaking to Melanie Herrick. She and her grandmother own the cottage, apparently, and hoped Draper would vacate it. Apparently he refused and they can't move him, which has caused a bit of friction.'

'Yes, that's basically it,' Worth continued. 'Old man Herrick was a friend of Draper's father from way back, you see, maybe even a distant relation in point of fact. Both were gentlemen of the old school, and old John Draper was supposed to live there unless a member of the Herrick family needed it. A tight-knit lot, the wealthy sorts around here, as you'll find out. The agreement passed to Charles, who set it up as a formal lease when old man Herrick died. I suppose you've met Edith Herrick? Nice old girl, but far too trusting. It's a pleasant spot, and Charles was well settled in there, so when the Herricks wanted it back he simply refused to vacate. His legal standing is unassailable. I should know, I set up the lease.

But I can't see the Herricks hiring a contract killer!'

'Why do you say a hired killer?'

'Well, you can hardly see them doing it themselves! What an idea! I mean, Edith must be eighty if she's a day and Melanie's as soppy as they come! She's got a tongue in her head, mark you, but a killer – never!'

'Yes, I must admit the idea seems unlikely. Thank you again, then, Mr Worth. Don't worry, I'll see myself out.'

Worth raised a hand in a casual goodbye as Blackheath left his office.

Anderson returned to the small office to which he had been assigned. The interview with James Draper had been far from satisfactory. His alibi had checked out. Uniform had picked him up for trying to start a fight outside the pub he had mentioned, the Matelot's Arms. Apparently it was a rough pub near the ferry terminal and Draper had tried to start the fight when he claimed that someone had removed his money from the edge of a pool table. The police had been called and Draper taken to the Devonport station to cool off. Draper, mouthy as always, had refused to accept a caution and had been held until nearly seven o'clock, finally being released without charge as his opponent had refused to press charges.

The alibi was perfect. Dr Wells set the time of death well within the period that Draper had spent in a police cell. In any case, Draper almost certainly lacked the strength to have dragged his half-conscious uncle across the mud flats and then drowned him. No, James Draper was innocent of murder. The perfect alibi. It seemed almost too perfect, and just the sort of flash stunt James Draper would have pulled if he'd known in advance that he needed an alibi for that period. Also, there was his super-confident, cocksure manner when interviewed, providing information, but only the information he wanted to give. Draper's involvement could certainly not be ruled out.

Anderson was mulling over his options and considering lunch when the phone rang.

'Anderson,' he replied promptly.

'It's me, Jo Blackheath, sir,' the caller said. 'I've got some information to exchange.'

'Good, go ahead, Jo. What have you got?' Anderson replied.

'Firstly,' Blackheath replied, 'James Draper stands to inherit the best part of a million pounds from his uncle and it seems likely that he was aware of this. I need to know if James Draper was hard up and whether he has an alibi for Monday night.'

'Monday night?' Anderson queried, setting aside the first part of Blackheath's request. 'That's irrelevant. Charles Draper was killed on Monday afternoon, definitely.'

'Oh,' Blackheath paused. 'I have a witness who claims to have seen him at around three o'clock on the Monday afternoon. Melanie Herrick, I interviewed her earlier.'

'Then she's almost certainly lying or mistaken,' Anderson replied. 'Charles Draper died no later than four, more probably three, and he died down here. Even if he had died at four o'clock, the latest time forensic will allow for, it would be impossible for him to have reached the Tamar in that time, it's very nearly two hundred miles. Even if we assume your witness is an hour out and that our forensics are also an hour out, it leaves three hours to get to Devon. I don't believe it could be done, or at least not without getting picked up for speeding. Use your judgement, but it seems most likely that she's not telling the truth, although I wouldn't want to speculate why.'

'Right,' Blackheath said slowly. 'That completely spoils my reasoning. Melanie Herrick is timid, a bit of a nervous wreck really. I'd swear she knew nothing about Draper's death. It's true that she has a motive, but I don't feel –'

'Don't go on feelings, Joanna, go on facts,' Anderson replied curtly. 'The fact is, she's probably lying, and if she is, then it's evidently with considerable skill. Do you have anything else?'

'Only Draper's possible motive,' she replied. 'He apparently inherited enough to live on from his parents. I really need to know how badly he wants money.'

'I don't know,' Anderson answered, 'and I'm not sure it's important. A million pounds would be a tempting prize even if he was well off, and he lives in revolting squalor on a hideous estate. Interview Herrick again, but make sure she's lying before you take any definite action.'

'Yes, sir.' Blackheath asked, 'Has the Cutts lead got anywhere?'

'I don't think so. Three officers are running house-to-house interviews and going over the records but I've yet to hear anything in the way of results. Keep in touch.'

Replacing the receiver, Anderson sat back in his chair. The case was becoming more complex. Cutts, he suspected, was merely a dead end. Draper could easily have borrowed the man's pen at some earlier date, it then falling from his pocket as he was dragged across the mud. Besides, the Cutts element appeared to be quite separate from the rest, while James Draper and Melanie Herrick might well link up. James Draper had not murdered his uncle, yet if he knew who had, then he would be likely to communicate with him after being visited by Krebs and himself. Not to do so would require extraordinary patience, a quality that seemed entirely lacking in James Draper.

The inheritance also tied in with the murderer's apparent desire to have the body of Charles Draper found. Having him merely disappear wouldn't be sufficient. He would have to be known to be dead for James Draper to gain promptly from his death. The case for James Draper's involvement was becoming increasingly strong.

Anderson tried to place himself in Draper's position. Assuming he knew about the murder, he would be expecting a visit from the police, and so would be primed to answer their questions. He had answered the questions as if reciting from a play, so that fitted the facts. Having got rid of the police without difficulty, and not having learnt of any complications, James Draper would surely be unable to resist passing the good news on to the theoretical accomplice. Would he do that in front of his girlfriend? Maybe, but much more likely not. James Draper was far from stupid and hardly likely to boast of his part in a murder to a girlfriend who might at some future time be an ex-girlfriend. His observations of the flat suggested that the girl didn't actually live there. So when she left he might be expected to try and communicate with someone. She had intended to come with him to identify his uncle, so he probably would not yet have had a chance to do so. If he did, then the itemisation for Draper's mobile phone might make worthwhile reading. Of course Draper might have considered such a possibility, in which case he would use a callbox. Anderson thought of the steep field that flanked Draper's block of flats. It was certainly worth a try.

Turning thought into action, Anderson got to his feet and strode from the room. There had been, he remembered, a large-scale map of the Plymouth area on the wall of the incident room, which should provide him with the information he needed. The room was empty except for DC Heath, hunched over a computer with a look of intense boredom on his face.

'Afternoon, sir,' Heath greeted him as he pushed open the door.

'Anything?' Anderson inquired casually.

Heath blew his cheeks out and settled back in his chair, stretching his long arms out above his head before replying.

'Plenty of Cuttses,' he replied, 'only one of them called Nathan so far, a builder in Lydford done for receiving in eighty-six. How about James Draper?'

'An unpleasant little man,' Anderson replied, 'but with a

perfect alibi. He was under arrest in the Devonport station when the murder took place. A fact that it would have been nice to have been aware of, even though he was released without charge.'

'Oh,' Heath replied, 'I'm afraid communication between us and Devonport's not that good.'

Anderson replied with a non-committal grunt and went to study the map. Following the lie of the land east from Crownhill, he managed to pick out the Leighdon Estate and the ridge opposite it. As he had hoped, a narrow track ran along the crest, leading to an area marked as allotments.

FIVE
Friday Evening

Anna Ferreira shrugged her white lab coat off her shoulders and stretched up to hang it on the peg. Glancing at her watch, she saw that it was still fifteen minutes shy of six o'clock. John Anderson should still be at the police station, with any luck, and although they had made no definite arrangement, she was sure that he would be more than happy to see her. The idea of carrying on their relationship as they had left it on the previous afternoon thrilled her. Dinner, followed by a long, sleepless night in either her flat or his room would make up for a long day thinking about their wonderful lovemaking while trying to concentrate on her work.

On the way out of the building she made a brief stop in the washroom. Her reflection showed a petite, curvy girl in smart, tight jeans and a bright red sweater. Pretty, yes, definitely pretty, she thought without a trace of self-doubt. Possibly she could do something with her hair, but a long plait had been practical for work and to let it out would just result in a mess, with no time to arrange anything more complex in case she missed John at the station. For a moment she considered playing coy or even being aloof, letting him do the running, then dismissed the idea as childish. A man of John's maturity and intellect could be approached frankly, as frankly as she had given in to him the day after they met. A delicious shiver passed through her as she remembered what they had done. Actually, she admitted to herself, 'given in to him' wasn't really fair: 'flaunted herself for him' would be more accurate, a description that produced an exquisitely rude thrill.

She left the building, noticing that Dr Wells's big old Rover was still in the car park. Wells, she knew, would be going out to dinner with Violet Krebs, the red-haired policewoman who had been on the flats where Charles Draper had been found. She wished Wells success, hoping that a new relationship would finally put an end to his pique at her own refusal of a second date. He was nice enough at heart, she decided, although he could be formidable and was something of a martinet when it came to precision at work. In fact she had nearly roused his ire earlier in the day, testing the ink in the pen she had found in the chromatograph without his permission and only just managing to hide the fact when he had re-entered the room.

The police station was a short walk away, the car park clearly visible from the road. To her disappointment there was no sign of John's silver BMW, but she determined not to give up so easily and made for the double glass doors that opened into reception. The desk sergeant recognised her and directed her up to the incident room, which contained only a bored-looking young man scanning a lengthy computer printout.

'May I help?' he asked.

'I was looking for John Anderson,' she answered, immediately feeling embarrassed.

'He went off at lunch time,' the man replied. 'You're Anna, the new pathologist, aren't you? I'm David Heath.'

'Hi,' Anna replied shyly, immediately remembering that it

was Heath who Dr Wells had mentioned as having said she had been bottomless in the river. A heavy blush rose to her cheeks. 'Do you know where he is?'

'Maybe,' Heath answered. 'He said something about checking on James Draper. He was looking at the map. I think he was going up to the allotments across from Draper's estate, but that was hours ago. I don't suppose he'll be there now.'

'Thank you,' Anna replied and quickly left.

Anna felt a weight of disappointment settle on her as she left the station. Not that it was rational, she told herself. After all, there was no particular reason why John should have been at the station. She considered her options, feeling suddenly lost. Carrying on with her normal routine of taking the bus back to her flat and cooking supper would be completely unsatisfactory. Could she seek John out? Impossible, unless she went back up to see David Heath and found out where Draper's flat was, and she couldn't face the idea. Even if she did, it would probably only lead to a useless trek around the suburbs of Plymouth. In all probability he had gone back to his hotel, the address of which she did not know.

Just as she was turning resignedly towards the bus stop, she noticed a familiar car pull up. It was Dr Wells, apparently indifferent to the white zigzag that prohibited parking and the fact that he was directly outside the police station. He was talking on his car phone, which he replaced as he saw her.

'Looking for someone, Anna?' he hailed her in a tone of mock innocence.

'I was –' Anna began.

'Hoping to find the wonderful Detective Chief Inspector Anderson?' Wells interrupted her.

'Yes,' Anna admitted, 'but he's not around. Are you here to pick Violet Krebs up?'

'Not in the least,' Wells replied. 'Unlike certain young ladies one could mention, Violet prefers to change before going

72

out for the evening. I, given that it would be pointless to spend the next two hours driving home to Peter Tavy and back, intend to drive down to the Hoe and take an invigorating walk.'

'But it's nearly dark,' Anna protested, ignoring Wells's dig at her casual dress sense.

'Ha! You have no romance in your soul.' Wells answered. 'What better than a walk on the front before a date with a beautiful girl? The sound of the sea, the calls of the gulls, the distant lights across Plymouth sound –'

'More like the sound of super strength lager cans being opened,' Anna interrupted him and immediately regretted it, feeling that she might have overstepped the mark.

Wells ignored her riposte, instead turning the key in the ignition so that the Rover's engine roared back to life before he spoke again.

'I shall be off then. I'm sorry that I am unable to enlighten you as to the whereabouts of your beau, but that's old man Walsh over there, he should know – after all, he's a Detective Superintendent.'

Anna turned to look back towards the police station as Wells pulled away from the curb. Walsh was walking towards her in his characteristically brisk manner.

'Excuse me,' she said as he drew towards her, 'could you tell me where DCI Anderson is staying?'

'John Anderson?' Walsh replied. 'Yes, certainly. The Royal, in Basket Ope, down by the old harbour. Do you know it?'

Anna shook her head.

'It's more or less on my way, I'll drop you off.'

Gratefully accepting the lift, she climbed into Walsh's car and was soon being dropped off in the tangle of tiny alleys that had once been the principal part of Plymouth. Locating Basket Ope, she found the Royal to be a timbered structure combining a restaurant and rooms. The receptionist told her that John hadn't been back all day and that she had no idea of his whereabouts.

Anna sighed and walked wearily into the bar area, ordering a vodka and lime and taking it to a corner. For ten minutes she sat sipping her drink, then finally decided to call it a day and return to her flat. As she approached the door it opened and John Anderson stepped in.

'Hi, John,' she greeted him, suddenly feeling silly for having made such an effort to seek him out.

He looked up, his expression at first one of annoyance and then fading to a smile. He had been unfastening the belt on an olive green trenchcoat which he wore over a suit of fine wool in a muted pale green, a different suit, Anna noted, to the one he had been wearing the previous day. He finished unfastening the belt and then looked back up at her.

'I'm rather busy, I'm afraid, Anna,' he remarked. 'Assuming, that is, that you were coming round to see me?'

'Yes I was,' Anna faltered. 'I'm sorry, I just thought –'

'Believe me,' Anderson replied, 'there's nothing I'd rather do than spend the evening with you. In fact, if you don't mind spending several hours sitting in a freezing cold car, you are very welcome to join me.'

'OK,' Anna answered, taking a spur of the moment decision. 'What are you doing?'

'Keeping an eye on a certain James Draper,' Anderson replied. 'Informally, of course, which is why I can invite you along.'

'James Draper? A suspect?'

'Charles Draper's nephew. DI Krebs and I interviewed him this morning. His alibi is absolutely watertight but the facts suggest that he is not as innocent as he appears to be. At present he is in his flat, eating a take-away curry with his girlfriend. I decided that it would give me long enough to nip back here and spruce myself up a little.'

'What do you expect him to do?'

'I expect him to telephone somebody as soon as his girlfriend leaves, assuming that she does. Unfortunately he may have already made his call, as he went for the curry on his own and I couldn't keep him in sight. Still, I intend to keep an eye on him for a while yet. Are you sure you want to come?'

'Fine,' Anna replied. 'After all, it's Saturday tomorrow. I'm hungry, though – what food do they do here?'

'I'm not sure, some good bread and ham or cheese perhaps. The food here is excellent, but it's not really designed to take out.'

They eventually managed to secure crusty rolls filled with ham and a bar of dark chocolate. Anna waited in the bar while Anderson went up to his room, returning in yet another suit, this time of a heavier wool in a rich, dark blue. A brief walk to Anderson's car and a fifteen-minute drive through thinning evening traffic and they had returned to the vantage point from which Anderson had been watching Draper's house. Anna leaned across the front seat, putting her arm over Anderson's shoulder.

'Which flat is it?' she asked. The idea of looking into the flat without the occupant's knowledge delighted her. It was not perhaps as good as a night spent in bed with John, but at least she was alone with him and who knew what the evening might bring.

'Tenth floor, the curtainless window above the flat with the maroon curtains,' he replied, retrieving a pair of binoculars from the back seat. 'They've finished eating, he's drinking from a large, green bottle, cider probably.'

Anna followed his instructions, quickly locating Draper's window. From their angle she was looking into the room from a few degrees above the horizontal, allowing a clear view of most of the room. Distance made detail indistinct, but it was possible to make out two figures, each slumped in an armchair.

'Try the binoculars,' John offered, 'but tell me immediately if Draper uses his phone.'

Anna took the instrument from Anderson and leant further forward, acutely conscious of her body pressed against his. The window swam into focus, Draper now distinct, a slight man a bit older than her, hair shaved at the sides and cropped close on top. His face was angular with loose features, perhaps a touch harsh. Blue jeans and a white T-shirt were all he wore, the jeans scuffed and threadbare in places. As she watched, he passed the cider bottle across, a slim white arm reaching out to take it.

Turning her attention to the girl, Anna found herself looking at someone of her own age, maybe even younger. A combination of dyed orange blonde hair, a short tight skirt in some shiny, bright red material and a plain, black top created a cheap impression. The girl was what her mother would call a tramp, the implication being that that style of dress implied loose sexual behaviour. A flicker of movement caught her attention. A door had opened, presumably the door to the main passage.

'Something's happening,' she said, quickly passing the binoculars to John Anderson.

Anderson took the binoculars from her and watched, saying nothing. Anna sat back, not wanting to intrude if what was happening was of any importance.

'He has visitors,' John commented. 'I fear we are in for a long stay. Here, you watch, I'll get some food together. Go round to the back seat so that you don't have to lean over me every time you want to look.'

Anna obeyed, feeling a twinge of disappointment that he didn't want body contact with her. He opened the driver's door, unwrapping the rolls very carefully to avoid any crumbs falling inside the car, apparently indifferent to the chill night air. She made herself comfortable on the broad back seat and once more turned to studying Draper's window.

'I'm really only interested in him making a call,' Anderson

told her. 'Here, have a ham roll, but lean out of the window while you eat it.'

With some difficulty she managed to position herself so that she could watch, eat the roll and keep him happy about the BMW's interior simultaneously. The night was cold, but not unbearably so, with no wind to speak of and a high layer of cloud blotting out the sky.

She studied the newcomers, again experiencing the thrill of spying on them. They were two girls of a similar age to Draper's girlfriend, one smartly dressed in a black pencil skirt and white blouse, the dress of a secretary or receptionist, the other in jeans and a tight green top that showed the shape of her breasts. The smart one had long black hair, her friend dyed blonde curls. Anna watched as they produced cans of beer from a plastic bag and passed them around, then went to sit on the sofa so that they were largely lost to her view.

'Hell,' she heard Anderson mutter, 'they're going to be here all night.'

Anna had been enjoying herself and her spirits were dampened by John's attitude, which showed that as far as he was concerned, anything that was not directly germane to the case was of no interest. She watched him take a bite of roll, the handsome, slightly stern face creased in a frown that might have been annoyance or perhaps distaste. All the vibrancy he had shown before was gone, along with the charm and the carefully manipulative flattery that she had taken such pleasure in going along with. He was clearly not in a good mood, she decided, determined to make the best of the evening in any case but unable to suppress a pang of disillusionment.

For well over an hour they sat watching Draper and his friends talk and drink, finishing the beer and cider and going on to vodka, drunk neat from the bottle. She and John talked quietly. She discovered his interest in gardens and drew him out a little before he steered the conversation to literary tastes,

77

expounding his philosophy that an individual's books gave a deep insight into their character. Anna listened with interest, impressed by his ability to order the world around him as he saw fit, his remarks only occasionally hinting at a high proportion of self-education. They took turns with the binoculars, each taking stints of ten minutes while the other rested their eyes. Anna was watching when Draper got to his feet and walked unsteadily out of her field of vision, returning with a small oblong package.

'I think he might have some drugs,' she commented.

'Let me see,' Anderson responded, quickly taking the binoculars from Anna and scanning the face of the block of flats. 'Oh, yes, I wonder what that could be. He's opening it, it's something solid. Playing cards, damn.'

He passed the binoculars back to Anna and sat back as she once more adjusted her view. The group had slumped on to the floor, the two girls leaning against the sofa, Draper and his girlfriend stretched out on the floor, only partially visible. Anna's initial hope that they might either do something criminal or sexual, and thus provide some excitement, began to fade as time wore on, to be replaced by boredom. She would have liked to flirt with Anderson, possibly even have sex, but his manner made it very clear that this was not an option, and suggesting it would clearly only lead to a rebuff.

Finally the group broke up, the girls rising and kissing Draper and then his girlfriend with light, friendly pecks. When the girlfriend was saying goodbye to the blonde girl, Anna noticed Draper give the dark-haired girl's bottom a squeeze as she bent to pick up a shiny handbag. Draper then went over to the door, turning the handle down and opening it a fraction.

'They're going,' she told Anderson.

'I see. Pass me the binoculars,' he replied. 'Thank you.'

Anna watched as Draper and the two girls left the flat, Draper's girlfriend going out of her field of vision.

'Look, on the stairwell,' Anderson instructed.

Three figures could be made out in the dull orange street light, descending the stairwell, briefly hidden and then emerging on to the area of grass that separated the flats. They walked slowly, disappearing behind another block. Some minutes later, Draper reappeared, now alone, walking fast and then breaking into a slow jog. It was immediately obvious that he wasn't aiming for Gaitskell House.

'I think he's heading for the phone box on the road,' Anderson said, once more full of life. 'Come on, but keep behind me.'

Despite her annoyance at his instant assumption that she would do as she was told, Anna followed, leaving the car and jumping the low earth barrier that ran beside the track. Anderson moved fast, dodging between the clumps of bramble that studded the steep field. Anna came behind more cautiously, scared that she might lose her footing in the feeble orange-brown light. Ahead of her Anderson had reached the black shadows of a thick hedge, stopping and vanishing in the gloom. She followed, sinking down beside him in a crouch. Draper was again visible, walking along the road towards the pale yellow light of a phone booth. He reached the box, paused, looked around and then went in.

Anna watched as Draper took a coin from his pocket and punched out a number. For a while he stood leaning against the edge of the phone booth, the receiver pressed to his ear, then he replaced it, only to dial again. Once more there appeared to be no answer, only this time Draper threw the receiver down, pressed at the coin return once, then again, before turning away and jogging back towards the estate.

'If that's an up-to-date phone box, he's just made a very stupid mistake,' Anderson remarked, speaking more to himself than to her.

The moment Draper disappeared from view Anderson rose and moved off down the slope towards the phone booth. Anna followed, her irritation with him pushed to the back of her mind in the excitement of the moment. Anderson reached the box ahead of her, hastily pushing a button. Anna saw a number appear on the LED screen.

'I've got him,' Anderson declared as he pulled a pen from his suit pocket and quickly scribbled down the number. 'Now let's see who's so clever, Mr Draper.'

Violet Krebs stretched and yawned, tensing her muscles in an effort to shake off the languor that the heat of the shower had brought on. The thick, soft bath towel in which she was wrapped tightened as her shoulder muscles flexed. It would be so easy to just let it slip off and crawl, naked, into her bed and drift into oblivion. The day had been long and frustrating. The combination of the calculated insolence of James Draper and DCI Anderson's self-confident, faintly patronising attitude had tested her ability to remain calm to the limit. Then there had been the afternoon – a series of house calls in the Calstock and Gunnislake area, made on the off chance that someone had information that might help with the case. Why, she asked herself, did so many people automatically switch on to the defensive when a police officer called? She had been polite, apologetic even, yet the great majority of people she had spoken to had given terse, uninformative replies, clearly wanting to get rid of her with the minimum of fuss. Dunning and Pentyre, moreover, had reported their findings directly to DSupt Walsh, a clear snub to her but nothing that put her in a position to complain. Not that there had been anything to report in any case. The entire population of both Devon and Cornish sides of the estuary seemed to have been asleep on the Monday. Every house within sight of the river from Thorn Point up to Gunnislake had been checked and nobody remembered a thing. A brisk work-out and the shower had lessened the head of aggression that had been building up all day, but she felt a smouldering resentment of most of humanity at a deeper level.

The evening at least looked promising. Morgan Wells appealed to her, both in terms of his extravagant personality and his powerful physique. More importantly, he was frank and open in his admiration for her, especially for the sleek muscularity that she went to so much effort to maintain. She walked to the wardrobe and opened it, considering her choice for the evening. Her kingfisher blue silk gown tempted but was rejected as too soft, too girlie. Intuition told her that Morgan would prefer a more refined look. Possibly the simple black velvet dress over stockings and high, black shoes, elegant, feminine, yet also comfortable.

Twenty minutes later she was admiring the effect in her full-length mirror. Her orange hair pulled up into an almost Edwardian style, the material clinging to the contours of her body – the effect certainly should be eye-catching. Possibly it was too daring, though. Station gossip being what it was, if anyone saw her, the lads would be making remarks until doomsday. On the other hand, why the hell should she dress to allay the criticisms of the likes of Dunning and Pentyre? Anyway, she could get Morgan to drive well out of town, which she wanted to do anyway.

As she was putting the final touches to her make-up the doorbell sounded, forcing her to forego the calming glass of wine she had intended to have before he arrived.

'Coming!' she called as the bell sounded again. She reached the door and opened it, revealing Dr Wells standing outside.

'Violet, good evening. Good heavens! You look divine!'

'Hi,' she managed, suddenly far from sure of herself.

'Ravishing, brilliant!' he enthused. 'I am honoured.'

'Thank you,' Violet answered. 'Come in. A glass of wine?'

'With pleasure, thank you.'

Violet closed the door and ushered Wells into the living room before pouring glasses of Shiraz and settling herself opposite him.

'How are things going with the unfortunate Mr Draper?'

he asked, sipping the rich, red wine carefully before placing the drink on the glass-topped table in front of him.

'Slowly,' Violet admitted. 'We interviewed his nephew James this morning. You probably remember him. The one who was selling icing sugar as cocaine a couple of years ago.'

'I remember something of the sort, not him specifically though. There are so many such sordid little incidents,' he replied. 'I take it you're no nearer to a result then?'

'Not really. He has the perfect alibi, being in the cells at Devonport station all Monday afternoon. The visiting DCI from Guildford, John Anderson, thinks he knows something because he was so smug, but he acted exactly the same before, when he knew he was innocent.'

'Yes, I agree, he sounds a horrible little tyke.'

'One thing I meant to ask you – would you agree that the murderer must have at least some medical knowledge?'

'Hardly,' Wells laughed, 'a chemistry A Level and a bit of common sense would be more than adequate. Anything with this Cutts chap?'

'Nothing. We're giving the search a fairly high priority as the name has come up twice in the investigation. Nathan Cutts's are fairly rare, but even so a broad-spectrum search and eliminate is going to take some time.'

'Discover Cutts and I think you will have your man,' Wells answered. 'I trust they don't have you on the search though? Not the most thrilling of jobs, I imagine.'

'No, that's Heath's responsibility, but I'm not much better off, doing house to house along the upper reaches of the estuary. You'd think they were suspects from the reactions I get.'

'Ah, Cornish mining stock, an insular and suspicious breed. Have any of them admitted to seeing anything, though?'

'Nothing, but then Monday afternoon was pretty horrible and the light must have been fading by the time poor Draper was killed. I expect they were all either at work or slumped in front of the telly. Anyway, let's not talk shop. I've had quite enough police work for one day. Where shall we go? I was hoping you might feel like going out of town.'

'I'd be delighted. Let me see, we need somewhere refined, elegant and far from the cares of the city. Quite by chance I have booked a table at the Cornucopia. Will that do?'

'Well, yes, I mean it would be perfect. Isn't it terribly expensive, though?'

'For you, my dear, only the best. Anyway, I hate to rush you, but time presses and there's always a demand for tables whose reservees fail to put in an appearance.'

Wells swallowed his wine at a gulp and rose to his feet. Violet looked up at him, admiring the swell of his chest and his impressive height. She judged him to stand six foot three or maybe more. His age was hard to guess, probably nearer fifty than forty, but still firm if not slim, and powerful, very powerful. His rangy build and mop of tawny hair with only the slightest touch of grey added to the impression of mature, forceful masculinity. There was also something primitive, almost animal about him, for all his refinement and knowledge. He was like a stallion, proud and strong. No, more like a bear, contemptuous of lesser creatures. She wondered how it would feel to straddle him, gripping his body between her thighs, her vagina engulfing his penis –

'Right,' she agreed, hastily finishing her wine, 'who's going to drive?'

'I shall,' he replied without hesitation. 'That way I shall be able to make you outrageously drunk while myself sipping at a small glass of mineral water with the unassailable pretext of not drinking and driving, especially when dining with an officer of the force. Also, your car is beautiful, mine is both spacious and robust.'

'OK, that suits me. Let's go.'

They left Violet's flat and drove out through the suburbs of Plymouth, Wells pulling onto smaller roads at Yelverton.

'The picturesque route,' he explained, 'or perhaps atmospheric would be a more suitable term as it is night time. You don't mind dining in this part of the county, I trust, the haunted feeling of the murderer's presence and all that?'

Violet reassured him. While it was true that she was sensitive to the atmosphere of a place, she had long determined not to let it affect her. The deep lanes through which they were driving, with the lights of Morgan's old Rover cutting a bright slash between banks and hedges, did give her a cold, gloomy feeling, and knowing that Charles Draper and his murderer could well have driven through these same lanes added to it. She shrugged the feeling off, only to have it return more forcibly as the car entered a wood, the headlights now illuminating tangled, leafless thickets and the stark, twisted trunks of windblown trees. She wondered how the murderer would have felt, driving to meet Draper, knowing what he was going to do. Of course it depended on his character, but she could easily imagine the bleak loneliness of the woods and lanes on a dim afternoon making it easy for the mind to slip away from sane, ordinary things. They crossed a narrow, grey stone bridge, the lights briefly illuminating a tumble of water, grey and white, broken by humps and ledges of black slate.

'Denham Bridge,' Wells was saying. 'It's beautiful in summer. You can walk from here all the way down to the top of the Tavy estuary.'

Violet gave a non-committal reply. The morose, unearthly atmosphere of the place obviously completely failed to reach him. Or more likely, she reflected, it simply didn't produce the same feelings in him. Places had always affected her mood strongly, intangible factors combining to create a distinct feeling. She had always been considered over-imaginative as a child, and now strove not to allow such feelings to influence her work, instead using the clear, precise logic of facts that Detective Superintendent Walsh was so keen on. Data and inference, that was what mattered, mood and intuition being relegated to an occasional tool, and not one the use of which she ever admitted to her colleagues.

Her mood broke as they climbed out of the woods and turned onto the main road as it emerged from Bere Alston. A grass verge, cat's-eyes and the central white line created an image that wouldn't allow for brooding introspection. Actually, she considered, chuckling to herself, it was far more likely that the murderer had driven this way. Why, after all, take the back lanes where meeting another car meant stopping and backing up or waiting for someone else to do so, thus destroying the anonymity of speed.

'You're speeding,' she chided Morgan jokingly as the needle of the speedometer touch eighty.

'Oh dear,' he replied, 'I'm terribly sorry, officer, I hadn't noticed.'

'Be careful, actually,' she continued more seriously. 'When I was in uniform we used to speed trap here sometimes. In fact, I wonder if they had one set up on Monday; it's worth asking.'

'You feel that a local beat-pounder will remember the passing of a blue Sierra Sapphire, recognise Draper and be able to describe who else was in the car with him? My dear, you magnify the skills of your colleagues out of all proportion to the reality.'

'Perhaps,' Violet replied, 'especially as we're assuming that the murderer came in another car, met Draper, killed him and then drove away.'

'Yes,' he answered, 'you are probably right. Anyway, we have arrived; let us give our full attention to feasting. Have you been here before?'

'No, never,' Violet admitted. 'It was too expensive when I was a WPC in Tavistock. I always thought of it as a place where terribly rich, important people went.'

Wells laughed and opened the door for her. He was greeted

by name and his coat taken by the doorman, who then turned to Violet.

'May I take your coat, madam?' the doorman asked, his tone carefully balanced between servility and hauteur.

She handed him the coat, feeling somewhat self-conscious. The decor of the restaurant was a simple but elegant combination of dark wood and white, relieved by a few modern landscapes, tasteful arrangements of flowers and the silver and crystal of the place settings. The Cornucopia had a reputation as the finest restaurant in the district, and certainly looked the part, making Violet feel privileged that Morgan had chosen it. The diners, on the other hand, impressed her less. Loud, ostentatious businessmen, well-to-do retired couples, the richer type of tourist – all they really had in common was money, with very little of the flair that set people like Morgan aside from the ordinary.

They were shown to a table in an alcove, largely hidden from view by delicate screens of carved wood. Menus, large and bound in deep green leather, were handed to them. It seemed ridiculous, Violet considered, that Morgan had gone to so much trouble merely to wine and dine her and then return her home. He undoubtedly hoped for more, but how would he play it? Morgan was not the type to wheedle and plead. Perhaps he would be urgent, fiery, protesting his love for her, hoping to overwhelm her resistance by sheer passion. Or maybe calm, humorous and affectionate, soothing her and relaxing her until she was ready for bed. In practice, though, the real control was hers. She could respond or not, play coy, tease or flirt openly. She decided that the experienced, sultry approach would be most to her liking. Also, she was dressed for it.

She turned her attention to the menu, which offered an extensive choice of dishes, mostly classics dressed in some distinctive manner, but with one or two exotic exceptions. Heavy dishes were best avoided, she decided, if there was a chance that the later part of the evening would get physical. A salad flavoured with herbs and then lemon sole seemed the best choice. She glanced across at her companion, who was completely absorbed in the menu.

A waiter approached, his timing perfect as Morgan lowered the menu and shot her an enquiring glance. They ordered, Morgan choosing a dish of wild fungi in pastry and wild boar, and the waiter left, to be quickly replaced by a tall, austere man, evidently the wine waiter.

'Good evening, Dr Wells, madam,' the man greeted them.

'And the same to you, Max,' Wells replied, taking the wine list and scanning it thoughtfully. 'I must be somewhat abstemious this evening, a half of Pommard will have to suffice. Violet?'

Violet took the list and studied it, determined neither to vacillate nor to make an eccentric choice. Most of the wines were unfamiliar, her own taste running to rich Australian and Chilean reds. Something John Anderson had said that morning came back to her.

'Do you have a Fourchaume?' she asked lightly.

The wine waiter paused, apparently desperately searching his memory. He clearly had no more idea of what she was talking about than she did herself. Finally he answered, 'I'm sorry madam, we have none in stock. May I recommend the Pouilly Fuissé?'

Violet accepted, noting the mischievous smile that briefly curved up the edges of Morgan's mouth. She smiled back, their eyes locking in a moment of intimacy. It was gone as suddenly as it had come, yet she knew that it could be retrieved and that there was plenty of time and no need to rush.

As the meal progressed they talked animatedly, sometimes disagreeing but more often finding shared ideas and opinions. Violet relaxed more and more, pouring from the full bottle of white Burgundy that had been served to her when she felt the need, her mood becoming ever more alive and flirtatious. She found herself increasingly admiring the combination of ease and self-control in his character. The depths of his experience and personality seemed without limit, leaving her with the feeling that despite his openness she was only seeing the upper layer of his character. This sense of hidden depth intrigued her, at once posing a challenge and adding to his aura of masculine strength.

By the time they reached the end of the main course, Violet felt completely at ease, sitting back comfortably in her chair, sipping wine while he described his impressions of drifting through central France in the early seventies. He had pushed his chair back, and was sitting in an attitude of absolute ease, one leg thrown across the other. Violet felt her eyes straying to the way this posture accentuated the bulge in his crotch, trying not to make her attention too obvious while wondering if the way her dress hugged the shape of her breasts was stirring similar feelings in him.

'– after the storm I took a souvenir,' he was saying. 'A good-sized tree had landed on the roof of one of the churches in Vezélay, you know, where the first crusade started from. I took the head of a gargoyle from the wreckage and managed to lug the damn thing across France and get it through customs. I've mounted it on the gatepost at home, you can see it later if you like.'

'Come back and see my etchings,' Violet thought, only delivered in Morgan's delightfully irreverent fashion. Now was her chance to back out gracefully, clearly given to avoid embarrassment later on.

'I'd love to,' she answered, the comment only a brief insertion into the flow of his story but creating an instant understanding. She immediately felt a familiar ache between her legs and a slight lump in her throat. It had been ages since she had had sex, and longer since she'd been treated with such a combination of courtesy and generosity beforehand.

She found herself moistening suddenly dry lips with the tip of her tongue, a gesture that was not lost on Morgan, who shifted his posture as his hand went briefly to his throat.

Violet accepted his suggestion of dessert and a glass of Armagnac, spinning out the delicious feeling of anticipation that was building in her. Morgan declined to join her, sipping coffee instead. The brandy made her head spin slightly after the wine, and when they left she found that she had to take care to place her feet correctly, the combination of high heels and her pleasant degree of intoxication making her careful. As they left, she could sense the gaze of the doorman on her legs and bottom, his eyes betraying a jealous glint for all his efforts at impassivity. His imagination was clearly speculating on what she and Morgan might be doing later, an idea that fuelled her excitement.

They climbed into the Rover, the ample front seat allowing her to stretch out her legs in a way that few modern cars permitted. Morgan started the engine, producing the same satisfying roar of power that her own car gave, so different to the high-tech purr of up-to-date engineering. That was Morgan all through, she felt, raw, effortless power. He turned out of the car park and set his course to the east, towards Tavistock and ultimately Peter Tavy where he lived. She knew he didn't need to ask now and would have been surprised if he had.

The road dipped and curved into a valley, the night absolutely black outside the glow of the headlights. In the dark of the car, Violet let a hand stray to her left breast, finding the velvet pushed into a little bump by the hardness of her nipple. She stroked the nipple gently through her dress, feeling a shiver of pleasure in response.

They passed through Tavistock, Violet feeling a pang of nostalgia at the familiar places where she had spent the first years of her time with the police. Peter Tavy itself she knew only faintly as a cluster of granite houses on the very edge of

Dartmoor, shadowed by the great bulk of White Tor. In her four years in the area she had never once been called out to the tiny village. Morgan crossed the bridge over the old railway and pulled off the main road, steering through lanes for a minute before pulling up in front of a cottage directly under the black loom of the moors.

As Violet got out she found herself shaking. Half of it was nerves, half excitement at the prospect of sex after such a long gap without a lover. Morgan turned his key and pushed open the door, apparently as calm as if coming home after a normal day. As he stepped inside, the hall light came on, the sudden brightness hurting her eyes. He opened another door and went in. She followed him, walking straight into a big square room still at ground level. The light from the hall illuminated a large bed set between four iron posts.

Violet felt a lump in her throat, unsure of what to do. He turned to her, taking the decision out of her hands as he took her gently by the arms and drew her towards him. She raised her head, his mouth meeting hers in a long kiss, her last doubt fading away as one of his massive arms encircled her back, the other sliding down, his hand stroking a path down her flank and on to her hip before cupping one cheek of her bottom in his hand. He sank backwards, pulling her with him until he was seated on the bed and she was straddled across his lap, her dress rucked up as her legs parted around him, his hand now stroking the naked flesh of her bottom.

She shivered against him, feeling like a toy in his hands, knowing that if he wanted to he could simply roll her on to her back and fuck her on the edge of the bed without bothering with preliminaries. She wanted something slower, though, taking her pleasure in his massive, heavily muscled body at her own pace. His fingers had moved into her panties, stroking down her crease and lifting her easily to slide underneath her bottom and on to her pussy. The movement pressed her pubic mound against his crotch, the rigid bulk of his constrained penis taut against her.

The fingers working against her vulva were starting to make her lose control, making her want to come like that, riding his lap. This wasn't what she wanted. Being held like a doll and brought off against his hand would be too passive, too quick. She steeled herself, fighting back her need for a quick orgasm, taking his jacket by the lapels and pulling it down his back so that his arms went behind him. He went with her movements, letting her push him backwards on to the bed, arms trapped behind his back, great chest straining out the front of his shirt. Violet sighed and steadied herself on top of him, her fingers working down the buttons of his shirt until it came open, revealing the heavy muscles of his chest, lightly grown with hair and utterly masculine. His fly button came next, popping open, the zip gilding down over the bulge of his penis. She pulled open the front of his pants, releasing the great swollen cock into her hand, the other making a good handful of his balls.

She began to stoke his penis, her hand encircling the shaft as his erection grew to full size, not exceptionally long, but wonderfully thick, heavy veins giving the surface a gnarled, irregular texture. She wanted to suck it very badly, but realised at the same time that kneeling on the floor to take him in her mouth would spoil her poise, making her his servant instead of the other way around. Still, feeling the solidity of his erection in her mouth was not something she intended to go without.

Violet dismounted, motioning Morgan to stay as he was as she stepped into the shaft of light coming from the hall. Locking her eyes with his, she slowly peeled her dress up over her hips and then her breasts. He lay still, his cock standing proud from his body, his eyes following her every move as she cupped her breasts in her hands and unsnipped the front catch, letting the two full mounds of flesh fall into her palms as her fingers stroked her nipples up to full prominence.

'Turn around,' he begged, his voice hoarse with wanting.

Violet laughed and turned, knowing exactly what he wanted. Well, if he was fascinated with her bottom, then he was about to get as much or even more than he bargained for. She turned to look over her shoulder, taking hold of the waistband of her knickers and sticking her bottom out to slide them slowly down. Morgan looked as if he was about to burst as the scrap of black lace came down to bare her bottom, falling to her ankles to be kicked off. Violet turned towards him again, now nude but for her stockings, suspender belt and heels, stretching her body luxuriously and then walking back to the bed.

'Did you like that?' she asked as her hand folded around his cock.

Morgan nodded and then gasped as she gave his penis a few rapid tugs, then swung her knee up on to the bed and straddled again, only this time with her bottom towards his face. She sat across his chest, most of her weight directly on his arms, which he accepted without protest. His cock reared in front of her, the meaty head so swollen that the skin was a glossy reddish pink. She took it in her hand and stroked it gently, savouring her ability to put it in her mouth when she wanted. Morgan tensed as her fingernails drew four slow lines along the length of his shaft, then shuddered beneath her as she dipped forward and crammed her mouth with cock, scooping his balls into one hand and taking him in as far as possible so that her whole mouth was filled, the tip pushed up against the back of her throat. She savoured the salty, meaty taste of excited male, squirming her tongue and cheeks around his shaft while she lifted her bottom to improve his view of her sex, relishing the feeling of him not being able to get at her.

Worried that he'd come in her mouth and finish too early, Violet drew back slowly from his penis, giving it a last kiss on the very tip before sitting back, now riding on his chest. She stretched, pulling her back in and lifting her bottom to present it to him, then looking down over her shoulder and smiling at him. It was time for her orgasm now, and she was going to get it from his tongue.

'Yes please,' he groaned as he realised her intention.

Violet breathed in deeply. She had always wanted to do this to a man, and now she was going to. She knelt up further, knowing that her naked bottom would be inches in front of his face, then she eased herself back and sat down, very deliberately, on his face, the cheeks of her bottom spread full over him, her pussy positioned directly over his mouth.

'Now lick,' she demanded. His tongue immediately beginning to lap at her. She sighed, her poise beginning to dissolve as her pleasure built. Her hands went to her breasts, leaving most of her weight directly on his face. The sensation was utter bliss, a full breast cupped in either hand, her naked bottom spread across his face, his tongue flicking at her clit, stopping to probe her vagina and then going back only faster than before. She knew it wouldn't be long until she came. Her nipples were hard between her fingers as she squirmed her bottom, the sensitive skin between her cheeks pressed hard against his face, her clitoris rubbing on his tongue. Her breath was coming fast and hard. A spasm shot through the muscles of her vagina, her back was arched, her nipples locked between her fingers, her bottom and vulva a mass of fire as she came, gritting her teeth in an ecstasy that seemed to go on for ever.

It finally stopped, Violet's body shivering with the after-effects. All she wanted to do was dismount and cuddle up to him, resting her head on the comforting strength of his chest. It wouldn't be fair, though, not with his cock standing up like a flagpole in front of her. Her hair had come loose and she was dripping sweat, her vagina too sensitive to bear another touch. She waited a long moment, letting the heat ebb out of her pussy as she regained her breath, then moved, preparing to swivel round and mount him, hoping that he would fuck her hard and fast, coming before too long.

'Other way,' he gasped. 'There's a condom in my pocket.' Violet understood and swung her legs back, patiently retrieving the condom from his jacket and peeling it onto his penis. So he wanted to see her bottom and back, well, fair enough. Her hand closed on his cock, a few careful strokes returning it to full erection. She lifted herself, placing the swollen tip against her vagina and sliding down on to it, impaling herself in just the way she had imagined at the beginning of the evening. He immediately began to thrust, bouncing her as if she were a doll. Violet stayed still, letting him do the work so that he could get his pace right for orgasm. His hands clutched her bottom, pulling her cheeks open. She shivered, despite her recent orgasm, realising that his eyes would be on her sex, with no detail hidden. For a while she rode steadily, her body bouncing to the rhythm of his thrusts, his breathing becoming gradually faster and deeper. Then his hands gripped hard on to her bottom cheeks and his strokes became faster, harder, then frantic, abruptly stopping, the last thrust driving his shaft to the hilt inside her.

'Violet!' he cried softly as he came. 'Oh, Violet.'

He relaxed and she lifted herself off him, turning and collapsing gratefully by his side, her head nestled into the crook of his arm. For a long moment they lay together in silence, then she felt him move and raised her head to let him rise. He walked into the kitchen.

'Would you like a beer?' he called out, once more his usual calm, easy self. 'Or I have some orange juice.'

Violet asked for orange juice and sat up on the bed, kicking her shoes free and peeling off her stockings before climbing under the covers and propping herself against the bed-head. He came back into the room and handed her the orange juice, the glass cold between her bare breasts as she relaxed, fully satisfied.

SIX
Saturday

Robert Walsh tapped his pencil irritably on DS Dunning's report. Every house on both banks of the Tamar estuary from Thorn Point to Calstock had been visited and a good many in Gunnislake and other less probable areas. No useful information whatsoever had come up. There was the normal scattering of supposedly suspicious men seen in woods, a couple of trespassers on farms and plenty of people who 'thought they might have seen a blue car on Monday afternoon but couldn't be sure where, when or what the make was'. None of it had any obvious bearing on the case, though. To make matters worse, there was a minimum of forensic evidence, Wells's report being no more informative than Dunning's.

On the positive side DC Heath was on his way to Lydford to interview Nathan Cutts, the builder and receiver of stolen goods, and the fact that the woman in Guildford was probably lying looked promising. What was her name? Melanie Herrick.

A sharp knock sounded at the door.

'Come in,' Walsh called, the door opening to admit Violet Krebs.

'This is my report from yesterday afternoon, sir,' she said, laying a single piece of paper on the table. 'There's not much of it, I'm afraid. I'd like to run a theory by you, though.'

'Fire away,' Walsh replied.

'OK,' she began, 'first the facts. Charles Draper's body was found at Thorn Point, his car near Hewton. He died at around 3 p.m. on Monday, drowning in brackish water after being sedated. Therefore we assume that he was drowned in the estuary near Hewton at 3 p.m..'

Walsh nodded. Krebs was about to continue when another rap sounded at the door.

'Yes,' Walsh called out. John Anderson came in, glancing from Walsh to Krebs.

'Are you busy?' he asked.

'Come in, John,' Walsh answered. 'Violet is explaining a new idea. Is it something important?'

'It can wait a few minutes,' Anderson replied as he took a chair to the side of the room.

'OK,' Krebs continued, 'we're assuming he was drowned near Hewton at 3 p.m. Against this we have the facts that there is minimal forensic evidence, no witnesses at all and at that point the tide was halfway out. We know it is possible to reach the water at half-tide, though, and it's a lonely area, so the absence of witnesses isn't that surprising.'

'I've been considering this,' Anderson broke in. 'I actually think that the absence of witnesses and forensic evidence constitutes important information in itself.'

'Exactly my theory,' Krebs continued, throwing a glare at Anderson. 'In fact I think that Draper could have been drowned in another body of brackish water and been brought to the quay near Hewton later in a deliberate attempt to make us misinterpret the times. The one problem is that Morgan Wells says that Draper's body was in the water for a good part of the time from his death to when we found it.'

'That is hardly likely,' Anderson interjected. 'It would mean that the murderer had to carry Draper's body down the steep track to the quay. Why would he do that? No, my idea is that Draper was actually drowned at Thorn Point and that his body remained caught in the small bay between the salt marshes and the shale ridge off the point. Nobody lives within a quarter of a mile and as it was raining nobody found him until the Tuesday morning. His car would then have been dropped near Hewton later. That covers all the facts and implies a carefully conceived attempt at staging an accidental drowning and throwing us off the scent. Violet's theory, on the other hand, assumes that the murderer left the body at the quay to be taken out on the tide and risk it just drifting out to sea and not being found. That would have meant that Draper only became listed as a missing person, while it seems likely that for some reason the murderer intended the body to be found. Now, we know the murderer is methodical and careful, so why would he take such a risk? Also, my theory covers Dr Wells's observation, as the body would have been in the small bay.'

'Excellent,' Walsh commented. John Anderson was proving a valuable asset, he considered, and it was unfortunate that he was only there temporarily. He felt a keen shortage of good officers. Violet Krebs had intelligence and enthusiasm but lacked experience, Heath even more so, while both Dunning and Pentyre had reached the highest rank for their competence.

'What about the pen?' Krebs asked.

'There are a variety of options,' Anderson answered. 'Firstly, it might be coincidence, and irrelevant, but I consider that a low probability. Secondly, it could be a deliberately left clue, designed to enhance the thrill for the murderer because it constitutes a risk. Given the rest of the MO, I consider this a very low probability. Thirdly, it could be genuine, having been dropped by the murderer when he was planning things out, which must represent a fair chance. Lastly, it could be a complex decoy, which I see as the second most likely option. We really need more facts.'

'Right,' Walsh continued, 'very neat thinking, John. Violet, you could take a hint or two from John's scientific method. Your theory is possible in that it covers all the known facts, but John's also takes into account considerations of highest probability. Do you see?'

'Yes, sir,' Krebs replied quietly. 'May I tell you my conclusion?'

'Go ahead,' Walsh answered, detecting the pique in her tone. Krebs's main fault as an officer was a lack of respect for her seniors, making her tend to ignore advice.

'Whichever theory we take, the murderer has clearly planned this very well,' Krebs said, then turned to Anderson. 'You said at the briefing that Melanie Herrick was probably lying in some way?'

'Yes,' Anderson replied, 'I spoke to DS Blackheath earlier, she'll be interviewing Herrick again today.'

'Then I suggest that Herrick paid someone to kill Draper and that she also agreed to confuse the timing to provide him with an alibi.'

Krebs sat back, waiting, her eyes focused on Walsh and not Anderson. Walsh weighed her idea in his mind. It fitted but was far from complete, yet it did provide a solid line of enquiry to be followed up, unfortunately in Guildford rather than Plymouth.

'John?' he asked.

'My own conclusion is similar but less simple,' Anderson replied. 'James Draper is also involved, and he's deliberately playing us for fools. You know I thought that there was a good chance of him calling any accomplice he might have after we interviewed him yesterday and that he would neither use his mobile nor do it with his girlfriend there. Well, he tried to make a phone call from a box last night, dialled twice and then left the phone off the hook. I got there in time to press redial and this is the number that came up on the screen.'

Anderson tossed a piece of paper onto Walsh's desk. Walsh took it and read the number, a local number. It was familiar.

'Devonport station's drugs hotline,' Anderson told him. 'He's taunting us deliberately. There's also his alibi, which is far too convenient. He has to be involved. I recommend that you put him under full-time surveillance.'

'I disagree,' Krebs broke in. 'James Draper would take any opportunity to play practical jokes on us. He probably saw DCI Anderson last night and decided to give him something to think about.'

'I'm certain he didn't see me –' Anderson began.

'John, please,' Walsh said. 'You may be right, but I have to think of manpower allocation here. DI Statham at Plympton has requested help with some sort of raid this evening and I've agreed to let him have Dunning and Pentyre. I need Heath on the computer and phones. Violet, you should be finishing off the questioning, or taking a new tack as you both seem to think we've been wasting our time. John, I'd imagine your time better spent chasing up your theory, but if you insist on watching Draper, then it's up to you.'

Walsh sat back in his chair, waiting for Anderson to reply. The DCI was certainly a good officer, but Graham Parrish had been right about him not being a good team player, preferring to work alone while other people followed his instructions. Seeing that neither Anderson nor Krebs had anything further to say, he made a gesture to indicate that the discussion was over.

Joanna Blackheath left the station at a fast walk. It seemed likely that Melanie Herrick had been lying all along, her pathetic girlie act exactly that, an act. Melanie had been out again the previous afternoon, probably at her grandmother's, but Joanna had had no intention of talking to the two women together, nor of allowing Melanie to realise that her lies had been seen through. Now, though, she would almost certainly be in, alone, and Joanna had no intention of being so easily put off this time. True, there was a chance that Melanie was simply badly mistaken about her meeting with Charles Draper, but it was a small one. In any case, the best tack on the interview was the assumption that Melanie was lying. Be assertive, be confident: that way she'd get the result she wanted and if Melanie was simply wrong then no great harm would have been done.

A few minutes' walk brought her to Guildford Park Road and a moment later she was ringing on the bell of Melanie Herrick's flat. Melanie answered, looking worried as she saw who it was.

'May I come in,' Blackheath asked.

'I – I suppose so,' Melanie answered. 'I thought we'd been through everything yesterday?'

'No we haven't, Miss Herrick. If you could sit down, I need to ask some important questions.'

Melanie did as she was told, clearly uneasy. Joanna watched her, trying to gauge her reactions. She just looked like a frightened mouse, big brown eyes wide and moist under a fringe of dark brown curls. Could it really be an act? Joanna found it hard to accept her on face value. She was a big, curvy girl, undoubtedly attractive to men. True, there had been the divorce, but could she really be so meek and insecure? Joanna doubted it. Melanie had, after all, had at least one shouting match with Charles Draper, who had been male and a lot older than her.

'First off,' Joanna began, 'we know you lied about seeing Charles Draper in the middle of the afternoon on Monday.'

'I didn't lie!' Melanie protested.

'There's no point in this, Melanie,' Joanna continued. 'When you claim to have been talking to Draper he was lying dead in the river Tamar in Devon. Now we know that, because we've had the time of death determined, scientifically, and you know it too, don't you?'

'No! I promise!' Melanie pleaded.

'Come on, Melanie, you're just making it worse for your-self. You do realise how serious this is, don't you? Being an accessory to murder carries a long sentence, ten, fifteen years, maybe more.'

'Yes, but I didn't do it! I'm telling the truth, I really am!'

'Melanie, we know you're lying. Now please tell me the truth, it's the only sensible thing to do.'

'But I am!'

Joanna looked at Melanie, who had begun to cry, big, oily tears running down each cheek. The sight triggered a flush of sympathy in Joanna. Melanie looked genuinely distressed, but then she had to be lying – there was no alternative. Joanna steeled herself. She had turned on tears herself in her day and knew how effective it could be. She had to remind herself that Melanie had in all probability helped plot the violent death of a perfectly innocent man. Still, she could continue the questioning later. Perhaps Melanie would try and concoct a new story, resulting in more complex and more easily broken pretences.

'I'm going to look round,' Joanna told Melanie, 'and you are to sit there while I do. OK?'

Melanie simply nodded miserably. Joanna glanced around what she could see of the tiny flat. Several boxes stood around along the corridor and under the table in the living room, presumably packed with things for which the flat had no room. Otherwise the living room was uncluttered. Melanie had clearly not troubled to try and make the room look pleasant at all. The kitchen was also pretty stark from what she could see. The door to Melanie's bedroom stood half open, a pale blue quilt and a laundry basket brimming with clothes visible through the opening.

Joanna decided that the bedroom was the best place to start looking for anything potentially incriminating. She opened the door, noting the contents. The furniture was cheap, mainly chipboard with a white plastic veneer, and had clearly come with the flat. Melanie's clothes showed a predominance of bright colours, reds, yellows and pastel shades. The bed clothes were the same pale blue as the quilt and a line of fluffy stuffed toys were propped neatly against the bed-head, with more along the top of the wardrobe.

The wardrobe was large but clearly cheap; one of the plastic handles was cracked, the other missing altogether. Joanna pulled the doors open, revealing rows of clothes on hangers. Like those on the floor and in the basket, most were bright and practical, jeans, sweat-shirts, leggings. A few items pushed to one end stood out as incongruous; a white dress, low at the front and so short that it could barely have covered the tall girl's bottom; scarlet trousers in some glittery, metallic material; a crop top covered in fake fur dyed a brilliant green, and several similar items. Probably the things the ex-husband had liked Melanie to wear, Joanna guessed. Melanie surely would never be so vulgar by choice.

As Joanna turned away from the wardrobe a biro lying on the bedside table caught her attention. She pulled open the single, flat drawer. Inside was a big notebook, the cover decorated with flowers. Joanna picked it up, ignoring the automatic feeling of guilt at looking at what was evidently something very personal and private to Melanie. She opened the book at random, finding the pages covered with a big, looping handwriting. There were no dates or any other apparent system of organisation. Melanie had apparently written her thoughts down as they came. Joanna flicked through the pages, stopping occasionally to glance at a paragraph. Most of it seemed bitter, hurt: comments on the behaviour of someone called Carl, presumably the ex-husband; lines addressed to someone called Duncan, at first loving, then angry rebukes that included the names of another woman, Sophie. Joanna skipped some pages, then turned back as an unusual page caught her eye. Two neat columns ran down the page, and across the top Melanie had written 'How to kill a rat' in large, careful letters. She scanned the first column. Stabbing, poison, shooting, electrocution and several more fanciful options, were each dismissed by a line in the second column. Then, at the bottom, 'hired killer' and opposite it a large tick.

Joanna snapped the book shut. Here surely was enough evidence to bring Melanie in and then the truth would come out – there was no way on earth that she would be able to resist a full-scale police interview. The money, of course, could not have come directly from Melanie and had almost certainly come from her grandmother, a fact which also would undoubtedly come out in the wash.

John Anderson placed the faxed sheet from Blackheath on his desk and turned to look at the map he had placed on his office wall, seeking inspiration in the complex array of contours, rivers and woods. Blackheath's logic for arresting Melanie Herrick seemed good, and was in no way at variance with his own conclusions. She had also been sensible in not immediately arresting the grandmother, a move that suggested a degree of tact.

Somewhere, though, there was a connection between Guildford and Devon, a connection that almost certainly involved James Draper. When Draper had punched out the first number at the call box, he was sure it had been ten, maybe eleven or twelve digits, and therefore not a local number. Nobody had replied, suggesting that the call had been made on the off chance. Could Draper be in collusion with Melanie Herrick? It was certainly a possibility, one the answer to which would probably come from Guildford before too long.

Thinking of the phone box diverted Anderson's mind to Anna. She had been so eager and affectionate at first, only to turn cold later. Had she been bored? Annoyed at his lack of affection? Surely she could hardly expect him to be sexually aroused in a distinctly chilly car during a surveillance?

He shrugged the thought off. He would take her out to dinner when he had some time, quite soon if things continued to move in their current direction. She was clearly genuine in her attraction to him and had none of the self-doubt that had damaged his relationship with Catharine Marshall. There was no doubt in his mind that he could win Anna round with a little care.

Returning to his earlier train of thought, Anderson considered maintaining his surveillance. Trying to keep an eye on Draper alone was hardly practical, and with events in Guildford developing so rapidly, it might also prove unnecessary. No, Robert Walsh was right: his time would be better spent checking up on his theory that Charles Draper had actually been drowned at Thorn Point. On the other hand, a visit to the Matelot's Arms might prove valuable. Turning thought into action, Anderson got up and swept from the room, pausing only to collect the address from the desk sergeant.

As he walked across the car pound a green Morgan sports car cut in front of him, pulling neatly into a space next to his own BMW. Violet Krebs emerged, her flame-red hair instantly recognisable.

'Did you get anything of interest?' he asked conversationally.

'No,' she replied in a terse, matter-of-fact voice.

'Which area did you do?' Anderson continued, entirely ignoring her defensive manner.

'I've been to the Lopwell Dam,' she replied, thawing slightly. 'It's one of the few easily accessible places where there aren't wide mud flats. Draper could have been drowned there much more easily than at Thorn Point. Unfortunately there's nothing to speak of there. I drew a blank. You should go to Thorn Point, you know; at half-tide there's at least a hundred yards of mud between any piece of land you can actually stand on and the open water, and don't ask your young friend Anna to go wading in it, she'll sink.'

'I've seen it,' Anderson replied, 'and the mud doesn't matter. There are channels in the salt marsh that would be perfect, deep, brackish and coming right up to the edge.'

'Can you get on to the salt marsh?' Krebs asked.

'I imagine so,' Anderson answered.

'So you didn't try?'

'No, it wasn't necessary at the time,' Anderson continued, irritated by her discovery of his lack of thoroughness and reluctant to admit that he had not carried out a full survey of Thorn Point because he was intent on seducing Anna Ferreira and hadn't wanted to ruin his suit.

'Well, shall we go and find out?' Krebs asked.

'It shouldn't take two of us,' Anderson replied, 'and besides, I was on my way to the Matelot's Arms to talk to the landlord. Take Heath with you, he's back from Lydford. The receiver of stolen goods proved to have a secure alibi.'

'I'll do it myself,' Krebs said, turning towards the door that led into the police station, 'just as soon as I've had lunch.'

'While you're there,' Anderson called after her as she left, 'try a few of the houses up by Bere Ferrers station. If I'm right, Draper's car was probably there at some point.'

Krebs shot him an unreadable look in reply. Anderson imagined that she would do as he had asked, though. She seemed thorough and efficient for all her disinclination to be led by anyone else. In a moment of insight Anderson realised that ten years previously his senior officers might have viewed him in the same light – an officer cut out for rapid promotion but not a good leader; efficient but remote; professional but refusing to allow the police to form the hub of his social life. Possibly Graham Parrish still viewed him in the same way.

Anderson climbed into the BMW and reversed carefully out of his space, now awkwardly close to Krebs's Morgan.

Glancing at the car to make sure his wing mirror was clear, Anderson noticed that the bright mid-green was a re-spray. He wondered if the colour had been chosen to make a dramatic contrast with her hair. If so, it revealed a streak of extravagant vanity in her that he had not suspected.

He pulled out of the car park and turned the car towards Devonport. Despite the confusing maze of little streets behind the docks, he quickly located the Matelot's Arms, a big, three-story building at the corner of two minor streets and less than a quarter mile from the Devonport police station.

The front of the pub was shabby, dirty brown brick with areas of paint that must once have been a deep yellow. The sign, showing a powerfully built sailor with his arms crossed over his chest, hung on a rusting iron bracket. Pink neon strip highlighted a new name, 'Penelope's', above either window. Anderson pushed open the door, the smell of beer and cigarettes immediately assaulting his nose. Smoke hung in wreaths in the air, gathering like a fog towards the high ceiling. The floor, part bare boards and part red linoleum marbled with a deeper red pattern, was worn in places and covered with marks from cigarettes dropped while still alight. A pop tune, unfamiliar to Anderson, was blaring out from speakers set high on the walls. The faces of the half-dozen men at the bar turned to him, unfriendly if not actually aggressive. He glanced across them, half expecting to find Draper sitting smirking in a corner.

Anderson turned to the bar, where a brassy-looking young woman with dyed blonde hair caught up in a bun was serving. He waited while she finished pouring beer for an obese, balding man, taking his money and returning change.

'May I speak to the landlord, please?' he asked.

'Bill, rep for you!' she shouted over her shoulder. 'Want a drink, love?'

Anderson declined, content to allow the customers to think he was a commercial representative rather than a policeman.

'Who from?' a deep bellow came from the back room.

'Don't know, new bloke,' she answered, still shouting and then turning to Anderson. 'Who you from, love?'

Before Anderson could answer, the man she had addressed as Bill emerged from a back room, rubbing his hands on a filthy towel.

'Come in here, mate,' he addressed Anderson. 'Who'd you say you were from?'

Anderson followed the man into the back room, only introducing himself and showing his warrant card when the door had shut behind them. The man showed little surprise and no disinclination to talk.

'Yeah, I know James Draper,' he began in answer to Anderson's question. 'He spends a lot, and he's mouthy, but not normally trouble.'

'Tell me what happened at lunch time last Monday,' Anderson asked.

'Oh, it's about that is it?' Bill replied. 'Let's see now. Yeah, Draper comes in at opening time. He's usually one of the first. Anyway, he's talking with some mates and playing pool –'

'Did he seem nervous?'

'No, he was the same as usual, drinking, mouthing off about his motorbike, his girlfriend, you know the sort. Anyway, after a while the pub starts filling up, busy for a lunch time it was. Draper and his mates are playing at one table, and a couple of lads at the other. Anyway, Draper starts getting mouthy with these two young lads, giving it all that 'cause he's in front of his mates like. I went over and told him to watch it, but then he puts down a coin on the table they're using, obviously just to wind them up. The bigger of the two lads was pretty pissed by then, so he takes Draper's coin and puts in on the other table. I could see what was coming, so I went over and told them to can it or they were both out. Draper wasn't having it though, and he puts his coin back on the table, telling the big lad that that's how it works in here.'

107

Bill paused. 'You sure you won't have a drink?' he addressed Anderson.

Anderson declined and waited while the landlord went out into the bar area and poured himself a pint of beer.

'Anyway,' Bill continued, taking a draught, 'I have enough trouble in here as it is, so I told Draper to get out. He did, but instead of going off elsewhere, he stands in the street shouting at the lad he'd been winding up to come out. The lad wasn't interested, and even Draper's mates were trying to calm him down, but he wasn't having any of it. Shouting, cursing and yelling at people in the street, he was. Eventually I had to call you lot in, what else could I do?'

'A sensible decision,' Anderson remarked. 'Would you consider this behaviour normal for Draper?'

'No way,' the man replied, 'he's all mouth is Draper. Sometimes he'll mouth off and end up getting one of his mates into a fight, but he keeps well out of it. Weedy sort of bloke anyway, ain't he? For all his mouth, he ain't that stupid.'

'So the police arrested him?'

'Yeah, Sergeant Mallows it was and another bloke I don't know. Draper ain't been in since.'

Anderson thanked the man and quickly left the pub, glad to be clear of the stifling atmosphere. What he had learnt reinforced his opinion. Draper had been very keen to be in the clear for Monday afternoon. He walked across to the BMW and drove the quarter mile to Devonport police station, reluctant to risk his new car by leaving it in the street.

'Afternoon, sir, how may we help you?' the desk Sergeant asked as Anderson entered the station lobby.

'DCI Anderson, Surrey Police,' he introduced himself, showing his warrant card and smiling inwardly as the Sergeant immediately straightened up. 'I'd like to see a Sergeant Mallows.'

'I think he's in the canteen, sir,' the Sergeant replied, 'left down the corridor and it's the double doors at the end.'

Anderson quickly located Mallows, a grey-haired officer who Anderson estimated must be nearing retirement.

'I want a few words about James Draper, who I believe you arrested last Monday?' Anderson asked as he took a seat opposite Mallows.

'Draper, yes, someone called about that the other day.'

'Yes – I need a little more detail though. I know Draper refused to accept a caution and that you eventually released him at around seven.'

'That's right, sir,' Mallows replied. 'I can check the exact time if you want.'

'That won't be necessary, Sergeant,' Anderson replied. 'I'm more interested in his behaviour while he was here.'

'Difficult, sir, that's what he was. Mark you, it's not the first time we've had him in – driving offences, drunk and disorderly, possession of cannabis, we nearly had him for dealing once. Mouthy, our James Draper. Aren't you one of the officers on his uncle's death? I was the first on the scene, you know, terrible thing –'

'Have you cautioned him before?' Anderson asked, breaking into the Sergeant's flow.

'Well, yes,' Mallows replied, 'more than once. Funny that, he wouldn't accept a caution on Monday, even though he'd have been out straight away.'

'Thank you, Sergeant, that's all I need to know,' Anderson said, rising from his chair.

Anderson left the station and walked back to the BMW, getting in but not starting the car. Instead he focused on the superstructure of a warship, visible between the houses where the street ran down to the water. He was now certain of Draper's involvement, the perfect alibi for the perfect crime, an image which he had no doubt would appeal to James Draper. What then should his next move be? Arrest Draper? But on what grounds? Get a warrant to search Draper's flat? Possibly useful but more likely futile. Draper was careful, even if he was too brash for his own good. Nevertheless, it was better than sitting around doing nothing, and it would certainly shake Draper up, at least a little. Anderson turned the key in the ignition, the engine instantly coming to life with a gratifying purr. He glanced out of the window again. The sky was a pale turquoise, high bands of stratus beginning to turn from white to pink as the sun settled towards the Cornish side of the estuary. The sight filled him with unexpected melancholy and the need for educated conversation and maybe sex. He should try and find Anna. Draper would have disposed of anything obvious. Anything else would keep, as would Draper.

James Draper gunned the Kawasaki out on to the A38. The old fool had gone for it again. Christ, it had been easy. A little push, a little shove and he got what he wanted, just like always. Now it was time to raise the stakes, and he had told the old fool so. Why not? You got respect from saying what you meant, being hard, never taking your foot off the gas; and anyway, the old fool had no choice. As long as he, James Draper, made it clear who was in charge, he would get what he wanted. Twenty-five per cent of old Charlie's money! He could fucking whistle!

As for the police, they didn't know shit. The one he'd called Mutt to wind him up had been a right stiff, trying to look hard and cool, but there was fuck all he could do and that was that. The girl had been attractive. Christ, she couldn't be much older than he was, thirty tops. Gorgeous hair, nice firm tits and a neat little arse. Christ, what would it be like to have her under him? Not that she'd go for it, too hoity-toity by half. But you never knew, sometimes the posh ones were gagging for it. After all, Lindsie fancied him, she never objected if he had a quick feel of her tits or arse when Sue wasn't looking, and her parents were loaded. There was something about Lindsie. Her body was pretty similar to Sue's, a bit less tit in fact but better legs, yet she could turn him on just by the way she talked. Still, who knew what the future might hold?

It was a pity about old Charlie, of course, but he'd had nothing to live for. What did he do? Sit in his house, drink tea, look at his clocks, fuck all. A million quid was wasted on old Charlie, but he'd know what to do with it, oh yeah. Nice house, nice bikes, nice cars, a swimming pool, booze, birds, you name it, he would just sit on it and do fuck all. No, Charlie was best where he was – same with all the old gits really, they had the money, but they didn't know how to spend it.

Shame the first plan hadn't worked. It should have been simple. Charlie decides to come and visit his beloved nephew. Charlie takes a detour on the way. Charlie gets pissed. Charlie trips and Charlie falls in the river. Bomp, dead. James gets the money. If some silly little bitch hadn't sussed out that Charlie had been done in, that would have been the lot. Still, the pigs had no chance. They'd arse around for a bit, give him some stress, but in the end they'd have to drop it and he'd be home free, and from now on the old fool would have to do exactly as he said.

He flicked the lights on when he reached the roundabout where the dual carriageway started, twisting the throttle to pull ahead of an old Maxi that was dithering around the inner track, and accelerating hard on to the A38. Some flash git in an Orion was trying to show off, driving close behind him in the outer lane. Draper put his head down and accelerated, seventy, eighty, ninety, and the Orion was left far behind. Oh yeah, this was good, maybe he should get the old fool to buy him an ZX1100 Ninja, that would burn off anything. Yeah, that would be the thing, with a custom paint job.

Draper left the A38, turned twice and then pulled off to read the map. Where was it the old fool had said? Near some village in the middle of fucking nowhere. Oh yeah, that was it. Sparkwell, the railway, yeah, a dead-end track, yeah. Christ, the old fool was full of shit. Never meet where you might be recognised, never call me on your mobile, always dial in several numbers in a call box. Fucking hell, it wasn't as if the police had the brains to figure it out anyway. So, straight up the lane, through the village, then a right, easy.

Four minutes later he pulled up by the side of a gravel track. Removing his helmet, he looked around, but saw nobody. In front of him the track rose in a hump to cross the railway, then stopped at a gate. Christ, the old fool couldn't have picked a lonelier place, fucking cold as well. The bridge was smooth tarmac, easier to walk on in the fading light. Nobody was there. If the old fool didn't hurry up it would be pitch fucking black. He waited, stamping his feet to keep warm, wondering why the old fool had to meet him instead of just talking on the phone. Beneath him the railway cutting was deep in shade, the tracks just visible in the gloom of late dusk.

Five minutes passed and nothing happened. His eyes slowly adapted to the fading light even as the last hint of colour gradually faded from the landscape. Losing patience, he pulled his mobile phone from inside his jacket and tapped in a familiar number. If the old fool wasn't here in five minutes, he'd demand something for his time. Yeah, that was a good idea actually: fines for being late, for not doing as he was told. They'd get paid – there was no choice.

Draper put his ear to the receiver, only to hear a soft, female voice telling him that the phone he was ringing was switched off. Christ, what a prat, Draper cursed, once more looking around for any signs of movement. Nothing. Then he heard a metallic tingle, gentle at first, slowly building to become a throb, then a roaring clatter as a train shot out from underneath him. He watched as one after another the carriages passed under the bridge, until finally the rear engine emerged with a low, powerful moan and the train rattled away in the direction of Exeter and London.

Draper heard a soft sound behind him, the scurrying of a pebble kicked across tarmac. He turned. A dark shadow loomed over him and then his head exploded with light.

SEVEN
Saturday night

DC Pentyre sat at the back of Plympton police station operations room. Around him clustered thirty officers, including an element of CID and a dog-handling team. At the front, DI Statham was conducting the briefing for the raid on the Red Barn to the north of the area. Good old Ernie Statham, Pentyre thought: here was a real police officer, someone who preferred direct action policing. Control the unruly elements of the community before anything happened, that was how things should be done.

Despite Pentyre's approval of Statham as an officer, he couldn't help but feel a pang of resentment at the other man's rank. They had been PCs together, nearly twenty years back now when he had joined the force, but while Statham had managed promotion at a reasonable rate, he had repeatedly failed his Sergeant's exams and now looked unlikely to ever rise above the rank of DC. The exam irked him. He had never been good at that sort of thing, but that shouldn't matter: he was the best driver in the area, without doubt, and he had made more arrests than some officers had had hot dinners. Surely a record like that should count for something?

But no, kids like Violet Krebs who could do their exams got promoted over his head. Mark you, with tits like hers it was no wonder she got favoured. Maybe old man Walsh wasn't such a dry stick as he made out.

Pentyre turned his attention back to Statham, who was outlining the details of the coming operation. The Red Barn, it seemed, had been using its out of town location to flaunt the licensing rules and soft drugs were also being sold and used openly in the club. Two DCs drafted in from Torbay to avoid them being recognised had worked undercover there for the last five Saturday nights, gathering evidence which Statham felt was now strong enough to justify a mob-handed raid. Pentyre envied the two undercover men. That was just the sort of job he was good at, instead of traipsing round farms and remote cottages to question antagonistic locals about something they almost certainly knew nothing about.

'We aim,' Statham was saying, 'for exactly five minutes past 2 a.m., OK? The five DCs are to go immediately to the two bar areas and take the till rolls out so that we've got proof of after-hours sales. The dog team stays outside until things are under control, then they bring down the sniffers. By that time, the rest of you will have dispersed around the building, each man standing by a group who will be told to stay still and wait. Myself and the two DSs will then come round each group individually and separate out the punters from the organisers —'

Statham's flow was cut off by a knock on the door. A constable responded to his annoyed shout, poking his head and shoulders around the door.

'Sorry to disturb you, sir, but we think we've got a jumper out at Sparkwell.'

'Isn't there a car?' Statham asked.

'None available, sir. Sorry, sir.'

'Hell. Bob, drive up there with a couple of men and sort it

115

out, would you. With a bit of luck you'll be back by two. OK?'

Pentyre got to his feet reluctantly. A jumper! That was all he needed. Why did the stupid bastards have to top themselves that way? If they couldn't hack it anymore, why not take an overdose or jump down a mine shaft? But no, they had to bring the whole railway system to a halt and of course it was the poor sodding police who had to clean up the mess.

'What do we know?' he asked the PC as he reached the door.

'Not a lot really,' the constable replied. 'A driver reckons he saw a body on the line in one of the cuttings as he was getting near Plymouth. We reckon it must be near Sparkwell. We've had the line closed until it's sorted anyway.'

'Shit,' Pentyre swore, then turned to Statham. 'Could I have more men, sir – we don't know exactly were the body is, or even if it was some bloody sheep!'

Statham eventually made up a team of ten, with Ted Dunning leading the group, clearly preferring to lose those officers not from his station if he had to lose any at all. Ten minutes later they were driving out of Plympton in three cars with blue lights going. The map showed the railway, with four or even six cuttings in the Sparkwell area. While a handful of roads crossed the railway, none ran beside it.

When they reached the bridge over the most westerly of the possible cuttings, Dunning split them into two groups, his own starting towards the east while Pentyre was to take the other and work from the far end of the possible area. When he got to the bridge he was to start from, Pentyre got out to find that the night was cold even for March and that the way on to the railway was barred by thick banks of thorn and gorse.

Eventually he reached the railway, his legs and arms badly scratched and one ankle in pain where he had twisted it on an unexpected stone.

'This had better not be a bloody false alarm,' he told the man nearest to him, who returned a heartfelt agreement.

They began to walk west, the double track of the Great Western railway vanishing in front of them into the gloom of the night. The first cutting was long and ran through woodland with no bridges from which a suicide might have jumped to the line. It had to be searched anyway. The body could, after all, belong to some lunatic who had decided to walk along the railway for reasons best known to themselves. Such things had happened, more than once with grim consequences.

The cutting opened out to a flat area, and then a short embankment where the railway crossed a narrow valley and a road. Beyond that it once more ran into a cutting, the map marking a small bridge supporting a farm track. They entered the cutting, the torches probing the darkness ahead. The light caught a black object by the track and Pentyre's pulse immediately quickened. They approached slowly, the torches converging on the object. Details became clearer, a black leather jacket covering something that had no right to be the shape it was.

'Jesus,' Pentyre swore.

DS Dunning could already see the lights from the other team's torches and was hoping that the whole thing was a false alarm when Pentyre's call came through. He relayed it to Plympton control, requesting an ambulance and the duty men from forensic. He then forced himself to carry on, despite his reluctance to spend his time standing over a corpse. After all, he was the senior officer there and so it was his job. Still, it was bloody unlucky. Normally he'd have been off at this time on a Saturday, watching telly with the wife and kids. At least the raid on the Red Barn had been something exciting to do, whereas this was just grim. Still, at least he'd get the overtime, maybe more, because it would probably take most of the night to sort this mess out.

117

He arrived in the cutting to find Pentyre and his team setting tape out near the bridge.

'You don't want to see, guv,' Pentyre informed him. 'It looks like he went under the wheels.'

'Whereabouts?'

'From the bridge for fifty yards or so towards Plymouth. We've covered everything with sheeting.'

'Right,' Dunning replied. 'Let's get the tape out before anyone else gets here.'

Within minutes the area had been taped off and set under arc lights brought out by the second group of officers. Dunning coordinated the setting up of the generator and the dispersal of lights, then returned to the cutting in case any lights needed to be moved.

The light of a torch caught his attention, crossing the bridge and coming towards where he stood.

'Are we ready?' he called out.

'I don't know, are we?' a familiar voice shouted back and the torch was turned up briefly to illuminate the face of Dr Wells, then flicked behind him to show his assistant, Anna Ferreira, pushing her way through the scrub.

'Sorry, Dr Wells,' Dunning said. 'I thought it was someone to tell me something was wrong with the lights.'

'Indeed not,' Wells replied. 'Merely your forensic team, as I was unlucky enough to be on call this evening. I understand it's a bit of a mess down here.'

'You're not wrong, sir,' Dunning replied.

'Lights!' a voice shouted from the blackness.

Dunning shaded his eyes from the sudden fierce glare as the generator hummed to life and the cutting was filled with brilliant white light, throwing the area around it into utter blackness.

The light revealed the full detail of the cutting, parallel tracks gleaming in the brilliant glare, the one on which they were standing marked by four pieces of white sheeting.

Dunning walked beside Wells as the doctor, serious for once, approached the nearest of the white covers and lifted it until the arc light shone underneath.

For a long moment he stayed still, then turned to Dunning. 'It's James Draper,' he said. 'You'd better call Walsh.'

John Anderson lifted his glass and studied the gleam of a light in the red depths of the fluid, then returned the glass to the table untasted. The Draper case, he felt, was rather getting away from him. The most he would be able to achieve now seemed to be establishing the connection between James Draper and the murderer, assuming that Joanna Blackheath in Guildford didn't get that piece of information from Melanie Herrick. He rather suspected that she would. The wording of her fax had suggested a confident, almost triumphant mood and it was entirely possible that by tomorrow the case would be effectively over.

He had also failed to find Anna Ferreira. The lab had been closed and she had not been at her flat. Once more he lifted his wine glass, this time taking a carefully measured sip. Above all, he hated the frustration of things not going the way he wanted them to. True, Jo Blackheath was only following her duty and Anna could hardly be expected to sit in her flat doing nothing on the off chance that he might call, but the failure of the world to be ordered to his preferences nevertheless irritated him. He swallowed the final bite of his lamb and wiped his mouth with a single, fastidious movement. A scattering of other people were eating in the restaurant and the main bar of the Royal was starting to fill up, exclusively with couples and small groups beginning their evenings with a meal or a drink. Anderson glanced at his watch. It was nearly ten.

Once more he sipped his wine, a rather astringent claret that had failed to live up to his expectations. As he returned the glass to the table, he noticed the receptionist entering the bar and looking from side to side, finally catching sight of him through the open door and approaching at a jog.

'A call, for you, Mr Anderson,' she said as she reached his table. 'It's from the police station – the man on the line says it's urgent.'

'Thank you,' Anderson replied, getting to his feet and following her back to the reception desk.

'John?' a voice sounded as he lifted the receiver from the desk. 'It's Robert Walsh. Could you come up here immediately?'

'Could you send a car?' Anderson asked. 'I've just had a half-bottle of claret with my supper. What's happened?'

'James Draper is dead,' Walsh replied. 'The car will be with you in five minutes.'

Anderson rang off. Further questions could be asked at the station. James Draper was dead and he didn't imagine for an instant that the death was accidental.

Pausing only to collect his trenchcoat, Anderson hurried out of the Royal, waiting by the door until a police Rover 114 pulled up. Anderson got into the car, the PC turning on his blue lights as they left the narrow street.

'Do you know anything about this?' Anderson asked as he clicked his seat-belt into place.

'Not really, sir,' the PC replied. 'From what I hear, Plympton got a call that someone had jumped onto the railway. Some of our lads were down there, and it turns out the bloke's that James Draper, so old Walsh – sorry, Superintendent Walsh says to get everybody on the team up here and that I'm to drive you out to Sparkwell. That's all I know, sir.'

Anderson sat back, pondering the significance of Draper's death as they sped through the suburbs of Plymouth and out on to the A38 towards the east. It seemed reasonable to assume that Draper had been murdered. To suggest suicide was ridiculous, given Draper's character and his impending wealth. Likewise, the idea that he might have fallen accidentally on to a railway track several miles from his flat on a cold Saturday evening stretched credulity. No, James Draper would have been murdered, and he would almost certainly have gone to Sparkwell to meet the person who became his murderer.

Why kill Draper then? Could the murderer have realised that Draper's over-flamboyant alibi would eventually lead to him? Other possibilities existed but that seemed the most likely. James Draper's death might cut the link between the murderer and Charles Draper, and it seemed reasonable that someone who murdered one man for gain would have no compunction about murdering a second to save himself from justice. The next question was, had the man been as careful with James Draper as he had with the uncle? The lack of worthwhile forensic evidence had been a major stumbling block in the case so far, but it seemed probable that this second murder had been less carefully planned than the first and so there was a higher chance of something pertinent turning up. Anderson had little doubt that the same man was responsible for both murders. Any other option was of a far lower probability – yet such options could not be ruled out until they had the full facts.

Anderson's mind was racing, constantly coming up against the barrier of not knowing exactly what had happened. He steeled himself to patience, instead looking out of the window at the lights of Plympton in the valley below them. Beyond that was the black loom of Dartmoor, with just two isolated lights showing against the darkness. What must it be like up there at the moment, he mused. Dank and cold, certainly, the distant lights of Plymouth and outlying villages serving only to deepen the loneliness. A beautiful place in summer, no doubt, but now steeped in melancholy.

The car pulled off the main road, turning towards the moor. A single hill, bigger than the rest, detached itself from the general skyline and loomed over him as the car drove through the village. Draper had been killed on a railway. It wouldn't be the first time he had been at the scene of such a death, and Anderson knew what to expect. Nevertheless, it was the sort of thing that he knew he would never become completely indifferent to and he had to steel himself against what he knew was coming.

The car pulled into a track, parking beside two other police cars, an ambulance and Dr Wells's massive Rover. There was also a large motorcycle which he guessed to be Draper's. Robert Walsh was standing by one of the cars, talking to a uniformed officer.

'Ah, John,' Walsh began, 'I'm glad you could get here so quickly. You'll find the rest of the team down in the cutting.'

'Do we know anything?' Anderson asked.

'Not really,' Walsh replied. 'Let me fill you in. At around five a driver called in to say that he thought he'd seen a body on the line. He wasn't sure exactly where it was, though, and it was half an hour before Dunning, Pentyre and some men from Plympton uniform found him. They assumed it was a suicide and it wasn't until Dr Wells got here just after eight that we found out who it was.'

Anderson nodded and turned away. Along the track he could see the brilliant lights of arc lamps set up in the cutting, illuminating the brown and green tangle of gorse and hawthorn and throwing the rest of the area into sharp, black shadow. Other lights covered the bridge and track, illuminating the twin ruts and scattered granite chips that ran between high stone walls. The bridge had been recently tarmacked, a glossy black arch which obscured the view beyond.

Anderson made his way to the bridge, stopping at the crest to peer down into the illuminated cutting. Beneath him was Dr Wells, crouching down as he closed a black body bag. Anna stood to the side, her arms crossed over her chest, her face white and drawn. Krebs stood next to them, her arm around Anna's shoulders, her expression set in restrained anger.

Some yards beyond them stood three men, Dunning, Pentyre and another man Anderson didn't recognise.

Anderson looked for a way down. Nothing was obvious, thick thorn growing on both sides of the cutting, broken only by stands of gorse. In both directions the cutting disappeared into the dark beyond the light. He cursed and began to climb the gate that cut off the end of the track and opened on to a field, eventually managing to push his way down the bank. Glad that he had missed the worst of it, he walked over to where the two women were standing.

Anna greeted him with a faint smile, Krebs nodding formally. Dr Wells looked up, for once without a remark. Anderson noticed the blood on his gloves and the anguished look on his face.

'I'm going to have the whole area vacuumed,' the big scientist said. 'It's been dry and there's hardly been a breath of wind. If there's a scrap of evidence this time, we'll get it.'

'He was definitely murdered, then?' Anderson asked quietly.

'What else do you think happened to him?' Wells asked. 'I'll need to check properly back at the lab, but at first glance I'd say his skull was crushed by a single, heavy blow and then he was thrown down on to the tracks. At the speed the trains come around this curve, there's no way one could stop even if they did see him.'

'What's the code for the Guildford area?' Krebs asked him.

'01483,' Anderson answered, 'Why?'

'I found Draper's mobile,' she answered. 'He hadn't cleared it. I've noted the last number he called, but it wasn't that code.'

'Check it,' he insisted.

'01297,' Krebs told him. 'I don't recognise it, it's not local.'

'It could be useful,' Anderson replied. 'With a bit of luck our man is getting careless. It has to be the same man, I can't see the two murders being unconnected.'

'I agree,' she said. 'It would be too much of a coincidence.'

Anderson moved aside to let two men past him.

'All done here, Dr Wells?' one asked.

Wells gave them the all-clear. They lifted the body bag on to a stretcher, walking away down the track in what Anderson took to be the direction of the main road.

'I take it you've been over the cutting?' he asked, unsure of what he could achieve after arriving when the initial flurry of activity was over.

'Several times,' Krebs replied. 'Other than the vacuum samples we've got everything we can for now.'

'I had to send someone back for the vacuum,' Dr Wells put in. 'It should be here in a moment. Even with the lights it's too dark to go through the undergrowth thoroughly, but when you do, the thing to look out for is some sort of club. It must have a rounded end, like an Indian club or a knob-kerrie, or maybe a piece of pipe with a bend at one end. He's probably disposed of it miles away, though.'

Anderson nodded, glancing with distaste at the rank tangle of gorse and thorn that cloaked both banks. It was not a place that he looked forward to searching. No suit would stand such treatment for five minutes. That, of course, was one advantage of rank. He would be able to handle some more civilised job while more junior officers tramped through the undergrowth.

'Is anyone at Draper's flat?' he asked Krebs.

'Heath,' she replied.

'I'd like to look it over,' Anderson continued. 'I discovered earlier that Draper's alibi was definitely contrived. He set it up carefully to cover the period in which the murder took place. It seems probable that he came out here to meet the murderer, perhaps to pay him off.'

'With what?' Krebs demanded. 'He hadn't received his uncle's money. I can't see a weekly DSS cheque hiring a killer.'

'He had some money from his parents' estate,' Anderson

replied. 'According to DS Blackheath in Guildford, he sold his parents' house when he inherited it. You saw the stereo system in his flat, and his motorcycle. He wasn't as poor as he looked at first glance. I think his finances will make interesting reading.'

'Maybe,' Krebs replied, 'but why kill him? OK, once the killer had the money he might have decided that he'd be safer with Draper dead, but then Draper would hardly have been in a position to shop him anyway and he'd be exposing himself to a new risk.'

'That is true,' Anderson replied thoughtfully. 'In fact, if it had been his intention to kill Draper, he would have planned it more carefully, as carefully as he planned the first murder.'

'Assuming it is the same man,' Krebs put in, 'the MOs are completely different. Charles Draper's body needed to be found for James Draper to get the money that was left to him. If the killer wanted James Draper out of the way, though, he would have been better off concealing the murder. As a fake suicide, this is far too clumsy.'

'I agree,' Anderson answered after a moment's thought. 'Unless, of course, some third person now stands to benefit. Joanna Blackheath said that there were no other relatives, though. We really have too few facts to go on. Maybe forensic will come up with something this time.'

'Maybe,' Anna spoke quietly, her face still pale with shock. 'Maybe we will, and maybe it'll be just what we're supposed to do.'

'How do you mean?' Anderson asked.

'The first time', Anna continued, 'there was nothing except the pen, and we could easily have missed that. This time it's much less well hidden. It just seems strange that someone so careful would be so clumsy the second time. I think the clumsiness is deliberate.'

'I'm afraid that's really a bit fanciful,' Wells answered her, his voice sympathetic, as if talking to a bright child who has made a clever, but misinformed, statement. 'In my experience even the most hard-bitten people find it difficult to remain completely calm in a crisis like this. Maybe Draper struggled, maybe a car passed the end of the lane and he panicked, we don't know.'

'It's not a bad idea,' Anderson put in, keen to show support for her but forced to agree with Wells. 'In my experience, though, the more carefully planned a murder is, the more carefully its nature is concealed. I suspect that what happened tonight was far less carefully thought-out than the original murder. To deliberately set up misleading evidence immediately after committing a murder would be the act of a man with an inhumanly callous nature.'

'It was just an idea,' Anna answered. 'You're right, it's silly.'

'I think we'd better get you back,' Wells said, again addressing Anna. 'I can see you're shaken.'

'Please, I'd like that, ' Anna replied. 'I'm sorry, it's not like me. I know I should be used to it, but this was different.'

'I'll see if one of the cars can go back now,' Anderson suggested. 'I'll come with you.'

Anderson and Anna Ferreira returned to the cars where Walsh readily agreed to allow a car to return to Plymouth. Both of them got into the back, Anna huddling against his side, shaking at first and then very quiet. He realised that in the cutting she had been trying very hard not to show the depth of her shock but that she now felt able to let her feelings go. Her reaction made him feel protective and also flattered that she should feel able to seek comfort from him. He squeezed her shoulder reassuringly, turning to catch a last glimpse of the black silhouette of the moors blotting out the detail of the place where James Draper had met his death.

EIGHT
Sunday

Joanna Blackheath hunched down over her coffee, which merely tasted thin and bitter and had done nothing to dispel her tiredness. The previous afternoon had been one of the most trying in her career, and although it had failed to shift her conviction that she had been right to arrest Melanie Herrick, it had given her a sharp and palpable lesson in the power of the establishment and the disadvantages of not doing things by the book. First there had been the discovery that the Herricks' solicitor was Sir Ralph Stukeley, one of the leading men in the county and a personal friend of Chief Constable Colin Farrell. Stukeley had then made mincemeat of her intention to keep the pressure on Melanie Herrick until she cracked. He had also managed to engineer the interview so that instead of her choice of DC Gerry Hart as her partner, she ending up having to give a carefully modulated and textbook interview with Detective Super-intendent Graham Parrish sitting next to her. Parrish, who she had already decided was more concerned with image than with efficiency, had quickly distanced himself from her decision to make the arrest, reminding Stukeley unnecessarily that each officer, whether a constable or the commissioner himself, made an arrest on their own authority.

The result had been the release of Melanie Herrick after an interview that made Jo look like a choice pupil of the Marquis de Sade. Melanie's pleas and tearful denials had impressed everybody else, but still rang false to Jo. However much she might protest her innocence, Jo considered, there remained the fact that she was claiming to have spoken to a man in Surrey at a time when the man was known to have been two hundred miles away in Devon and dead. Stukeley had been unimpressed, pointing out that the evidence was both circumstantial and highly tenuous. They had ended with the conclusion that Melanie Herrick was simply not recalling her facts correctly, an explanation that Melanie had gratefully accepted. As for the 'How to Kill a Rat' revelation in Melanie's diary, her assertion that the idea was aimed at her ex-husband Carl and that it had been done during acute depression brought on by his violent and humiliating behaviour, seemed to impress Parrish more than Jo's insistence that it could as easily relate to Charles Draper. In the end she had had to admit defeat.

She took another sip of the still harsh and now also cold coffee, reflecting bitterly on Mr Worth's warning about the local bigwigs sticking together. On discovering that she had searched Melanie Herrick's flat without proper authorisation, Stukeley had pushed for a formal complaint to be brought, which Melanie would now be doing. The last half hour had been spent listening to Graham Parrish berating her for slipshod, heavy-handed policework, and there would be more to come, the least damaging outcome of which she could expect to be a black mark that would do nothing for her career prospects. It had to be pretty bad for Parrish to have dragged himself in on a Sunday. Also, she had been told to drop the line of enquiry for the time being, with the implication that somebody more senior would be put in instead of her if further enquiries were needed. She cursed silently to herself. For goodness sake, she had only been trying to get to the truth. Didn't Charles Draper's life count for more than Melanie Herrick's sensibilities? If Melanie had been some girl from one of the estates instead of the grand-daughter of a wealthy old landowner, would it have gone this way?

Clearly not, she reflected sullenly, especially with Melanie being so obviously gorgeous. Parrish had been close to drooling. Unfortunately there was nothing she could do about it, and her inner conviction that catching people who killed, especially those who killed for personal gain, was infinitely more important than the niceties of procedure provided minimal comfort.

'Jo?' a masculine voice cut into her brooding.

She looked up to see DC Gerry Hart and smiled bravely. He at least seemed to have some sympathy for her. His colleague and girlfriend, WDC Carrie Vickers, stood behind him, also looking concerned.

'You all right?' he asked.

'No,' she admitted frankly.

'I'm sorry,' he said, putting his hand on her shoulder.

Jo smiled and raised her eyebrows in a gesture of resignation.

'Fax for you,' he continued. 'It's pretty heavy. It'll take your mind off things, I guarantee.'

She accepted the fax, reading it once and then again. It was from DCI John Anderson in Devon. James Draper was dead.

She quickly scanned the details. James Draper had been murdered, killed with a blow to the head and then thrown under a train in a clumsy attempt to make it look like suicide. The assumption was that the murderer was the same man who had killed Draper's uncle. They had new leads and she was to call the solicitor, Worth, and find out what would now happen to Charles Draper's money.

Simple enough, except for the fact that it was Sunday and Worth would not be in his office. Waiting was out of the question – John Anderson expected a rapid response.

In the event, Worth's home phone number proved easy to find. Worth himself answered, informing her that as Draper had died after his uncle, the details of Charles Draper's will became irrelevant and that the disposal of the money would now be in accordance with any will James Draper might have made. Had James Draper died intestate, the money would go to his closest surviving relative. Worth promised to look into the matter.

Jo thanked the solicitor and put the phone down, glad that at least for once the situation was simple, with Worth's answer effectively throwing the ball back into the Devon court. The next step then was to discover whether James Draper had had a will. A fax to DCI John Anderson in Devon would hopefully provide the answer.

Violet Krebs rang the bell marked *Ferreira* and then glanced at her watch. There was no great hurry: the trip she was making to Charmouth was almost certainly merely an exercise in ensuring that all possible avenues of exploration had been dealt with. When Anna had left the previous night, she had clearly been deeply distressed, although doing her best to hide it. As the only other woman on the team, Violet felt a responsibility towards Anna, who was both younger and less experienced than herself. It was true that John Anderson had taken her home, but Violet had little faith in Anderson's ability to soothe a distraught woman. In fact she had only a moderate opinion of Anderson in any case. Intelligent and charming he might be, but he was also patronising, pompous even, and seemed to expect the entire world to run to his personal scheme of things.

The door opened to reveal a dishevelled Anna dressed in a towelling bathrobe.

'I just dropped by to see if you were OK,' Violet said.

'Thanks,' Anna replied. 'I suppose I'm all right. I don't know what came over me last night. Would you like to come in?'

'OK, just for a minute. Don't worry about last night, it happens to most of us.'

'I bet it never happened to Dr Wells, or John Anderson for that matter.'

'Don't count on it. Remember, it was a long time ago when they were juniors.'

'I suppose you're right. I was three when John joined the police.'

'That makes me ten,' Violet laughed, 'but I already wanted to be a policewoman.'

They went into Anna's flat and sat down to coffee, the conversation quickly drifting to their respective relationships.

'You don't resent me for going out with Morgan, do you?' Violet asked.

'No,' Anna assured her, 'I'm really glad, actually. Ever since I turned him down for a second date he's been a bit sarcastic, but since he went out with you he's improved.'

'Oh,' Violet replied, 'I though he gave you the push. At least that's what he said.'

'No,' Anna answered, 'it just didn't work between us. I liked his maturity and intelligence, but we – we didn't get on in bed, if you see what I mean.'

Violet noticed a faint blush come to Anna's face and couldn't resist a smile. She could guess why Anna and Morgan hadn't hit it off, and was also amused by his vanity in pretending that it was he who had decided that the relationship was not worth pursuing.

'You prefer John Anderson, then?' she asked.

'Yes,' Anna replied. 'He's really sweet but very strong.'

'He annoys me rather,' Violet admitted, 'but then I don't like to be fathered.'

'I do,' Anna admitted. 'He makes me feel really secure. He

131

can be cold, though. I don't really understand him; in fact he even scares me a bit sometimes. I know that sounds like a contradiction, but –'

'Not at all, I understand. Possibly Morgan's similar. It's as if he never really lets himself open up completely. Anyway, I had better get on or old man Walsh will want to know why I'm so slow. I'm going to stop at Sparkwell to see if anything new has come up. I'll say you're OK.'

Anna thanked her as she drained her coffee, accepting a friendly squeeze of the hand as she left.

Detective Sergeant Dunning looked down at the line of policemen making their way slowly along the cutting, pushing their way through the dense undergrowth and prodding at the ground with sticks, one or another occasionally bending to examine something. In the light of day the cutting at Sparkwell had lost its sinister atmosphere, although the fact that he wasn't expecting to come across a mangled corpse at any moment did make things easier. He had seen too much to be over-sensitive anyway and knew that he would never react the way the girl Anna had done. Actually, he considered, forensic science was no job for a young girl: she'd have been better off going into law or something.

The area of search which he had allotted to himself had proved barren, containing nothing more interesting than a rusty iron stake that was not only far from the shape that Dr Wells had told them to look out for but had also obviously been buried in the turf for years.

Dr Wells himself was standing on the bridge, not taking part in the actual search but collecting in any samples that might prove relevant. Rumours in the station suggested that Wells had got it together with DI Violet Krebs. The thought of Krebs filled Dunning with jealousy. She had come into the Plymouth CID unit as a DC fresh out of uniform and he had watched as she was promoted to equal rank with him and then to Inspector over his head. Not only, that, but while half the male staff in the station lusted after her physically, she had remained utterly aloof to all of them, not so much as accepting a date. He had begun to wonder if she was completely cold or even if she might prefer other women. There was no evidence for it, though, and she didn't fit the image he expected of lesbians – dumpy, short-haired viragos, while Krebs was fanatically fit to the point of being over-muscled and dressed like something out of a fashion catalogue. Now she was with Dr Wells, the lucky bastard! He found himself wondering how her full, round breasts looked bare and what Dr Wells liked to do to her.

'Over here, sir!' a cry went up from one of the searching officers. Dunning snapped out of his envy-inspired erotic daydream to look at the man. He walked across to where the PC was holding up something white and the shape of an upside-down meteorological balloon. On coming closer, Dunning saw that the object was a piece of white cloth, stained with blood at the bottom where it contained some heavy, round object. He held out a specimen bag. The PC carefully dropped the object into it.

'Dr Wells!' he called, turning to see the scientist already starting towards them, pulling on thin rubber gloves as he came and meeting Dunning halfway to the bridge.

'I think this is what we've been looking for,' Wells said, holding the bag up to better examine the grisly contents. The blood was clearly only recently dry, the short, dull brown hairs exactly like those of the unfortunate James Draper. It had to be the murder weapon, Dunning didn't need Dr Wells's scientific analysis to tell him that, but he had to admit that it would certainly help with a jury. He watched as Dr Wells opened the top of the bag and peered inside the linen, revealing a black-painted sphere the size of a small orange.

'Iron, by the look of it,' Wells remarked to Dunning as they peered into the bag. 'Very neat, fits into the pocket of a jacket, and you could fell an ox with it.'

'Why do you think he threw it away so near?' Dunning asked him. 'I mean, he didn't even really try and hide it.'

'That, my dear chap, is a question for you clever detective fellows,' Wells replied. 'I, a mere scientist, hesitate to speculate, but I will hazard a guess that if you were standing out here in the middle of the night with a body at your feet and this in your hand you might be disinclined to simply put it back in your pocket for later disposal.'

'I dare say you're right,' Dunning replied. 'Any road, I'm not one to look a gift horse in the mouth.'

'Precisely,' Wells replied. 'A sensible attitude. Would you care for tea and a biscuit?'

Dunning accepted gratefully, walking back to Dr Wells's car with him and taking the Thermos lid full of hot tea that was passed to him after Wells had placed the object in the boot with the other sample bags. He was still drinking the tea ten minutes later when a familiar green two-seater pulled on to the track and parked next to Wells's old Rover.

'Morning, Violet,' Wells greeted DI Krebs as she swung her legs out of the car and walked over to him. 'I had thought you well on your way to Charmouth by now. A charming little town, by the way, if a little unfashionable for the last century or so.'

'I am going there now,' she replied, kissing Wells through the window and then settling herself on the bonnet of the Rover, acknowledging Dunning with a restrained nod. 'As I pass here anyway I decided to drop in. Seriously though, I was hoping some more evidence might have turned up, as, frankly, this Charmouth trip isn't likely to be much use.'

'You're in luck,' Wells replied, 'not ten minutes past, your boys found an item which, I think I can say without contradiction, is the murder weapon.'

Wells climbed out of the car and went to the boot, taking the sample bag and holding it up for Violet to see.

'There is blood, there is hair identical to that of the unfortunate Draper, and inside the material is a small, black iron ball, possibly a large bearing or an old cannon ball. I can tell you that the shape and size fit the depressed fracture in Draper's skull without even troubling to open the lab. Possibly more pertinently, why would such an object be where it was if it were not the murder weapon?'

'That's true,' she admitted. 'Could you spare some of that tea? I didn't get to bed until two o'clock and then I couldn't sleep. Doesn't the atmosphere here get to you?'

'No,' Wells admitted frankly. 'I pride myself on being a rationalist. I always have been, by inclination rather than experience. In my misspent youth I once found myself stranded in one of the least salubrious parts of Detroit. Lacking money and concerned for my safety, I slept in a graveyard with my sleeping bag rolled out on a conveniently flat section of a mausoleum. I slept well.'

'I don't think I could do that,' she replied, accepting the tea he had poured for her. 'I'd find it impossible to ignore the atmosphere.'

'It's not a question of ignoring it,' Wells continued. 'For me there simply is no atmosphere. Not that I'm unaware of it as a concept. I concede that this place, with the dark bulk of the moor and the light fading over Cornwall, might have inspired some people to melancholy, but not me. Also, it doesn't mean I don't enjoy beauty, both natural and man-made, but perhaps I miss abstract elements that you would take for granted, or possibly my perception is simply different.'

'You seem to appreciate good food, wine, civilised things. I mean, those Nigerian sculptures of yours give out an atmosphere you can almost touch.'

'Yes, but all those things are reassuringly solid. I am by no means insensitive to physical sensations, nor yet visual stimulation. The sculptures have a sinuous grace and an exquisite texture. Those I enjoy, but you clearly have a different, maybe deeper appreciation of them than I do. No, I take my pleasures at a straightforward level. "In your face" is the modern expression, I believe.'

Violet laughed softly and took another swallow of tea. Dunning shifted uneasily on his feet, feeling somewhat left out of the conversation and sure that he was missing some sort of private joke.

'No,' Wells was continuing, 'to me this is simply a field with a railway cutting in it and a bridge which happens to be a murder site.'

'You're lucky, in a way,' Krebs said. 'I suppose I'll become used to it, or maybe I should have gone into something else.'

'Not at all,' Wells assured her. 'Sensitivity such as yours is all too rare in the police, not to mention intelligence. You have your place, as does our good Detective Sergeant Dunning here, and as do I.'

Wells gave Dunning a good-natured prod in the ribs, a comradely gesture that lessened the Sergeant's feeling of being out of place.

'I should be going,' Krebs remarked as she drained the last of her tea and passed the cup back to Wells. 'Thanks for the tea. Oh, I called in on Anna on the way. She's a bit shaken but she'll be OK.'

Dunning turned away as she kissed Wells again and then looked back as she walked away, jealously admiring the elegance of her walk and the neat shape her bottom made under her coat.

John Anderson stood at the window of James Draper's flat, looking across to where he and Anna Ferreira had parked in order to watch Draper. If only he had maintained his vigil he would have seen Draper leave and in all probability either been able to prevent the murder or catch the murderer literally red-handed. Of course he had spent his time in the way he judged most valuable, and suggested to Robert Walsh that Draper be kept under surveillance, yet he couldn't escape the feeling that he had let slip an important opportunity. One small decision on his part and James Draper was dead. True, he reminded himself, Draper was almost certainly an accessory to a carefully premeditated murder, yet to Anderson's way of thinking that did not in any way justify Draper's subsequent murder.

The flat had proved barren of obvious clues. This had come as no surprise to him, yet the various samples that had been collected might yet yield something of significance. His own survey of the flat had also revealed very little. Draper's tastes had been simple and materialistic. Motorcycle magazines and pornography of a laddishly blatant style appeared to have been his sole reading interest. The kitchen was virtually bare, coffee, sugar and various sauces being the only sign that he ever ate in his flat. The refrigerator contained several bottles of strong lager, canned beer, cider and a half-empty litre bottle of vodka, nothing else. Everything he had learnt about Draper suggested a lifestyle devoid of depth and a greedy, selfish attitude with little or nothing to make up for it. What, he wondered, had his girlfriend, Sue, seen in him? Humour perhaps? Company? Or simply an improvement over her home life?

She had come round to the flat on Saturday evening, dressed for the town and clearly expecting James Draper to be there. DC Heath had had the unpleasant task of telling her that Draper was dead. Her response had been both hysterical and irrational, transferring the blame to the police for no apparent reason. Anderson couldn't help feeling privately glad that it was Heath rather than himself who had dealt with the hysterical girl, eventually getting a WPC to escort her back to her parents' flat in a different block of the estate.

Anderson pondered her value to the case. Undoubtedly she would have a better knowledge of Draper's movements than anybody else, even if she was unaware of his involvement with Charles Draper's death. On the other hand, her attitude to the police had been uncompromisingly antagonistic, to the point where she had scratched DC Heath's face and all but accused him of killing her boyfriend. Interviewing her was not going to be easy and was certainly a task for experienced officers. First they would have to convince her that they were acting in her best interests and intended to catch her boyfriend's killer. After that she might well prove a valuable asset to the investigation.

He sighed deeply, annoyed at the attitude of automatic antagonism to the police that some people took. They could do no right, but were always the first to be blamed if some tragedy did occur, as had happened now.

Violet Krebs yawned and stretched as she got out of the Morgan. The steep, narrow streets of Charmouth had left her no option but to park in the area that fronted the beach. In front of her the river ran out across the coarse sand, splitting into dozens of shallow channels. A couple of children were braving the cold, splashing in the water in brightly coloured boots, their attempt at damming the torrent swept instantly aside. Otherwise the beach was deserted, the hills rising on either side of the little town to form imposing cliffs, the fossiliferous strata for which the town was famous showing clearly in bands of dull blue-grey, off-white, and a deep red-brown. Behind her the huddle of houses and shops straggled up the shallow valley, the pines and cedars of the old gardens producing a picture reminiscent of postcards of Edwardian spas – which, she reflected, was exactly what it was.

Despite the fact that the trip to Charmouth was almost certainly a wild goose chase, she had been glad to volunteer for it. Driving across Devon and half of Dorset had been a far preferable option to spending the day in close company with her colleagues. True, the fact that Draper had telephoned a call box in Charmouth shortly before his death was likely to be significant, but then at best it implied that his murderer had been in Charmouth before driving to Sparkwell. It proved the murderer had arrived by car and had parked somewhere near Sparkwell, as it would have been impossible to get there from Charmouth by any other reasonable means than driving. Unfortunately, the chances of being able to show that a given vehicle had been in two places at distinct times were close to zero, even if they made a television appeal. As it was, all she expected to find was a call box in which the unknown prime suspect had been at some time the previous day.

Where was it the phone company had said? Close to the beach, near a restaurant. Violet looked around her, immediately finding the only call box that fitted the description. She walked across to it. There it was, a call box. On a summer afternoon, anybody using the box would have been right next to the outside tables of the restaurant. Now, however, it was unlikely that anybody would have noticed the phone ring. The restaurant was worth trying, of course, as were the shops on either side of it.

She decided to try the restaurant first. The retracted awning and empty hanging baskets gave it a rather forlorn look from the outside. On the inside it was warm and bright, polished wooden furniture, brass fittings and old photographs of sailing ships and heavily bearded tars giving it an atmosphere that she recognised as more or less standard in West Country seaside resorts. Only the use of fossils as ornaments seemed to give it local character, until a tap on an enormous ammonite proved it to be plastic. Violet coughed and then called out, eventually attracting the attention of a large, cheerful-looking man who emerged from the kitchen.

He had heard nothing. Indeed, the restaurant wasn't actually open, it being the closed season, but he had been decorating in preparation for spring. He had been around on Saturday afternoon, painting at the back most of the time and could easily have missed it had the phone in the call box rung. Also he had noticed nothing unusual over the last few weeks. Indeed, the town had been exceptionally quiet.

Violet thanked the man and left. She had expected nothing better. The two small shops between the restaurant and the car park were both tourist shops and firmly shut, her raps on the shuttered doors producing no response. To the other side of the restaurant the shops curved back in a line so that the last few were out of her line of vision. All of those which she could see were shut, narrow, two-story buildings the upper windows of which had obviously not recently been cleaned and appeared to open from storerooms for the shops rather than residences. Finding a witness was clearly a hopeless task, yet she determined to walk to the end of the line, if only for her own satisfaction at having checked as thoroughly as possible.

She walked across to the railing that separated the street from the beach and turned. A shop sign immediately caught her eye – 'George Cutts – Antiques and Curios'.

Violet walked across the intervening space, her pulse quickening. The door was locked, the interior of the shop showing dark, the grey winter light illuminating a rag-tag collection of paintings, military curios, *objets d'art* and fossils. Beyond the window display were larger pieces, cabinets set against the walls, tables and chests covering most of the floor, each one littered with smaller pieces, books, old albums, a globe, filing drawers that were themselves antique. A small cannon caught her eye, smart in polished brass and black paint, the mouth stoppered with a red-painted cannonball. Beneath the barrel stood more of the iron balls in a carefully stacked pile, each painted in glossy black. A lump came up in Violet's throat. She stood back. The upper window was clean and bordered by deep green curtains, nets obscuring her view of the inside.

She rapped loudly on the glass door. Nothing happened

and so she repeated the process. A creak drew her attention to the window above her. She looked up to see a large, callused hand lifting the frame, and then a heavy, bullet-shaped head being thrust out, bald except for a fringe at the rear like the tonsure of a monk. He looked puzzled. Violet flashed her warrant card at him, failing to change his expression.

'Are you Mr George Cutts?' she asked, stepping back further so that she didn't have to crane her neck to talk to him.

'No, no,' the man replied, 'George Cutts was my father. I'm the new owner, Nathan Cutts.'

EIGHT
Monday

Violet Krebs leant back against the railing and looked up at the banks of houses rising up the hill. Nathan Cutts's shop and house stood in front of her, no longer the peaceful place it had been the previous day but a hive of activity. Police tape held back a crowd of onlookers, two Dorset constables ensuring that everything stayed in order. Morgan Wells was inside, as was a man from Dorset forensic and John Anderson. Cutts himself was in Plymouth, awaiting his interview.

From where she stood it was possible to see which houses looked down on the front and the area around Cutts's shop. One, painted a pale blue and a story taller than its neighbours, had a exceptional view and she decided that it would make a good first port of call – moreover a woman was looking out of an upstairs window at the activity below. She walked along the line of shops, doubling back to find the entrance to the house. 'Sea View Guesthouse', the sign on the gate proclaimed with a marked lack of originality.

Krebs ascended the steps and rapped at the door, her warrant card already in her hand to prevent any misconceptions. After a moment it was opened, a sharp-faced woman in her late middle age looking out with an air of disapproval that quickly changed when she saw the warrant card.

'I'm Mrs Smith, Lilian Smith. Come in, dear,' the woman answered when Krebs had introduced herself. 'So I see you've finally got Mr Cutts. I can't say it's not before time either. Well, if you want a witness you know where to find me. I thought it would come to this for years, mark you, but old Prosser never would take any notice of me. Said I was making it up, he did. Well, we'll see who's so clever now, shan't we.'

'Perhaps you could go a little more slowly, Mrs Smith,' Krebs interrupted, feeling lost. Mrs Smith had entered what appeared to be a communal sitting room and was indicating an armchair. Krebs took it and accepted the woman's offer of tea. Prosser was one of the Dorset PCs guarding the house, but otherwise Mrs Smith's monologue meant nothing to her at all.

'So,' Krebs began as she accepted her tea, determined to get a grip on the conversation before Mrs Smith's flow resumed, 'first of all, can you confirm that you know Mr Nathan Cutts who owns the house directly between yours and the sea?'

'Certainly I can,' Mrs Smith announced. 'Weird he is, not like his old father, no, he was a gentleman, but not Nathan, oh no.'

'Right,' Krebs broke in, 'and you're not surprised that he's been arrested?'

'Not at all, I've been expecting it for years. Nasty piece of work.'

'Why exactly?'

'Eh? Surely you know, else why arrest him?'

'No, Mrs Smith, I'm afraid I don't. Mr Cutts is helping us with our enquiries on a very serious matter, and I'm hoping you can throw some light on this.'

'Oh,' Mrs Smith continued, now sounding somewhat

nonplussed. 'So you're not arresting him for what he does on the beach? What's he done then?'

'I'm afraid I can't tell you why we are talking to him, but it's nothing to do with the beach. Anyway, what does he do on the beach?'

'Well, he's pretends he's collecting fossils for his shop, but of course he's not really –'

'So what is he doing?'

'Why, looking at the girls of course. Tries to watch them change, he does. Old Prosser won't believe me, though –'

'Mrs Smith,' Krebs interrupted, her last hope that the woman had any interesting information fading. 'That's a concern for the local police, if that. My interest is in knowing whether you have any idea of Mr Cutts's movements, or whether you've noticed a blue car, a Ford Sierra Sapphire to be exact, near his house.'

'No,' the woman answered, shaking her head, 'I'm afraid I haven't, but I can tell you what he's been up to all right. I keep notes so that old Prosser can see that he goes out when there are girls on the beach –'

'Might I see your notes?' Krebs asked, suddenly hopeful again.

'Why, certainly,' Mrs Smith replied with absolute delight.

Krebs took a sip of tea and smiled to herself as Mrs Smith left the room. Hopefully this would prove useful, providing evidence of Cutts's movements. Then she thought of how Mrs Smith would look on the witness stand and quickly lost her smile.

The woman returned with a large notebook, which she proudly handed to Krebs. The notation was erratic but legible. Monday the tenth contained only the statement 'out all day'. Saturday the fifteenth had no entry. Krebs cursed under her breath, noting that the entries for some of the days covered pages of writing. It proved nothing, but on the other hand it also failed to provide Cutts with an alibi.

'What about last Saturday?' Krebs asked.

'Oh, I'm afraid I was out, shopping in Lyme,' Mrs Smith answered. 'He was in in the evening, though. I saw him, sitting at his window like he always does, pretending to do things but really he's watching the guest house. About ten at night it would have been.'

'OK, thank you, Mrs Smith. You've been very helpful,' Krebs replied. On the whole, she reflected as she finished her tea, the woman's information weighed against Cutts, her assumption that he was a pervert being fortuitous if irrelevant. It was, however, circumstantial at best. But if other neighbours were like Mrs Smith she could expect to build up a solid bank of evidence.

Krebs left and continued her questioning, receiving two views of Cutts. Most of the men thought of him as a rather pathetic figure, lonely, dull and socially inept. Women tended to be more antagonistic, weird, creepy and sneaky being some of the adjectives used to describe him. Hard fact was less easy to come by, and she returned to his shop without anything concrete to discuss with Wells and Anderson.

John Anderson paced slowly across the floor of Nathan Cutts's main room to stare out of the window at the beach and the sullen grey-green of the sea beyond. For a moment he watched the crash of waves on the shingle beach and the constant ebb and flow of water where the river drained into the sea. He then turned back to the room.

The house was tiny: one small bedroom, an attic dormer, minimal facilities and the shop. It was also entirely cluttered with antiques, curios and souvenirs, ranging from pieces worth a few pence to fine pictures and furniture the value of which it was beyond his ability to assess. A strong believer in the character of a person being reflected in their environment, Anderson had studied Cutts's flat at leisure once Dr Wells and a forensic scientist from Dorchester had removed anything that might be valuable as evidence.

There had been no shortage of evidence. The cannonballs in the shop exactly matched the one used to murder James Draper. Dr Wells had discovered old linen kept under the sink for use as rags. One piece had a cut-out exactly matching the piece in which the cannonball had been wrapped. An ink bottle had been taken, hopefully to match the ink in the pen found in the Tamar. A wide variety of other samples had been taken, each with the potential to add one more dram to the weight of evidence building against Cutts. True, nothing that had been found suggested a motive, but that would undoubtedly become clear in the longer term.

On his return to Plymouth in the afternoon, Anderson was to be present at the interview with Cutts and now sought to provide himself with an insight into the man. In another house, the range of antiques would have been a valuable indicator, but as Cutts had taken over the shop from his father, Anderson felt them to be of limited significance. The house was also crammed with books, which he judged to be more telling. Many were old and could well have predated Cutts's occupancy. Tide tables and books of local marine information also abounded, some series going back several years. Many, however, were new titles, which showed that Cutts's main interests lay in natural history. Books on the taxonomy and identification of plants, birds and wildlife in general made up the majority of the collection, while others dealing with geology, palaeontology and evolution were also common. Novels were scarcer and mainly classics from the last century, Dickens, Trollope, Saki and Conan Doyle among them. Cutts appeared to be quiet and scholarly. There was nothing one might associate with aggression and nothing more murderous than a book on poisonous fungi.

Everything about the house supported this assessment. The fittings in the bathroom were china, the glaze fractured into mosaics by age. The taps were brass and green with verdigris.

An ancient water heater provided for both kitchen and bathroom. Wood, linoleum, glazed tiles in a pattern that was probably Victorian – everything about the place suggested a total lack of concern with modern convenience. While not exceptionally dirty, and cluttered rather than messy, the flat had a slightly stale smell, mixed with aromas such as moth-balls, wax polish and carbolic soap, none of which had been commonplace for years. The choices of colour and decoration were in all cases understated, dark, rich browns, muted greens and blues, black and slate-grey. All in all, from the appearance of his surroundings, Cutts appeared to have been a thoroughly old-fashioned, quiet man.

Interviews with neighbours had also created a picture of an intensely lonely man, both meek and unobtrusive, a man who preferred not to hold a conversation even with trades-men with whom he had dealt for years. True, one or two of the women who Krebs had talked to had spoken of finding Cutts creepy, saying that in the summer he spent a lot of time on the beach or walking in the countryside, ostensibly looking for fossils, birds or flowers but in their view spying on girls. A Mrs Smith in particular had been antagonistic towards Cutts, although from what Krebs said she had lacked firm evidence. Her notebook, however, might prove a useful contradiction should Cutts attempt to create a false alibi.

Violet Krebs had also been going over the house, and was now in the bedroom. Thinking that she had been a remarkably long time, he crossed the main room and pushed open the dark oak door, finding her kneeling on the floor to examine the escritoire that had been placed under the window close to the bed. She was running her fingers over the woodwork, paying particular attention to the details of veneer and carving. Her face was set in an expression of absolute con-centration, her brow furrowed and her lips pursed.

'What have you found?' he asked.

'There's a false bottom in this writing table,' she answered.

'I'm trying to find the way to open it.'

'How do you know?' he said, sinking to his knees beside her, briefly catching the faint musk of her perfume.

'If you open the top,' she continued, 'the well isn't deep enough to account for the full depth of the table. I'd say a space has been built in big enough for a will or title deeds, that sort of thing. It's well concealed, though.'

Anderson considered the table. A complex pattern of carved scroll work and veneer inlay decorated the front, which Krebs was assuming concealed some sort of catch. The sides were similar, the back pressed against the wall, dust and cobweb showing that it was clearly not moved regularly. He bent down to examine the underside, which proved to be a featureless plate of wood. Each leg rested on a small brass wheel, the back pair dull and clogged with dust, the front pair with little dust and showing areas of brighter brass on the actual wheels.

'I think I have it,' he reported, placing a hand on each of the front legs and twisting. At first nothing happened. Then there was a sharp click and the front panel swung open to reveal a flat drawer no more than an inch deep.

Krebs took hold of the tiny brass handles and pulled gently, the drawer sliding out smoothly. Inside, neatly stacked in eight groups placed with careful attention to symmetry, were piles of fading photographs, each depicting a naked woman.

Anderson selected a pile. The top picture, the style of which suggested to him a date prior to the turn of the century, showed a young woman in the act of undressing in front of a long mirror. It struck him as more artistic than pornographic, although scarcely an article of high art. He turned to watch Krebs, interested in her reaction to their discovery. She was smiling, looking at a picture with an expression of tolerant amusement.

'Amazing that this sort of stuff used to be thought of as deeply shocking,' she commented, passing him her photo.

Anderson took it from her, finding that it showed a girl on a swing, her skirts flying up to reveal full drawers pulled tight over a fleshy bottom.

'Amusing,' he remarked, 'but hardly a valuable clue. We should be making for Plymouth – let's leave this to the local men.'

He placed the photo carefully back on its stack and got to his feet, turning to the door.

'Hang on,' Krebs said, 'they get saucier. Actually I think you ought to see this.'

Anderson turned back, taking the photo Krebs was holding out for him. It was more recent than the last, possibly from the twenties, and showed a woman naked except for impractically high heels and tied to a tree. Another woman stood to the side, also near naked and wielding a short, many-thonged whip. The one Krebs was holding depicted two young women in old-fashioned pyjama suits, one bent across the other's knee with her trousers tangled around her knees while her companion spanked her with a hairbrush.

The next down in the pile was similar, as were each of the others. When they had laid each out on the floor, only a minority of the pictures proved to show simple nudity, far more being devoted to flagellation and other sado-masochistic practices.

John Anderson drew the BMW to a halt in the police station car park. DI Violet Krebs's green Morgan was already there, which meant that they should be able to interview Nathan Cutts more or less immediately. He strode across the car park with a stronger feeling of energy and purpose than he had had since coming down to Plymouth. Finally he had an opportunity to handle the case on his own terms, instead of pursuing frustratingly vague leads. He entered the building and made his way to the interview rooms where both DI Krebs and DSupt Walsh were waiting.

'Is his solicitor here yet?' Anderson asked.

'The duty solicitor's with him now,' Walsh answered. 'Oddly enough Cutts has no solicitor, or at least he says he doesn't.'

Anderson shrugged, his interest lying only in being able to start the interview. With the weight of evidence they had accumulated, who acted as solicitor for Nathan Cutts was unlikely to be important. He motioned Krebs into the interview room ahead of him, taking his place leaning against the wall. His role, by prior agreement, was to watch Cutts's reactions and ask occasional questions to break the flow of Walsh's questioning.

Nathan Cutts was sitting across the table, slouched into his chair, his face a picture of nervous misery. Despite his posture, Anderson could see that he was a powerfully built man, short but broad and heavy-set. His barrel-like build suggested natural muscle rather than the better defined results of planned exercise. At fifteen, maybe sixteen stone, Cutts was certainly powerful enough to have handled the big but fleshy Charles Draper, while James Draper would have been a toy in his hands, even with youth in his favour. Actually, Anderson decided, Cutts was not as old as he initially appeared. His almost totally bald cranium, weather-beaten skin and shabby brown tweed suit suggested a man of fifty, yet on closer inspection he seemed no more than forty, possibly as young as thirty-five. Next to Cutts sat the duty solicitor, a thin, grey-haired man whom Anderson had not previously met.

Robert Walsh cleared his throat and depressed the button on the recorder.

'Interview commencing 14.22,' he began. 'Present are the suspect, Mr Nathan Cutts and Mr Giles Goulding, representing Mr Cutts. Officers present are Detective Superintendent Robert Walsh, interviewing, Detective Chief Inspector John Anderson and Detective Inspector Violet Krebs.

'Mr Cutts, you have been charged with the murder of Charles Draper of Guildford and of James Draper of

Plymouth. Do you understand the charges?'

'Yes, but this is some sort of terrible mistake! I've never even heard of these people!' Cutts stammered. Anderson noted his educated accent, almost certainly denoting public school, and also the high pitch of his voice, more probably the result of stress than a natural trait.

'Mr Cutts,' Walsh continued, ignoring Cutts's protestations of innocence and laying a sample bag containing the cannonball and its linen sheath onto the table, 'do you recognise this object? For the tape, I am now showing Mr Cutts exhibit A, the presumed murder weapon.'

'No! I mean yes, I know what it is,' Cutts squealed. 'But it's nothing to do with me!'

'Please describe it, Mr Cutts,' Walsh asked.

'It's – it's a piece of cloth, like a bit of old sheet. There's something heavy in it, like a ball and there's blood, and – and – look, I've never seen the horrible thing before in my life! You've got to believe me!'

'So you recognise the material as a piece of linen bedsheet?'

'Yes – I mean no – well maybe. I don't know, it was a guess. I mean, what else would it be?'

'A sheet of linen was found in your house, Mr Cutts. The fabric exactly matches this piece, as do the dimensions of the piece cut from one corner. Do you admit that you cut this piece from the larger piece in order to make a club which you subsequently used to murder James Draper?'

'No! Look, I give you my absolute assurance, this has nothing to do with me whatever!'

'Mr Cutts,' Krebs remarked, her voice soft and reasonable, 'there is overwhelming evidence to link you with the murder of James Draper. Should you admit the crime, it will ultimately save you considerable trouble, while a guilty plea will result in a shorter sentence. Now –'

'DI Krebs, that sounded not dissimilar to a threat,' Goulding broke in. 'Please keep your questions pertinent.'

'I apologise,' Krebs replied. 'I worded that poorly.'

'Very well, Mr Cutts. Let us put that aside for the moment.' Walsh said as he placed another sample bag containing the gold fountain pen on the table. 'I am now showing the suspect exhibit B, a gold fountain pen engraved with the name Nathan Cutts. Mr Cutts, do you deny that this pen belongs to you?'

'Yes,' Cutts protested, 'I've never seen it before in my life!'

'Mr Cutts, it has your name engraved on it,' Walsh continued.

'I don't care,' Cutts answered, the volume of his voice rising to approach a shout. 'It's not mine!'

'Perhaps', Anderson spoke from his position by the door, 'Mr Cutts can provide alibis for the two murders.'

'Yes, yes,' Cutts said hastily, snatching at the verbal bait Anderson had thrown for him. 'I'm usually in my shop. My till receipts will show when I served customers. I don't employ anyone, I'm always there.'

'Very well,' Walsh replied. 'First then, can you account for your movements during the afternoon and early evening of Saturday the fifteenth?'

'Saturday, Saturday,' Cutts answered. 'Let me see. Yes, it was low tide in the afternoon, so I went looking for fossils on the beach. Yes, and I didn't get back until it was nearly dark. Then I had some tea and stayed in.'

'Can anybody confirm this?' Walsh asked.

'Well, er – no, I don't suppose they can. I mean, there were a few people on the beach near the town, but it was rather a cold day.'

'Do you recall anybody seeing you when you returned to your house at dusk?'

'No, I'm afraid not. It's right next to the beach, you see.'

'Very well,' Walsh repeated. 'How about the afternoon of Monday the tenth?'

'Last Monday, well, let me see. I don't open the shop on

152

Monday, not in the offseason. Yes, that's right, I remember. Someone rang to ask if I was interested in buying some old maps, West Country maps, you understand. The price was very attractive, so I went to see them, but I'd copied the address down incorrectly or something, so I never did get there.'

'And where was this appointment?'

'Ah, in Okehampton, yes, but when I got to the road the gentleman who had phoned me was supposed to live in, the numbers didn't go up far enough. In the end I had to come back. It took most of the day.'

'And can anybody confirm this?'

'No, I'm afraid not. You see I work alone, and I'm not married or anything, but I assure you it's the truth.'

'I'm afraid we need a little more than that, Mr Cutts. Think carefully: could anybody have seen you on either occasion?'

Cutts paused to think, giving Anderson a further opportunity to study him. When the questioning had changed tack he had relaxed visibly, his air of tension only returning as his alibis proved difficult to establish.

'Yes,' Cutts began suddenly. 'I might have been seen. I stopped for petrol before driving back. It was the garage outside Okehampton as you go towards the A30. It's a new garage, they've probably even got a security camera.'

'What time would you have been there?' Walsh continued, his tone as bland and even as ever.

'Let me see, quite early in the afternoon. Perhaps two o'clock, maybe a little later.'

'Thank you,' Walsh answered, 'we will of course need to confirm that. Now, when did you meet Herrick?'

'Who's he?' Cutts answered.

'She, Melanie Herrick, a neighbour of Charles Draper.'

'I assure you I've never met her. I tell you, you've arrested entirely the wrong man. I've never heard of either Draper, or this Herrick woman.'

'What about Sparkwell?' Anderson put in.

'I don't know anybody of that name either,' Cutts protested, making a frantic gesture with his hands. Anderson considered the answer. If Cutts had murdered James Draper, then the fact that Sparkwell was a place rather than a person should have been engraved deeply in his mind. Cutts had failed to fall into his trap, and had also failed to make a mistake when answering Walsh's questions, many of which had been designed to make the suspect slip up by giving a detail which he should have had no way of knowing. Either Cutts was genuine, or he had a far cooler head than he was letting on. Anderson preferred the second choice. Cutts lacked a firm alibi for either murder and the forensic evidence was clear. Cold, hard facts were preferable to any amount of intangible evidence such as not being caught out by carefully worded questions.

'I think that will do for now,' Walsh was saying. 'Interview terminated, 14.46. Violet, John, can I have a word with you.'

Anderson left the interview room, followed by Walsh and Krebs, the duty sergeant escorting Cutts back to his cell.

'My impression,' Walsh began as soon as they were out of hearing, 'is that the evidence is strongly against him. Also, I feel he is a great deal tougher than he makes out. We're assuming he was paid, which provides his motive for killing Charles Draper, so I think that if we can find a link between Cutts and James Draper we're home and dry. What do you think?'

'What about Draper having the call box number on his mobile, sir?' Krebs asked.

'At the end of the day, that's circumstantial,' Walsh replied. 'We need something firmer.'

'I agree with your analysis,' Anderson told Robert Walsh. 'I also feel that his ability to answer questions without making mistakes is in accord with the careful planning of the first murder.'

'I agree too, sir,' Krebs added, 'but – no, never mind.'

'What's on your mind, Violet?' Walsh asked.

'Nothing really, sir,' she replied. 'It's just that his personality, the atmosphere of his house, his lifestyle – they just aren't in accord with my image of the murderer. Still, as you say, the facts speak for themselves. In the end, I have to agree with you.'

'That's the right attitude,' Walsh answered her, 'especially as evidence based on vague hunches is worse than useless in court.'

'I can see the sense in your uncertainty,' Anderson addressed Krebs, 'yet it's clearly a carefully contrived front.'

Krebs nodded and for a moment seemed lost in thought. Then she suddenly brightened, stating that she, for one, was sorely in need of a coffee. Anderson followed her from the prisoner reception area.

Anna Ferreira sat on the hulk of a fallen pine, gazing out over the mud and water of the Tavy estuary. It was one of the loneliest places she knew, a sheltered enclave of slate beach that could only be reached by a muddy scramble along the shore from the Lopwell Dam, itself a place that most people would have considered quiet. Behind her the thickly wooded hillside rose at such a rate that it acted as a cliff, barring any risk of intrusion from that direction, especially with the last twenty feet a sheer wall of wet slate. Across the river a flat expanse of marshy ground bordered the mud, giving way to flat meadow and then a slow rise, with the hamlet of Maristow set against thick woods.

She felt that she had failed by letting the horror of James Draper's death get to her so much. She hadn't expected the shock to affect her, which had been part of the reason that it had, when normally she could manage seeing and handling bodies without difficulty. The main reason had been the situation – the brilliant arc lights, the utter blackness surrounding the cutting, the bloody mess that had once been a man, and the knowledge that short hours before a man capable of such a foul act had traced the same path she had. Dr Wells had insisted that she didn't return to the lab until at least Tuesday, which she also felt unreasonable as it might harm her record when she had in fact completed her work in the cutting, only accepting a comforting arm from Violet Krebs when the bulk of the work was finished. Actually, it hadn't been until she was in the car with John Anderson that she'd really let her feelings show, her irritation after the events of the previous evening quickly forgotten in the comfort and reassurance of being held by him.

Meanwhile, with time to kill and no desire for company, she had taken the train out to Bere Ferrers and walked down to her private place. It was perfect for simply sitting and thinking, and far enough away from the site where they had found Charles Draper's body not to be tainted by the first murder. Unfortunately she had been unable to take her normal pleasure in the beauty and solitude, her mind constantly going back to the murders.

Maybe she had chosen the wrong place to come; perhaps it was, after all, too similar to the area of the murder investigation. The moors might have been better from that point of view, but they would also have been colder, windier and much harder to get to without a car. Anyway, here was more enclosed, sheltered both in a physical and emotive sense, a better environment for her present mood than the bleak emptiness of Dartmoor.

She lay forward, resting her chin on her hands with the length of her body supported by the tree trunk. With her eyes closed she let her other senses work, taking in the sharp salt smell of the mud with its hint of decay, a distant trill of birdsong and the faint rustle of the breeze, the rough bark of the pine trunk underneath her and the faint warmth of the winter sun on her back. Another sound came, strident and intrusive in the peace and solitude, the sound of a human voice. She looked up, annoyed at what she felt was an intrusion, then saw that the voice came from the far side of the river where a young woman with two children was calling to one of them who had strayed too far ahead of her. Anna stayed still, keen not to be noticed for no rational reason, watching the three figures across from her.

After a minute she grew bored, instead turning her attention to the glossy black shape of a waterlogged branch that was drifting lazily down stream on the falling tide. Maybe not so lazily. It was going as fast as the woman who was moving at a brisk jog, maybe faster. She estimated its speed at around eight miles per hour, pushed mainly by the flow of the river in the centre of the channel. Of course it would be slower going up, with the weight of river water pushing against the tide. It was five, maybe six miles to the open sea, so the branch would probably get to the sea before the tide turned. No, it certainly would, unless it got caught. Charles Draper's body had been floating like that, possibly for as much as eighteen hours before it was found. Why hadn't it drifted out to sea?

Anna sat up, keen to iron out the apparent inconsistency. A copy of the tide table was in her back pocket, an essential item when walking along a narrow shore with a cliff behind her. She pondered a minute. Draper had been drowned at the quay at 3 p.m. – that was the assumption. If that was the case, the rising tide would have taken his body up river for the next four hours until the tide turned at 7 p.m. No, it would have been later, as the tables were for Devonport, perhaps 7.15 p.m. The tide would then have turned and run out for six hours. Even if the body had been at the very top of the tidal reach, twenty or more miles up river at Gunnislake, it should have been taken out to sea. Unless, of course, it caught on the shale ridge off Thorn Point, which was evidently what had happened.

Then again, that only put the body on Thorn Point at 1 a.m. on the Tuesday morning, although admittedly near the top of the beach, where it had been found. Could the morning's high tide have failed to reach the body? Definitely not, both because if the body had arrived at Thorn Point on the top of the high spring tide it would have gone clean over, and because Tuesday morning's tide had actually been twenty centimetres higher than Monday evening's and so would have caught the body.

So, Tuesday morning's tide would have picked the body up and moved it upstream briefly and then back. Yes, it could easily have been stuck near the high tide mark on Thorn Point to be found in the morning. On the other hand, the whole theory rested on the body getting caught on Thorn Point, which, if it had been initially dumped in the current on a rising tide, there was no reason that it should. No, the wind must have blown it into the bay that Thorn Point guarded to the seaward side. It did make sense, but then why shouldn't it have done?

Anna wryly admitted to herself that she had been hoping her chain of logic would provide a different answer, an answer that might have stirred the case up a bit and made her look a little less useless. Oh well, there was no harm in thinking. Actually, she reflected, the wind on Tuesday morning had been cold and quite strong. She remembered putting her hair up to stop it blowing in her face. It had been blowing up river, from Plymouth, which meant from the south-east. Yes, that was definitely right, so when the tide was right up and the shale ridge covered, anything floating in the bay would have been pushed out into the channel and then swept out to sea.

What of Monday afternoon, though? If the wind had been the same, the body should never have stuck on Thorn Point in the first place. She thought back to the Monday. Was it the day Dr Wells had been away all day, extending a weekend in

London with a day's holiday? Yes, that was right. She had spent the day in the lab, improving her skills with various instruments. It had been wet most of the day, maybe all day, and windy, but she was unable to remember the wind direction.

She decided to look at it another way. The body had been there, so how could it have got there if her reasoning was right? It would have to have stuck on the shale ridge as the tide fell, therefore arriving there after high tide on the current, without the chance of being pushed out by the wind during slack water. That meant it would have been washed up after 7.30 a.m., more likely 8 a.m., a couple of hours at most before it was found. To have reached that point at that time, it would have to have been dropped at the quay not on Monday afternoon when he had been drowned, but in the early hours of Tuesday morning, after low tide and maybe as late as 7 a.m.

No, there were too many ifs and buts, the only sure facts being that Draper had died on Monday afternoon and been found on Tuesday morning. She wouldn't dare present her ideas to Dr Wells, who would dismiss them as unscientific speculation. She ought to talk to somebody, though, as the idea would suggest that Draper had been drowned earlier and then dumped in the river in the middle of the night, a supposition that fitted the absence of witnesses for Monday afternoon and made much more sense as a time to dispose of a body. Also, it cleared up the difficulty of dragging the body across the mud if it had been dumped shortly before high tide. Detective Superintendent Walsh was in charge, of course, but perhaps too senior and too remote for her to talk to easily. John would be better, or perhaps Violet Krebs, who seemed both intelligent and sympathetic. In any case, they would be busy with the second murder and best not approached until later. Also, she wanted to look at Thorn Point again and think a bit more before speaking to anyone.

Anna climbed off the log, slid the tide table into her back

pocket and set off along the shore, looking for an easy place to climb the hillside and so cross the Bere Peninsula to Thorn Point.

Following the interview with Cutts, John Anderson requested the go-ahead from Walsh to interview James Draper's girl-friend. Walsh agreed, also agreeing that an interview by a single officer might prove less intimidating. Following Krebs's advice, Anderson requisitioned an unmarked car from the pool and drove out to the Leighdon Estate, parking immediately by Attlee House, in which Sue lived with her parents. The block was identical to that in which James Draper had lived, but set across from it in mirror image.

Anderson stood for a moment in front of the lift, pondering his line of questioning. When told of her boyfriend's death, Sue had become hysterical, for some reason managing to transfer the blame on to the police in her mind. She seemed neither rational nor intelligent, with an unremitting hostility to the police presumably derived from her upbringing. A sudden thought occurred to him and he turned back to the car, calling in to control on the radio.

'This is DCI Anderson,' he said to the constable who answered. 'Could you get me information on a Sue Walker of 37, Attlee House on the Leighdon Estate, or more specifically on her parents.'

The PC acknowledged his request and asked him to wait. Anderson replaced the radio and sat back, watching the passing residents with a feeling of detached distaste.

After a while a call came over the radio for him with the information he had requested. There was nothing on Sue or her mother, Gloria Walker, while her father, Saul Walker, had no recent convictions but a record of burglaries and assaults across a period of over twenty years. Anderson drew his breath in. This was clearly not going to be a simple case of asking questions and receiving direct information. He climbed out of the car, contemplating the best slant to take on the interview.

It would be an hour or more until anybody with a conventional job returned home, which increased his chances of not having to face the entire Walker tribe at the same time. Therefore it was best to interview now, and to tread softly. Anderson entered the lift, winced at the unpleasant odour and decided to take the stairs instead. The third floor proved to contain larger flats than the one James Draper had occupied, 37 facing out from the bulk of the estate. He knocked gently on the door, which was answered by a worn-looking blonde woman in whom an older version of Sue was immediately recognisable.

'DCI Anderson, Surrey Police,' he introduced himself. 'Are you Mrs Gloria Walker?'

'Yeah,' the woman replied resignedly. 'Come in. What is it this time?'

'Nothing to worry about, Mrs Walker,' Anderson replied in his most casual manner. 'I was hoping to ask your daughter Sue a few questions, that's all.'

'Oh, right,' Mrs Walker answered. 'I suppose it's about that James Draper. Sue! There's some copper here to see you! Do you want a tea, love?'

Against his normal habit, Anderson accepted the offer of tea, hoping that by being as informal as possible he would maximise his chances of obtaining the information he wanted. He took a seat in the kitchen, waiting patiently while Mrs Walker made the tea. Presently Sue came in, looking more slatternly than ever, her make-up smeared down her face where she had been crying. She threw Anderson a look that combined hatred and misery, hunching her back and folding her arms across her chest in a gesture at once defensive and wary.

'What do you want?' she demanded.

'I realise this is a very difficult time for you,' he began, 'but

161

I was hoping to ask you some questions that may help us to catch the man who killed James.'

'What do you care?' Sue answered coldly.

'Sue,' Anderson replied, 'I realise that in general you regard the police as being against you, but in this case it really would be in your best interests to help.'

'I don't know anything,' Sue replied. 'All right? Now you can go.'

'Sue –' Mrs Walker began, only to be silenced by a look from her daughter.

'Please,' Anderson began, 'it really is very important and surely you want the man caught?'

Sue didn't reply, instead biting her lip and looking away. Her resolve was apparently weakening. Appealing to her desire to see her boyfriend avenged was clearly a worthwhile tack to follow. As he was about to ask for her help again, Anderson heard the key grate in the lock.

'Oh God,' Mrs Walker said, 'your dad's back early.'

Mentally, Anderson cursed, certain that the presence of Saul Walker would not make things easier.

'Hello Saul, love,' Mrs Walker said in a tone of apology as a heavy-set man entered the room. 'This is Mr Anderson, from the police – he's here to ask about James.'

'Got a warrant?' Saul Walker demanded.

'No,' Anderson admitted. 'This is purely informal.'

'Then get out,' the man said tersely.

Anderson felt his skin prickle at the man's aggression but kept his face carefully expressionless. Interviewing Sue in the presence of her father was clearly impossible and there was nothing to be gained by staying. Nevertheless, he was determined not to be rattled by the man and so drank the rest of his tea before leaving.

'And if you want to know what I think, Draper got what he fucking deserved!' Saul Walker bellowed as the door closed, a wail of distress from Sue following her father's heartless

162

statement. As Anderson walked away down the corridor he could hear the beginnings of what promised to be a major family argument. He blanked the noise out, instead considering the possibility of Saul Walker as a suspect. He was certainly big and powerful enough to fit the known characteristics of the murderer, better in fact than Cutts. If Cutts was innocent, however, then he had clearly been set up, and Anderson could neither imagine Saul Walker doing that nor arranging the carefully planned murder of Charles Draper. Still, in the unlikely event that Cutts proved innocent, Saul Walker would certainly need further investigation.

Anderson only glanced at the lift before taking the stairwell down, arriving at the bottom to find a young woman waiting outside the lift doors. She immediately struck him as familiar, especially her dress of a smart, if plain, secretarial suit and carefully applied, understated make-up. This was the smarter of the two girls with whom James Draper and Sue shared so much drink when he and Anna had been watching Draper's flat.

'Excuse me,' he asked, 'are you a friend of Sue Walker?'

'Yes,' the woman answered in a tone no more defensive than any woman might be expected to use when addressed by a strange man in public.

'I'm Detective Chief Inspector Anderson,' he continued, producing his warrant card to allay her suspicions. 'Would it be possible to ask you a few questions?'

'I suppose so,' the woman answered. Anderson noted her accent, a typically neutral BBC English without apparent regional or class intonations. 'I was just going to see Sue, actually.'

'I've, er – just been there,' Anderson replied, deciding on an attitude of slightly conspiratorial friendliness. 'Her father wasn't too pleased to see me.'

'Is he back already?' the woman asked. Anderson nodded and grinned.

'Then I'll wait till he goes out to the pub,' she continued. 'How about buying me a drink?'

'Very well,' Anderson answered, for the sake of professionalism ignoring the streak of brashness that he found so distasteful in women. 'May I ask your name?'

'Lindsie,' she answered, 'Lindsie Gibbs.'

'Did you know James Draper well?' he asked.

'Fairly,' Lindsie answered as he opened the car door for her. 'He was all right.'

Anderson avoided the temptation to ask what it had been about James Draper that she considered 'all right'. Obnoxious, arrogant, dirty, crude, all came to mind when considering Draper, but nothing complimentary.

'Take me to the Bull, up near the airport; I'll tell you where to turn,' Lindsie said. 'Detective Chief Inspector, that's pretty high up isn't it?'

'Fairly,' Anderson admitted.

'You don't look old enough,' she answered as she clipped the seat-belt into place.

'You'd be surprised,' Anderson said, realising that Lindsie was trying to flirt with him. Although her status as someone involved with suspects put her out of bounds and she simply wasn't his type anyway, especially with Anna around, the idea amused him. What would she think, he wondered, if she knew that he had spent an evening watching her in Draper's flat.

They drove out to the Bull, which, to Anderson's relief, proved to be a small, quiet pub frequented by airport staff, travellers and business types from the nearby industrial estates. He bought her gin and orange and a mineral water for himself, choosing a quiet corner to sit in.

'So you knew Draper well, then?' he repeated as he sat down, keen to steer the conversation in the right direction.

Lindsie nodded and sipped her drink.

'I take it, then, that you know what happened?' he continued.

'Sue said something about a train,' she answered. 'She's really upset. I didn't like to push.'

'I understand,' Anderson said. Clearly his attitude was working and being open seemed the best way of inspiring trust in her. Lindsie probably watched TV police dramas and was likely to be flattered by apparent confidences from a senior policeman. 'I'm not at liberty to say a great deal, but I think I can safely tell you that James Draper's death is regarded as suspicious.'

He paused, watching the interest in Lindsie's face. She was undeniably pretty in a rather straightforward way, straight, glossy dark hair and an oval face giving her the sort of look that might be expected of a girl in an advertisement for cheap cosmetics.

'The thing is,' he continued, 'Sue is really too distraught to be of much help at the moment, but we urgently need to know if James Draper's movements had been in any way unusual recently, particularly in the period from immediately before his uncle's death. You do know about that, I take it?'

Lindsie nodded and took another sip of her drink. Anderson sat back, letting her think. Her expression suggested uncertainty, nervousness even, an impression backed up by the way she was rubbing her fingers on her glass.

'Is this in confidence?' she eventually asked.

'Absolutely,' he answered without hesitation.

'Complete confidence?' she said.

'Yes,' he replied, 'even to the extent that I need not tell my colleagues my source of information unless it becomes essential to the investigation.'

'Well, for starters, James used to deal drugs,' Lindsie said quietly. 'Mainly just black but some hard stuff. He used to go on about how he'd never get done, but he was always like that anyway. In the end he did get done, but got off because what he had in the bag was just sugar. He's never stopped bragging about it since.'

'Did he often do that?' Anderson asked.

'I don't know,' Lindsie went on. 'He was really tight about his dealing, never even told Sue where he got it or anything. He always went to make calls in phone boxes and sometimes used to go and meet people secretly. He thought Sue and I didn't know, but we did.'

'How long had this been happening?' Anderson asked.

'Nearly four years, I think,' Lindsie replied. 'The stuff he got was really good too, we —'

Lindsie stopped abruptly, turning her eyes to Anderson with a worried look, clearly thinking he was about to arrest her for drug abuse.

'Carry on,' he said gently.

'We reckoned he was getting it from someone who was bringing it straight in,' she continued. 'He was always down the docks, you see, around where the yachtsmen come in and stuff.'

'Good,' Anderson broke in, feeling that the interview was straying from the point, 'but has this behaviour been more frequent recently?'

'Yes,' Lindsie answered. 'Last month he was always sneaking off. Then he went off to his uncle's for a bit and when he came back it was worse. Then it stopped, and the next thing was his uncle was dead and then him. He was killed, wasn't he?'

'Yes,' Anderson admitted, keen not to damage the level of intimacy he had built up, 'I'm afraid so.'

'Poor James,' Lindsie answered in a subdued voice before taking a long pull at her drink.

'Lindsie,' Anderson asked, placing a hand on top of hers where it lay on the table. 'Do you have any idea of who might have wanted James dead?'

'Not really,' she answered, 'but maybe he hadn't paid his supplier or something. He was like that, he'd do anything to get one over on someone else.'

'Is there anything else you can tell me about the supplier? Anything at all, however trivial it may seem.'

'I'm sorry, I really don't know.'

'Anything, Lindsie. Was it one person or several? Old, young, whatever? Local or not, any little detail.'

'Oh, definitely local,' Lindsie answered. 'James was never gone for long. Nothing else though.'

'Thank you, Lindsie,' Anderson answered, 'you've been extremely helpful.'

She proved to have no further information of value, but hinted that his presence would not be unwelcome for the rest of the evening. Anderson declined, citing pressure of work as his reason so as to let her down gently. As he drove away after dropping her back at the Leighdon Estate he couldn't help feeling pleased with himself, partly at his success in extracting the information he wanted and partly because, although he had declined the chance of sex with her, the situation had nevertheless been entirely under his control.

The immediate question seemed to be whether, assuming Cutts was the murderer, he was also Draper's drugs contact or whether the two situations were unrelated. Given Lindsie's certainty that the contact was local, it seemed likely that Cutts and the drugs suppliers were at best loosely connected. Her information, while useful, had in fact posed more questions than it answered.

Violet Krebs pushed open the door of Dr Wells's laboratory, her feelings mixed from the interview with Cutts. While the evidence did seem entirely clear, everything about him suggested a character quite different from what she had been expecting. The style of the murders, particularly that of Charles Draper, suggested a sharp mind, a callous nature and nerves of steel. Cutts appeared to have none of these traits. Indeed, he seemed intelligent in a rather bumbling fashion, insecure rather than callous and shy to the point of being neurotic. The evidence, if it could be called evidence, that he tended to perverse tastes in sex and was something of a local bugbear, she considered unimportant. Indeed, if anything, it reduced the plausibility of him as a hired killer. On the other hand she was only too aware of the influence implications of sexual depravity could have when presented to a jury by a skilled prosecution lawyer. It was not so much that she distrusted the evidence of Cutts's guilt, as that she was intent on ensuring that if he were convicted is would be on the basis of solid fact without room for uncertainty. Throughout her career, and with increasing force as her rank and the consequent responsibility increased, she had been exceptionally aware of the chance of unsafe convictions. The idea of innocent people being imprisoned was almost as abhorrent to her as that of the restoration of the death penalty. If she was going to be giving evidence against Cutts, she was determined to ensure that it was cast-iron.

Of course it was just possible that Cutts was shielding someone else, someone who could scare him into doing exactly as he was told. It was not a possibility Violet had cared to bring up in front of Walsh and Anderson, neither of whom she felt a particular rapport with. Morgan Wells, on the other hand, could not only be relied on to debate any idea she might have without patronising her, but might also be able to provide hard fact in support or denial of her theory.

'Ah, Violet,' he greeted her. 'You must excuse me if I do not greet you with appropriate fervour; my gloves are in no fit condition for such intimacies. In any case, I fear that you are rather early if you are seeking my report. There is a positive mountain of information here and I have given poor Anna the day off. Ah, the tribulations of the generous and the concerned. Oh, did the good Nathan Cutts squeal, as I believe the expression is?'

'No,' Violet replied, 'he denies everything and managed to evade every trap that Walsh and Anderson set him. If it wasn't for the hard evidence, I'd swear he was innocent.'

'Innocent he is not,' Morgan Wells replied. 'While I have yet to conclude my work, I think I can tell you informally that both hair and fibre samples found in Cutts's house match those picked up by the vacuum on the bridge over the cutting. Also, the blood and hair on the most inventive murder weapon are those of the late James Draper. Sadly we are without prints, possibly the reason Cutts felt able to dispose of his little cannonball so casually. He wore gloves. We do, however, have a chromatograph of ink from a bottle on Cutts's escritoire, which, as you can see, is an exact match for that from the pen found in the Tamar, thus tying him in with the murder of the uncle as well as that of the nephew. *Et voilà!*'

Morgan flourished the two chromatographs, which were clearly derived from the same ink, a deep blue-black that contained a strong element of orange.

'Anyway, I would be flattered if you had come simply to socialise,' he continued, 'but I don't imagine that you did.'

'I was going to ask a question, actually,' Violet answered. 'You've just answered it, though.'

'Ah ha!' Morgan responded. 'In that case I wish to ask you a question instead. Would you care to join me for dinner at my humble abode tomorrow evening? I would say this evening, but I imagine we shall both be occupied with paperwork until quite unreasonable hours.'

She accepted his invitation cheerfully and left the room feeling considerably more at ease than when she had come in. The added weight of the new evidence was enough to push any doubts she had of Cutts's guilt from her mind. He had been on the bridge near Sparkwell and he had been on the Tamar quay. Those two facts were clear, and damning. Cutts still seemed an odd hired killer, but then what did she expect? A tall, shady figure in a black trenchcoat with a Homburg hat pulled well down over his face, the red glint of his eyes showing in the dark? That was ridiculous, like the gang who had recently robbed a warehouse without being noticed only to get picked up because they were speeding in the getaway car. Idiots. Cutts, on the other hand, was the sort of man who got dismissed as a nobody, a bit weird, but harmless, and certainly not 'cool' enough to be a hired killer. The ideal man, therefore, to hire as a killer.

In theory, yes, but how often did things work so neatly? Besides, how would James Draper, a Plymouth wide-boy, have known that the owner of an antiques shop in Charmouth could be hired as a contract killer?

NINE
Tuesday

Melanie Herrick ran her hand down the iron pole that made up one corner of the swing in the cottage garden. Her touch was a caress, stroking the rust-encrusted metal as if it were a favourite pet. Here and there on the iron frame scraps of paint remained – bright green, the original colour of the swing when it had been first installed for her father and her uncles and aunts when the cottage had been a disused cow shed; and rich yellow, like the daffodils that grew around it, from her own childhood when old John Draper had let her play in the garden as much as she liked.

In fact it had been John Draper who painted the swing for her when the green paint began to flake. He had been such a nice old man, teaching her the names of flowers and birds, telling her stories about the garden and woods, and letting her sit on his knee when they had tea on the lawn. Then he had died and Charles Draper had moved in, by which time she had been a shy, gawky teenager. He had quickly made it clear that he wanted the cottage entirely to himself and that had been the last time she had been where she now stood.

Melanie took hold of one of the chains and lowered herself

on to the old wooden seat, her hips now snug against the fittings on either side. OK, she thought, maybe she was a bit too big for it, but at least nobody could tell her she couldn't use it, and when the police had finished with their investigation the cottage would be hers. Knowing that was such a beautiful feeling and even made up for the trauma of being interrogated by the police and all but accused of Charles Draper's murder. Thank God for Uncle Ralph, who had put the terrifying Detective Sergeant Jo Blackheath on her best behaviour and had even had the senior man who had been with them running in circles to please him. Jo Blackheath had been so harsh with her, stern and unyielding, even putting her in handcuffs to take her to the station.

The thought of Jo Blackheath locking the handcuffs on her wrists sent a shiver right through Melanie, a shiver that she now recognised was not entirely fright. The discovery that she could be sexually attracted to a woman frightened Melanie and filled her with guilt. Yet there was no denying it. Although a woman, Jo Blackheath had all the tough resilience and assurance that had always attracted Melanie in men and had been an important part of both Carl and Duncan's characters. Sex with Carl and with Duncan had always involved her being underneath, sometimes even on her knees. It had also been rough and fast, with her giving all the attention, dressing nicely for them, doing striptease, sucking cock. Carl's favourite kink had been to make her wear short dresses with no knickers in public. He would then drop something so that she had to pick it up and risk people seeing her bare bottom, which had embarrassed her furiously, the bastard! OK, so maybe it had turned her on later, but still. Maybe Jo Blackheath would be kinder, kissing her tummy, her breasts, maybe even between her legs –

She caught herself, only too aware of what her train of thought was leading to. She wasn't going to do it, especially when the woman had arrested her and had her locked in a cell. Her feelings for Jo Blackheath were something she had no control over, but she was determined that she was not going to give in to them. Besides, the idea of actually making a pass at the policewoman was absurd. She would never have the courage, and if she did Blackheath would probably arrest her for it or something.

Melanie had been swinging slowly backwards and forwards, keeping her momentum with little kicks of her feet. In front of her the cottage stood as it always had done, the first buds on the laburnum that ran over the big patio doors beginning to break through. Although the cottage was out of bounds until the police had finished, she decided to walk round the outside. After all, they had been over it again and again and if there was anything to find, they must have done so by now.

Pulling herself up from the swing by the chains, Melanie rose and walked towards the cottage, brushing the bits of leaf and lichen from the seat of her jeans. The cottage garden was as pretty as ever, the lupins and delphiniums beginning to grow, just as she always remembered them in spring. At least Charles Draper had looked after the garden, his only crime being to install the horrid little statue in the middle of the pond, a deliberate act of insolence towards her and granny, with the statue pointing a diminutive penis in the direction of her granny's house. She rounded the corner of the house to find the statue, as vulgar as ever, but instead of being sideways on to the cottage so that it faced the hedge and by implication Edith's house, it was facing away from the cottage.

Melanie paused. The statue had been in its normal position on Monday afternoon when she had had her last argument with Draper. She remembered demanding that he get rid of it. Could he have felt remorse and turned it to a less offensive angle? It seemed unlikely, as she had left him red-faced and furious. Much more likely was that the police had moved it during their search. She shrugged. It was no concern of hers.

173

Anyway, as soon as she could she intended to take a hammer to the beastly thing.

Anna Ferreira took her lab coat from the peg and slipped it on. Dr Wells's car was parked outside, so she knew he would already be there. Although she felt rather belittled by his insistence that she didn't assist him on Sunday and took Monday off, she had to admit to herself that he had acted from kindness and that his attitude to her had improved since he had become involved with Violet Krebs. He greeted her with his normal expansive good humour when she entered the lab and she returned the greeting.

'I trust you feel better?' he asked solicitously as she crossed the room, still buttoning her lab coat.

'Yes, thank you,' she answered. 'What should I do today?'

'Very little, my dear,' Wells replied. 'I have been up until a quite ungodly hour, assembling the Draper evidence and writing a report. The work is now all but done, only one or two of the more tedious tests remaining to be completed. One or two things might prove instructive to you, though, James Draper's head for instance. Are you up to the task?'

Anna nodded. Wells was clearly keen to make sure that she could now handle her work without becoming ruffled.

'Good,' he said, 'then to the morgue we go.'

She followed him out of the lab, Wells striding along the corridor at such a pace that she had to hurry to keep up.

'The murder weapon,' he was saying, 'was a cannonball of three-inch diameter wrapped in a square of linen, thus making a most effective club that could be easily concealed in a coat pocket. It is currently over at the police station, where they showed it to Cutts yesterday in the hope of browbeating him into a confession. They failed, so it is up to us scientists to help the poor dears out. Here we are, the morgue.'

Anna followed him into the room and watched as he drew the sheet back from the table that supported the remains of

James Draper. She shuddered at the sight, steeling herself not to look away.

'Note the skull,' Wells remarked. 'This severe depressed fracture on the right parietal plate was what killed him. The bowl-like shape is typical of a club wound. More usually it would be less regular, the handle of the weapon distorting the impact site. In this case it is round, and fits the cannonball a treat. I'll remove the skin for you at a later date and you'll be able to see the characteristic cobweb-like shatter pattern. It was a very heavy blow – death would have been near instantaneous.'

'What about the damage to the frontal and malar bones?' Anna asked.

'Intercity train,' Wells answered, 'which also accounts for the rest of the damage. As far as I can see, Draper was struck a single powerful blow from behind and then thrown on to the tracks. There is extensive bruising, but all of it occurred after death. Note the distinctive coloration, here on the arm and here and here on the abdomen.'

Anna nodded, listening intently to Dr Wells's remarks, observing his demonstration of the damage done to the mangled body that has once been James Draper as calmly as she could. When he finished and pulled the sheet back up, she congratulated herself on retaining her professional detachment but gave an internal sigh of relief.

Wells led the way back to the lab, indicating to Anna an array of equipment spread out along the bench that ran around the interior walls of the lab.

'Evidence, evidence,' he said. 'Here's the chromatograph, a simple but effective toy. Note the identical dye components of the two examples, one the ink taken from Cutts's pen, the other ink taken from a bottle in his house. Have a chair, take a microscope. The slides in tray A are fibres from Sparkwell, those in tray B from Cutts's flat. The ones marked with an asterisk match, have a look at each.'

175

Anna followed his instructions, gradually going through the evidence. As she did so, she felt a degree of pride in her job. True, it was Dr Wells who was doing the actual work in this case, but it was their evidence that was going to have the murderer convicted, while John and the others had done little more than legwork.

At length Dr Wells finished his demonstration, then went to his office and returned with a sheaf of papers.

'I dare say old Walsh will be champing at the bit to see these,' he told her. 'Would you mind dropping them over to the station?'

Anna willingly accepted, hoping for an opportunity to see John Anderson. Instead, however, she found Violet Krebs getting out of her car.

'May I have a word?' Anna asked, keen to discuss the ideas she had been considering the previous day with someone she felt she could talk to.

'Certainly,' Krebs replied. 'I'm on my way up to the incident room, come with me.'

Anna fell into step beside her, explaining her theory of why Charles Draper's body could only have been on Thorn Point if it had been dumped in the river shortly before high tide early on Tuesday morning, and how the idea fitted both the lack of witnesses for Monday afternoon and bypassed the problem of the murderer having to drag the half-conscious Draper across a calf-deep mud flat.

'Thank you, Anna,' Krebs answered with surprising intensity when Anna finished. 'You're brilliant. I had reached the same conclusion myself, assuming that Draper was drowned elsewhere and then taken to the quay in the night. I tried to explain it to Walsh and Anderson on Saturday. Anderson thought that Draper might actually have been drowned at Thorn Point, though, which seemed to fit the facts better. But as you say, the wind and the high tide would almost certainly have carried the body out and over the bar.

Sadly, we've just about got Cutts now, so it's a bit late to be important. I've got a security tape here that was supposed to be his alibi but will actually make things worse for him. Still, I'll discuss your idea with Morgan this evening and see what he thinks. I'm sorry you don't feel you can talk to him easily, but I won't have any difficulty with that. Actually, I still feel uneasy about the whole thing. Cutts just doesn't fit, for all the facts. I'm not going to say that in front of all the men, though, I'll discuss it with Morgan this evening. He's going to cook for me.'

'That's nice of him,' Anna replied. 'Thanks for helping – I'll talk to you tomorrow.'

They had reached the interview room, in which the majority of the team were sitting, discussing the evolution of the case. John Anderson was there, but she couldn't bring herself to talk to him socially in front of the other officers. Instead she contented herself with a smile and a deliberately coy look when the attention of the others was distracted. She finally handed Dr Wells's report to Detective Superintendent Walsh and left, uncertain whether she had managed to convey her meaning to John Anderson.

John Anderson smiled to himself as Anna left the room. His feeling that she wished to distance herself from him vanished on the instant, to be replaced by a pleasant sensation of anticipation. An evening of intense, passionate sex with Anna Ferreira was something very much to be looked forward to. Pigeonholing his intentions for Anna for the time being, he turned to where Violet Krebs was placing a video into a machine that stood in the corner of the incident room.

'Fortunately', she was saying, 'the petrol station keeps its tapes for two weeks before rotating them in the hope of being able to spot potential raiders casing them. Before we look at them, you should know that the petrol station is to the west of Okehampton. Cutts, driving from Charmouth, would have arrived on the A30 from the east and had no reason to go out to the west at all if he was simply returning to Okehampton. Also, even if he's on the tape at 3 p.m. on the dot it doesn't completely exclude him from the inquiry. When I drove up to Okehampton I went via Hewton. The journey might take as little as forty minutes.'

Krebs began to run the tape, fast forwarding and then stopping so that the team could examine each customer as they came in. The time counter in the corner of the screen showed 2.10 p.m. when a short, bulky man with a bald head came in.

'Mr Cutts,' Krebs said, making no effort to hide the delight in her voice.

Anderson watched the image of Cutts as he walked to the counter, moving in jumps as the frames had been taken at one second intervals. He wore the same shabby suit of brown tweed that he was now wearing. Cutts placed a bottle of water and a Cornish pasty on the counter, dug in his pockets and then made a gesture that suggested apology to the cashier. He then opened his coat and took a cheque book and a pen from his inside pocket.

'Stop,' Anderson ordered. 'Wind that back; now stop, there.'

The frame of Cutts clearly showed the pen as he took it from his pocket and there were no other pens next to it.

'There's no gold pen,' he remarked. 'If I were him I would use my fountain pen to write a cheque.'

'Fallen down inside his pocket? In a brief-case in his car?' Krebs suggested.

'Maybe,' Anderson conceded. 'Carry on anyway.'

The tape continued to run, showing Cutts paying and then leaving the garage.

'Other than the small inconsistency with the pen, that does us more good than harm,' Krebs said as she ejected the video. 'I think we can fairly say that Cutts is our man.'

There were general nods of agreement. Anderson rose,

considering the implications of the mounting evidence. Cutts's guilt seemed beyond doubt, the facts coming together well, with only minor details still unresolved. Indeed, he reflected, it would be a rare case where every single minor point was fully explained. He noticed that Robert Walsh was approaching him, scanning the sheaf of papers which Anna had delivered.

'Ah, John,' Walsh began, 'pretty convincing in all, I think. By the way, I've got the answer you wanted about James Draper's will. He died intestate, so it looks like that's that for the inheritance side of things.'

'Thank you,' Anderson replied. 'I'll fax the information to Guildford.'

Joanna Blackheath opened the door to Detective Superintendent Parrish's office with a sinking feeling that she had not known since facing the headmaster at school.

'Joanna, take a seat,' Parrish said as she closed the door behind her. 'Right, well, I'll cut straight to the point, shall I.'

Jo Blackheath sat down, her feeling of trepidation undiminished by Parrish's matter-of-fact manner. She was certain she was about to be suspended, maybe worse.

'You are a very lucky young woman, Joanna,' he continued. 'Both myself and Chief Constable Farrell were considering suspending you pending a full investigation of your conduct. Had Sir Ralph insisted, we would have had no option. However, you have support from an unexpected quarter.'

'Sir?' Joanna asked.

'Yes, Edith Herrick, who is apparently Sir Ralph's mother-in-law, feels that you were simply over-enthusiastic and has exerted her influence on your behalf, for which you may be suitably thankful. The complaint has been withdrawn, subject to you apologising to the Herricks.'

'But, sir,' Joanna replied, her relief mixed with a good measure of indignation, 'the Herricks are still under suspicion.'

'Joanna,' Parrish continued patiently, 'you would be well

advised to accept their offer. Personally I am extremely surprised that it was made. Sir Ralph's reputation is not one for forgiveness. If, and this is extremely unlikely, any further evidence against the Herricks comes to light, then we can reconsider our position. Until then, you will tread very, very lightly.'

'Yes, sir,' Joanna replied quietly.

'Also,' Parrish continued, 'I've just received a fax from DCI Anderson. They have arrested a man called Nathan Cutts, against whom there is strong evidence. The assumption is that he was paid by James Draper to kill Charles Draper and then killed James Draper for a reason we have not yet established. He also says that James Draper died intestate and that you are to close off that line of enquiry by finding out if any remaining relatives exist.'

'There aren't any, sir,' Joanna broke in.

'Nevertheless, Joanna,' Parrish answered, 'you are to go back to Mr Worth and confirm that. DCI Anderson does not like loose ends, and nor do I. Oh, and another thing, Cutts has an alibi for 2.00 p.m. on Monday but no later, so the idea that the Herricks are covering up for him becomes not just unlikely but absurd. They are no longer suspects, and that's final.'

'Yes, sir,' Joanna replied meekly while seething inside. Parrish, Anderson, Edith Herrick, Sir Ralph bloody Stukeley, they all treated her like a child. Still, she had to admit that the withdrawal of the complaint against her was very welcome.

She left the office and telephoned ahead to make an appointment with Worth, giving him an outline of what she wanted to know in the hope of keeping the interview with the bombastic solicitor to a reasonable length.

On her arrival at Worth's office, he proved as garrulous as ever, greeting her enthusiastically and motioning her into a chair.

'Well,' he began, 'you will be glad to hear that I have managed to uncover at least a measure of detail on your problem. As James Draper died intestate, the money left to him devolves upon his nearest surviving relatives, to be apportioned according to a complex system with which I shall not bore you. Draper, as you are aware, had no close relatives and so my assumption would be that the money would devolve to the crown.'

Worth looked up, peering at Joanna over his spectacles. An answer was clearly expected so she nodded to indicate that she had understood.

'But,' Worth continued, 'after some excavation into the records of the practice, I find that the faint and ailing memory of an old man, which is to say me, is not always inaccurate. No, you may remember that I mentioned the possibility that old John Draper was in some way related to the Herricks. Yes? Good girl. Well, old man Herrick, George Herrick as was, proves to have been the first cousin of John Draper, sharing mutual grandparents. Edith Herrick is therefore the third cousin twice removed to James Draper, or something of that order, I'm never sure quite which way it goes. A claim for the money might therefore be made by a fair-sized tribe, the extent of which I have no inclination to define for you. Nevertheless, it includes Edith and Melanie Herrick, and Sir Ralph and Lady Stukeley. As a piece of professional advice, my dear, delivered *gratis*, I would not recommend seeking a motive for the murder of Charles Draper along these lines.'

'I don't intend to, Mr Worth,' Blackheath replied, privately noting that the information in fact strengthened the Herricks' motive for murdering Charles Draper. 'Thank you for your trouble, you have been a great help.'

'Not at all, my dear, not at all,' Worth replied. 'You grace my office in a manner calculated to gladden an old man's heart. Drop in any time you need some advice.'

Jo left the office feeling calmer but in no mood to go and apologise to the Herricks. That could wait until she was off duty.

TEN
Tuesday Evening

Melanie Herrick sat in her grandmother's kitchen sipping a glass of red wine. She was slightly, pleasantly drunk, her grandmother having taken a single small glass of wine while she drank her way slowly down the bottle, which was now two-thirds empty. It had come from the cellar laid down by her grandfather and had a strange, earthy, slightly sweet taste. She had needed two glasses to get used to it but was now thoroughly enjoying the flavour. Her grandmother was talking blithely of this and that, apparently oblivious to Melanie's noncommittal answers. Melanie's mind was on other things, mainly her impending move into the cottage, which could now be only days away. Also, following a brilliant piece of legal manoeuvring by her uncle Ralph, she looked like getting a decent alimony and a settlement that would wipe the smile off Carl's face for good. The crunch of tyres on the gravel of the carriageway broke into her reverie, and a moment later bright lights swung across the window and then died with the car's engine.

'Whoever could it be at this time of night?' her grandmother said. 'Perhaps you could answer the door, dear?'

Melanie went to the door, opening it at the same instant that the bell rang. Outside stood Joanna Blackheath. Melanie's heart sank as she saw visions of another night in the cells and further questioning flash in front of her eyes.

'Hello,' she managed, making no move from her position in the open doorway.

'May I come in?' the Detective Sergeant asked, stepping past Melanie as she moved aside. 'Thank you.'

'What's the matter?' Melanie asked.

'I won't disturb you for long,' Blackheath replied. 'I'd just like to speak to you and your grandmother for a minute. This is purely informal, I'm off duty.'

'Oh, yes, OK, I suppose. Granny's in the kitchen.'

Melanie watched as the policewoman went into the kitchen, following her and resuming her seat. Blackheath remained standing.

'Oh, good evening, Miss Blackheath isn't it?' Edith Herrick said as she turned in her chair to see who the visitor was. 'I expect you've come to apologise.'

'Yes, Mrs Herrick,' Blackheath answered, her manner contrite but formal. She then turned to Melanie, 'I understand that I may have acted with undue haste –'

'Yes,' Melanie answered, trying to sound indignant but in fact elated. Not only was the terrifying Jo Blackheath not going to arrest her, she was actually going to apologise for her previous behaviour.

'– and I apologise for this,' Blackheath continued. 'I hope you will appreciate that I was only trying to do my duty and accept my apology in the same spirit in which it is offered.'

'Well –' Melanie began, intent on passing at least a couple of remarks on Blackheath's behaviour.

'Of course we accept, my dear,' her grandmother interrupted. 'Don't we, Melanie? I realise how very difficult your job must be, Miss Blackheath, and I do hope you have found whoever killed Mr Draper.'

'Yes, we have, Mrs Herrick,' Blackheath continued, 'but there are still some conflicting pieces of evidence to clear up. I might in fact want to talk to both of you again if that's OK.'

'At the station?' Melanie asked sarcastically.

'Do be gracious, dear,' her grandmother addressed her, then turning back to Blackheath. 'Now would be as good a time as any, my dear, especially as we are both here.'

'Are you sure?' Blackheath asked.

'Certainly,' Edith Herrick continued. 'Will you have some tea, or perhaps a glass of wine? Melanie has brought something up from my late husband's cellar. I daren't go down there myself, you see, not on my own – it's the stairs, you know.'

'Thank you,' Jo Blackheath answered. 'I'll have a small glass of wine as I'm off duty. May I sit down?'

Melanie, feeling slightly sulky, fetched a glass for Jo Blackheath and filled it a third full, then refilled her own to the brim.

'Thank you,' Jo Blackheath addressed her. 'The thing is, Melanie, we still can't understand how you could have seen Charles Draper so shortly before he was killed on the Monday before last.'

'I would help if I could,' Melanie replied, a tight knot growing in her stomach as she once more began to feel under suspicion. She had seen Draper when she said she had. What should she do, lie? The answer had to be no, because if she did she was bound to dig herself into an even deeper hole than the one she had got out of. She decided that if she told the policewoman about the statue she might seem more helpful. 'I promise I would, but I've told the truth and that's all I can do. I can tell you one thing though.'

'What's that?'

'Did you move the statue in the pond outside the cottage?'

'No, absolutely not, we will have left things exactly as we

184

found them. Besides, isn't it cemented in?'

'No, he just stuck it in the middle, facing us so it was like it was peeing towards granny's house.'

'A most vulgar man,' Edith Herrick put in.

'Well, it's not any more,' Melanie continued, 'and it was when I last spoke to Draper.'

'I think I'd better see this,' Blackheath answered, getting up from her chair. 'Could you come over with me?'

Melanie agreed, now with the new feeling of excitement at helping.

'I shall go to bed, if you don't mind,' her grandmother said. 'Goodnight Miss Blackheath, goodnight Melanie, and don't forget to lock up.'

Melanie swallowed her wine, wished her grandmother goodnight and followed Jo Blackheath out into the night.

'I've got a torch in the car, let's walk,' Jo Blackheath said. 'Besides, the moon's bright enough to see by.'

They walked along the lane, quickly arriving in front of the cottage where Melanie showed Jo the statue.

'You see, it's moved,' she said.

Melanie watched as Jo Blackheath pushed at the statue, finding it loose on its base and unstable. The policewoman then stood back, lost in thought.

'And you're certain it was facing the other way on Monday afternoon?' she asked after a while.

'Yes, absolutely. I asked Mr Draper to turn it back or get rid of it, but he wouldn't,' Melanie replied.

'Melanie,' Jo Blackheath asked her, 'on Monday, you spoke to Charles Draper and then did what? Walked back across the field?'

'Yes,' she replied, 'it's much shorter than going round the lane.'

'And remind me at what time you left your grandmother's?'

'I'm not sure, maybe four o'clock or so. You're not going to arrest me again, are you?'

'No, don't worry, I just wanted to check something. So you didn't see anyone or hear a car?'

'No, I swear I didn't.'

'But Charles Draper's car was here when you argued with him?'

'Yes.'

'Thank you.'

'Why?'

'It's complicated,' Jo Blackheath replied, 'and I shouldn't really go into it. It's just that if you're right, then other facts simply don't add up.'

'I promise I am right,' Melanie replied. 'Really, truthfully, I just wish I could show you.'

'Don't worry, Melanie,' Jo Blackheath replied, 'we think we know who killed Charles Draper and we think he was paid to do it. One thing I can guarantee, if you catch a hired killer, he's not going to keep the name of the person who hired him secret.'

'Oh, good,' Melanie replied. 'Oh, I'm so glad. You know, I really thought you were going to arrest me again!'

Melanie laughed, finally sure that she was no longer suspected of being involved with the killing of Charles Draper. The light of the torch only showed Jo Blackheath's face faintly, yet Melanie immediately noticed her expression soften. If meeting her off duty made her seem less tough, then now she seemed positively sympathetic.

'You really don't know a thing about it, do you?' Jo was saying.

'No,' Melanie answered honestly, 'only what I've told you.'

'Oh you poor thing, I am sorry,' Jo answered. 'I must have put you through hell.'

Melanie shrugged, suddenly finding a lump in her throat and a moment later she had burst into tears. She felt Jo's arm close around her shoulder and a tissue was pressed into her hand even as she tried to stifle her sobs.

'Come back to your gran's and sit down,' Jo said, her voice, always so hard, now full of sympathy.

'No, she'll be in bed,' Melanie managed through her sniffles. 'Can't we go into the cottage?'

'I suppose so,' Jo replied. 'We shouldn't really, but we'll stick to one room and we should be OK.'

Melanie followed Jo to the cottage door, still dabbing at her eyes as the policewoman dug out the keys and opened the door. It was the first time she had been inside the building since her childhood and the familiar layout seemed smaller. The atmosphere was not dissimilar though, many of Charles Draper's things having been taken over directly from his father.

'Come and sit down in the kitchen,' Jo told her.

Melanie followed Jo and sat down on one of the heavy oak seats that surrounded the kitchen table. The table and work surfaces were as she remembered them, as was the arch into the main room. Charles Draper had added a fine sideboard for use as a bar and a great many clocks, but very little else.

'Do you think I could have a drink?' she asked.

Jo hesitated but then shrugged and walked over to the sideboard. Melanie watched her as she surveyed the selection of bottles and decanters uncertainly. She couldn't deny it to herself, there was something horribly attractive about the blonde woman, a forcefulness, a determination not to let things get the better of her. Melanie pushed the feeling back but without any real fervour. The wine made her feel daring, as if she might actually have the guts to do something. But what? Besides, the idea of rejection was even more terrible than the idea of acceptance.

'What would you like?' Jo said.

'Vodka,' Melanie replied.

'You're out of luck,' Jo answered. 'How about brandy?'

Melanie accepted, watching Jo pour a glass and then another for herself.

187

'I shouldn't be doing this,' Jo remarked in a tone that indicated that she wasn't really bothered. 'It's a little thing, though, and anyway, it's your brandy as much as anyone's.'

'Eh?' Melanie asked.

'According to Mr Worth, Charles Draper's solicitor, your family has the best claim to Charles Draper's money, so far as there is a claim.'

'Why?' Melanie demanded.

'You're distantly related, apparently,' Jo continued. 'I can't remember the details.'

'Are you sure?'

'That's what Worth says. I suppose he's right.'

'Gosh, nobody ever told me that. We used to call Charles's father Uncle John, but I thought it was just a way of saying things.'

Melanie accepted the glass and took a sip of her brandy. It was fiery but smooth, warming her mouth and throat as it slid down. She sighed as she took the second sip, thinking of how she would change the cottage when it was hers. Everything that reminded her of Charles Draper would have to go, then she'd redecorate in bright, simple colours. She'd fix the swing and paint it yellow, as it had been when she was little.

'You're very lucky,' Jo said, as if divining her thoughts.

Melanie nodded her agreement and began to talk about the swing as she refilled her glass and then Jo's. Jo listened to her with pleasure, comparing what Melanie was saying with her own childhood in a suburban street in Croydon.

For a long space the two women sat together, drinking and talking, the level in the brandy bottle gradually falling as eleven o'clock and then midnight passed. As the night became colder the need not to disturb anything was forgotten. Melanie turned on the gas fire in the main room and then sank back on to the sofa.

She looked at Jo, watching her lower herself carefully on to the floor, tummy down so that she was full length on to the fire. Its light reflected on her face, which was flushed and bright-eyed from the brandy. Melanie leant forward to fill the glasses. Jo held out a restraining hand, but only laughed when Melanie ignored it. The conversation had become more intimate, Melanie expounding on Carl's faults.

'The bastard used to make me flash in public,' Melanie admitted.

'Sorry?' Jo giggled.

'You know, he'd make me wear a little short skirt and then bend over so my bum showed. It was so embarrassing!'

'Where?' Jo asked.

'Anywhere. Not usually in Guildford because people knew us. But he'd take me up to London and then make me show off in the train on the way back.'

'Why'd you let him?'

'Oh, you know how it is. I loved him, and he was really forceful.'

'Didn't it turn you on at all?'

'Maybe, a little bit,' Melanie laughed. 'Yes, all right, but it was still embarrassing.'

Jo didn't reply, but sipped her drink instead. Melanie watched her, focusing her eyes on the pretty golden bob of hair with some difficulty. Jo was lying face down, supporting herself on her elbows, her back dipping elegantly to rise at the swell of her bottom under the smart, business-like skirt. One leg was raised, the shoe dangling negligently from one toe and then falling to the ground.

Melanie felt compelled to reach out and touch Jo's shoulder, gently rubbing the muscles with her fingers. Jo made no protest but dipped her head forward to expose the nape of her neck, the short, blonde fluff like kitten fur under Melanie's fingers as she massaged Jo gently. Her head spinning and a familiar ache beginning to build up between her legs, Melanie slid off the sofa to kneel over Jo, massaging the woman's back in the way Carl had liked, pressing firmly with her fingertips and moving gently across the shoulder blades and then down either side of her spine.

Jo sighed, making no attempt to stop Melanie as her fingers eased the knots out of the muscle of her back. Melanie carried on, working up and down Jo's back, knowing exactly what she wanted to do but not daring to go any further. A piece of Jo's blouse came loose from the waistband of her skirt, revealing a small slice of pale flesh. With her heart in her mouth despite the brandy, Melanie tugged more of the blouse out, pulling it up Jo's back to her neck and starting to massage again, only this time on bare flesh.

'That's nice,' Jo said softly. 'Undo my bra, it gets in the way.'

Melanie snipped the little catch open, pulling the strap to either side, noticing the bulge of Jo's breasts where they were flattened against the floor. She could feel her breath coming faster, her pulse hammering. Did she dare slide her fingers on to the soft curves of Jo's breasts? Would Jo get angry, or gently push her fingers back into less intimate areas? Or would she lift herself up more, allowing Melanie's hands to cup each little round tit and squeeze the nipples between her fingers as she did with her own breasts when she masturbated?

She let her hands curve around Jo's ribcage, sliding a half-inch lower with each slow circle, until her fingertips finally brushed against the silky smooth skin of Jo's boobs. On the next circle her fingers touched the carpet, a clear invitation to Jo to rise and let them cup her breasts. Jo didn't move, but sighed again, a throaty little sound that was certainly not an objection.

'Please,' Melanie whispered as her fingers touched the carpet again.

Jo lifted her body. Lust and triumph welled up in Melanie as her hands slid under Jo's chest and she took a handful of soft flesh in each, lowering her own body to hug Jo and press her own, bigger breasts against Jo's bare back. This time Jo moaned as Melanie squeezed her nipples, Jo's head turning, her mouth open, seeking Melanie's. Their tongues met, Melanie tasting the softness of Jo's mouth as she pulled the smaller woman to her.

Their kiss signalled the collapse of their last shred of restraint. Jo turned and pulled Melanie into her, their mouths locked together in a frantic kiss, eyes tight shut and tongues deep in each others' mouths. Jo's blouse was pulled off, her bra following even as Melanie pulled up her own top, leaving it in a tangle around her neck in her haste to give Jo access to her breasts. Jo sat up, her hands coming up to Melanie's big, heavy boobs, her eyes wide as she ran her hands over them, the big nipples jutting out in response to her touch.

'They're lovely, Mel,' Jo said, looking up into Melanie's eyes. 'Oh, you're so lovely.'

Melanie hugged Jo to her, pushing the smaller woman's head into her cleavage, nestling her breasts against her face, her hands on Jo's back. They fell back, Melanie letting her hands roam, inhibitions now completely lost. Her hands slid down Jo's back and over the gentle curve of her bottom, frantically tugging the skirt up, finding the silky feel of tights and hooking her thumb into the waistband. Then her hand was down Jo's pants, squeezing a small, firm buttock, her fingers sliding down the cleft, trying to reach Jo's pussy but unable to get her hand far enough round to do more than just reach it.

Jo gasped as Melanie's fingers brushed against her bottom hole, her hands pulling at Melanie's clothes. Melanie felt her jeans wrenched open, the zip pulled frantically down. Her grip on Jo's bottom slipped as her jeans and knickers were pulled down, Jo rocking back into sitting position to pull Melanie's shoes, socks, jeans and knickers clean off in a single tangled mess. Melanie felt the cool air on her bare legs, the fire hot on one thigh. Nude from her neck down, she rolled on to her back, Jo kneeling between her legs. Melanie watched as Jo peeled of the remains of her clothes, watching the blonde's firm little breasts and flushed face. Jo finished her strip and Melanie spread her thighs to the gentle pressure of Jo's hands, letting her head fall back on to the carpet as Jo's hair brushed her inner thighs and a tongue began to lap at her.

'Oh, Jo,' she moaned, taking a handful of the blonde girl's hair and pulling her face on to her vulva. Melanie bit her fingers to stop herself from screaming as Jo's tongue lapped feverishly at her. There was no calculation, no careful judgement of each other's needs, just blind, desperate lust, fuelled by drink and a long time without a lover.

Melanie felt she was going to come when Jo suddenly stopped licking and swivelled round.

'Please, yes,' Melanie managed as she realised what was happening. Jo straddled her, legs spread wide across Melanie's chest, neat little bottom poised in front of her face as she once more buried her face in between Melanie's legs. Jo's hand reached around under her bottom, spreading her cheeks, two fingers entering her pussy.

Melanie's head swam with pleasure and drink, Jo's tongue grinding against her sex, the fingers moving inside her. Jo's bottom was directly above her face, the hole tight and puckered, the pink purse of her vulva wet and open in a nest of dark blonde hair, inviting her attention. She was going to do it, lick another woman between the legs, she had to, and she desperately wanted to. Her arms curled around Jo's thighs, her head lifted and her lips met Jo's vulva, tasting the salty, musky feminine taste. Her tongue lapped out, touching the flesh and flicking against the hard little button at the centre. It felt so rude, so utterly dirty, every detail of Jo's most intimate parts spread out in front of her. She wanted to lick it all, to make Jo come with her pussy pressed against her face. Jo gave a muffled squeak and suddenly it was Melanie who was coming, her whole body going into spasms as Jo's tongue pressed hard against her clitoris.

'Oh, God, Jo!' Melanie screamed as the peak of her orgasm

hit her, her mouth coming away from Jo as she arched her back and subsided on to the carpet, her breath coming in ragged pants.

'Don't stop!' Jo demanded.

'I –' Melanie began, only to have Jo rock back on her heels, smothering Melanie's face under her bottom, her pussy pressed determinedly against Melanie's mouth, her cheeks spread wide over her face. Melanie began to lick again, Jo squirming her bottom on to her face, rubbing herself against Melanie's lip, pressing hard, then harder as she began to gasp, giving sharp, regular pants then suddenly letting out a long, loud moan of ecstasy.

Jo held her place on Melanie's face for a long moment and then subsided, turning to hug her lover, kissing soft and long before Melanie drifted into oblivion.

The microscope light faded from brilliant white, through orange, to a dull red glow and blackness as Anna flicked the switch to off. Two hours spent collecting and matching fibres from samples had made her eyes hurt but the result was a full range of matches to complement Dr Wells's original set.

'Time to go, young Anna,' Wells said from across the room. 'Chop, chop, young lady, I have a date.'

'What are you cooking for her?' Anna replied.

'Ah ha! So you have been cultivating Violet, with whom I trust you will not seek to besmirch my image.'

'I wouldn't dream of it,' Anna answered with mock sarcasm.

'In that case,' Wells continued as he pulled his lab coat off, 'the answer is oysters in champagne, local lamb served in the traditional fashion and *crème brulée* done in my personal style. Simple, perhaps, but then I lack the time for anything grander.'

'It sounds excellent,' she answered.

'What then are you doing with your evening?' he asked.

'Seeing John Anderson,' she answered quietly.

'Ah ha! I might have guessed. He will be returning to

Guildford soon and plans a last night of fiery passion with the delectable Anna. A sensible move in my opinion.'

'I'm sure it's not really like that,' she answered.

'No? Well perhaps not. Still, take my advice and make the best of it. What was your personal predilection? To be spanked if I remember rightly?'

Anna blushed furiously. Wells immediately saw the colour in her cheeks and began to laugh as he moved to the door. Anna followed and he ushered her out, planting a firm smack on her bottom as soon as her back was to him. A bitter retort rose to Anna's lips but she choked it back, knowing that it would only cause him further amusement.

The worst thing was, he was right. She had spent a good part of the afternoon thinking about how to broach the subject with John. More or less continuously in fact, since they had met at lunch time and he had suggested dinner. She fully accepted that he liked to be in control of a sexual situation, or in fact in any other situation, but it was a big step from allowing him to take the lead to getting him to actually take physical command of her body. Probably he would do it, but so many men seemed to think it was somehow wrong, even if she actually asked for it. In fact, it would be best if he did it without knowing how desperately she wanted him to, yet any man who did it without her consent would lose her respect immediately. To get precisely what she wanted was going to take a metaphorical juggling act and even then she would have to trust John's maturity and experience. On the other hand, her knowledge of his potential for coldness frightened her. Honesty between lovers meant a lot to her and she would have preferred to fully understand John's character before making such an intimate request. Still, the notion of being put firmly across his knee and spanked was far too exciting not to take the chance of him being cold to the idea.

* * *

Anna left the building and set off towards the police station, leaving Dr Wells behind her to finish setting the security system. Actually, she considered, maybe Dr Wells had the right idea. Offering to cook for John might well get things off on the right foot. As she approached the station, she saw him come out of the door and hailed him. He was his usual dapper self, dressed in a suit of fine wool in a mid-blue tone, immaculate shoes, a white shirt that looked freshly ironed even at the end of the day and a tie in tones of silver-grey and dark blue. For a moment she wondered if he wouldn't think her unreasonably scruffy, dressed in her normal combination of jeans and a brightly coloured jumper, then decided that this was something that could be adjusted easily enough.

He returned her greeting and they talked for a while by his car. John cheerfully accepted her suggestion that she cook for him. Their conversation continued as he drove, avoiding the topic of the investigation by unspoken agreement. She corrected him only once on the route to her flat, despite the web of similar-looking roads in her area of Plymouth. On arrival they entered the house and she went up the stairs ahead of him, opening the door to her flat and casting a quick eye around, glad that it was tidier than usual.

'Would you like a drink?' she asked, suddenly feeling a touch nervous now that they were actually in the privacy of her flat.

'Wine if you have any,' he replied. 'Otherwise just fruit juice.'

'Wine it is,' she replied, 'but nothing as grand as we had the other day, I'm afraid. Have a seat in the main room, I'll bring it in to you.'

Anna chose a bottle and poured two glasses, coming into the main room to find him glancing over her bookshelves.

'Mainly things from college and reference books,' she said shyly.

He nodded and took the wine glass, swirling the purple liquid, sniffing and then sipping.

'It's good, strong and heady,' he commented. 'Spanish?'

'Portuguese,' she answered, 'Douro valley, where my dad comes from. It's like port but unfortified, so it's dry and not quite so strong.'

'It's excellent,' he answered taking another sip. 'What are you going to cook to go with it?'

'You'll see,' she answered. 'Anyway, relax for a bit, look through my books if you like. I just need a shower and a change of clothes.'

Anna went through to her bedroom, stripped quickly and crossed over to the tiny bathroom, hoping that John would catch a glimpse of her nakedness as she passed in front of the door. Stepping into the shower, she twisted the control, the sting of cold water making her skin tingle before it became warm and then hot and soothing. She took the soap and rubbed it on to her tummy, working up a good lather before running her hands up each arm and then over her breasts, feeling their weight in her hands and running her thumbs over the nipples before rubbing the soap in. Her eyes were shut, the water cascading over her hair and down her body. Anna bent forward, soaping her calves, knees and thighs and then moving up between her legs, massaging the warm soap into the fleshy folds of her pussy and sliding the soap bar between the cheeks of her bottom before letting her fingers follow. She shivered with pleasure, tempted to call out, to ask for John to come in and make love to her in the shower. It would be nice, but it wouldn't be everything, and if she behaved so demandingly then he wouldn't really be in charge, which she sensed was very important to him.

Stopping the exploration of her body that had almost become masturbation, Anna rinsed the soap away and stepped out of the shower, suddenly cold as her wet skin made contact with the cooler air of the flat. She scampered into the bedroom and pulled a towel around her, the big rectangle of soft fabric covering everything between her neck and her knees. She dried herself quickly, powdering herself and spraying on a touch of perfume much faster than she would have done normally. The next question was what to wear. She knew John didn't like what was conventionally considered sexy clothing, short tight skirts, low tops and so on – not that she had anything like that anyway. Jeans and plain tops were too ordinary, although she felt they set her figure off as well as anything. Serve him nude? It was a nice thought, but impractical as hot oil or boiling water on her skin was likely to bring the evening's romance to a rapid halt.

She opened the wardrobe, eyeing her selection of clothes with dissatisfaction. Quite unexpectedly, the gentle touch of a hand on her shoulder made her start.

'John!' she protested. 'You made me jump!'

'Let me choose,' he said in reply as if he had divined her thoughts.

'OK,' she answered, thrilled at the idea. She hoped he would choose something uncompromisingly naughty, something that would make her feel like his plaything – wanted, protected, yet indisputably under his command.

John paused to consider her wardrobe, and for a moment she thought that nothing at all was to his taste. Then he reached out, his arm still draped loosely across her shoulder, and took a plain white cotton blouse by the hanger. Anna took it and looked up at him, knowing her eyes would be big and moist, looking into his deep blue, sensitive eyes and wondering if hers were as attractive to him. He bent down, pulling open a drawer and choosing right first time. Anna shivered as she watched him sort through her underwear, piling brightly coloured briefs to the side until he found what he wanted, a pair of lacy white panties that would come up to her waist.

He stood back, leaning against the door frame. She knew

he had no intention of going, so she let the towel drop to the floor to stand naked in front of him, feeling, as she had before, the delicious vulnerability of her nakedness in contrast to his fully clothed body. She pulled on the panties he had chosen, adjusting them in the mirror so that each full cheek of her bottom was evenly covered with the delicate lace pattern. The blouse followed, Anna doing the buttons up one by one from the bottom, waiting for him to tell her to stop. When he did the blouse was done up as she would normally have worn it, except that with no bra underneath the dark circles of her nipples showed clearly through the fabric, each one creating a little hump in the cotton.

She looked up at him expectantly, but he just smiled and turned back to the main room. Anna realised that she was now wearing all that he intended her to, a combination at once innocent and flirtatious. She followed him into the room, her skin tingling with anticipation.

'More wine, sir?' she teased as he resumed his seat.

He held out the glass, which Anna filled before taking a swallow of her own wine. Did he want her now? Or would he make her wait, teasing her to a peak of excitement before having his way with her? Most importantly, would he know how best to handle her without her having to ask? Despite the wine her throat felt dry. She wanted to ask him what to do, but he was sitting casually sipping at his wine, the picture of relaxation.

He got up and came towards her, her pulse quickening, expecting his arms to go round her, to move on to her most personal places with an easy familiarity as he kissed her.

'Come on, then, let's sample your cooking,' he said casually as he passed her and moved on down the passage to the kitchen.

The bastard, she thought. Sex, then dinner, then more sex was what she had been hoping for, but he clearly intended to prolong the build-up as long as he wanted. They moved into the kitchen, John sitting at the table while Anna prepared a salad of fried spiced sausage, greens, herbs, sun-dried tomatoes and olive oil. Her feeling of sexual expectancy dropped off slowly as they ate, and he seemed to be deliberately avoiding anything that might excite her in the conversation. By the time they had finished, she was wondering if he had lost interest. Perhaps she had done something wrong, to change his attitude to one of polite restraint. He took his last forkful and pushed his chair back from the table, Anna taking his plate and her own and carrying them to the sink. Surely he wasn't just going to get up and go? If he did, that was going to be the end of their relationship.

'Anna,' he said as she passed his chair on the way back to her own, 'could you fill my glass?'

'Oh, sorry,' she said, reaching across him for the bottle.

As she stretched, he took hold of her arm, folding his hand around her wrist and pulling forward. In an instant she found herself across his lap.

'John!' she squeaked in mock protest but he had already transferred his arm to hold her around her waist, his other hand touching her at the back of her knees and moving slowly upwards, his fingers stroking the sensitive flesh of her inner thighs. Anna whimpered with pleasure and hung her head in total submission to his will. His fingers carried on, touching the crease where her bottom joined her thighs, making her whimper again as one finger traced a slow line up the crease of her bottom, pushing the lacy material in so that it tickled her between her cheeks.

Her shirt-tail was lifted, his hand taking a hold of her knickers by the waistband, then relenting and returning to explore her bottom, cupping her cheeks as if to test their weight. His hand moved clear of her bottom and she tensed, expecting him to begin to smack it, wanting desperately to ask for it but knowing that if she did it would ruin the pleasure of being spanked. Nothing happened. John's hand went between her thighs instead and motioned gently for her to open them. She obeyed, knowing that she would be damp and ready for him. Her hopes of being spanked faded, but the disappointment was small as he responded to the way she was squirming into him by cupping her pubic mound in the palm of his hand and grinding the heel of his palm into her vulva through the material of her panties.

'Pull them down, John, I'm ready,' she gasped as she pushed herself against his hand, trying to get a better contact with the hard muscle.

'Well, I'm not,' he replied, his voice calm and steady. 'Just relax.'

He lowered her back to lie fully across his knee and once again hooked his hand into the waistband of her panties. Anna waited, trembling. This time they were coming down, there would be no remission and then he'd take her and fuck her over the table with her bottom bare without the slightest shred of modesty. He began to pull, the lace brushing against the small of her back and then the sensitive skin of her bottom as she savoured every inch of exposure until the panties were tangled around her thighs. Her bottom felt huge and very vulnerable. John's hand once more caressed the cheeks. She sighed as his other hand came to rest on her other cheek. Then her bottom was being opened, his strong, masculine hands pulling apart the soft globes of flesh, his fingers moving in between them, stroking her fur, loitering on her anus, touching her pussy, penetrating her and then moving down to her clitoris. She knew exactly how she would look, blouse up, panties pulled down, her thighs shamelessly wide, her bottom cheeks open, every detail of pussy and bottom-hole open for his inspection.

'Please, yes!' she begged as his finger began to trace a slow circle on her clit.

Without warning he stopped, his hands moving to her

hips and pushing her gently. Anna let him guide her, unsure of what he wanted her to do.

'Go down on your knees,' he instructed her.

Anna obeyed, crawling off his knees and going into a kneeling position on the hard, cold tiles of the kitchen floor as she positioned herself to face him, her eyes raised to look into his. He was looking down at her, the deep blue eyes cool and stern, his excitement only betrayed by the slight flush of blood on each cheek.

'Take off your shirt,' he told her. 'Then your pants.'

She began to unbutton the blouse, opening it to bare her breasts and then shrugging it down off her shoulders. Her panties followed, wriggled down her legs and pulled off to be discarded in a heap on her blouse. Naked, she went back into her kneeling position, watching in fascination as he slowly drew down his fly and pulled his penis out. It was already half stiff, smooth and smelling hot and male. She knew exactly what she was going to have to do, take it in her mouth and fellate him, maybe until he came in the back of her throat. His hand locked in her hair, gently but brooking no resistance as he guided her mouth towards his penis. Anna parted her lips, let her tongue touch the tip of his cock and then kissed it. He pulled her head forward on to him, her mouth filling with salty cock which stiffened quickly as he fucked her mouth, drawing her head back and forward by the hair.

She raised her eyes to find him looking down at her, his expression showing his pleasure, yet also tenderness. A detached, rational part of her mind told her that he was enjoying her response to him as much as the actual physical sensation of having his penis sucked. Otherwise, her thoughts ran with her fantasy that she had been spanked for mis-behaviour and that he now wanted to be sucked without thought for her. She only wished it was true, but the idea was too much in any case – she had to come without waiting any longer.

Anna took her hands off the floor, one going behind her to feel the smooth skin of her bottom, the other going between her legs to open the damp lips of her vulva and find her clitoris. She began to rub herself in little circular motions, faster and faster as his penis stiffened to iron hardness in her mouth, making her choke and gasp for air. As her pleasure began to approach a peak she imagined how she must look, on her knees in front of him, stark naked with her mouth full of his penis, her bottom stuck out, bare and vulnerable. Anna began to come, working frantically on his cock as her climax hit her and her muscles tensed, one finger sneaking between her bottom cheeks to touch her anus, popping into the little hole as the full fire of her orgasm came over her, coming up her spine to explode in her head.

She had expected him to come, prepared to accept the salty mouthful for the sake of his pleasure. Instead he waited until her shudders had fully subsided and then helped her to her feet, taking her by the hand and leading her into the bedroom. She followed, concious of how her nudity contrasted with him being fully dressed and wondering delightedly what John had in mind for his own pleasure.

On entering her bedroom he steered her gently down on to the bed and began to undress. Anna sat back, leaning on her hands as she watched, admiring the firm muscularity of his body. His skin was mainly smooth, with just a little hair around the nipples and in a line down to his stomach. Naked, he looked younger than she had expected, the outlines of his muscles showing clearly. He must be really quite strong, she thought, not with the massive, irresistible strength of Morgan Wells, but strong enough to handle her the way she liked.

Anna's finger went to her mouth in anticipation. John noticed and smiled at her in response. His erection had subsided while he undressed, and she reached out to take hold of him as he came close to her. He took hold of her wrist, but instead of guiding it to his penis he lifted her arm, taking the other wrist as he placed a knee on the bed. Anna complied with the gentle pressure he was exerting, allowing her arms to be raised above her head. She wondered what his intention was, then realised as he put her wrists together and reached out for a bright red ribbon that she had left on the bedside table.

He looped the ribbon around her wrists. Anna smiled and tried to wriggle over into her preferred, bottom-upmost position, only to have John resist her movement as he tied the ribbon on to the ironwork of the bed. She squirmed and sighed, delighting in the pressure of his firm belly against her breasts as he tied her in place. He drew back, kneeling on the bed, watching her breath quicken with the delicious help-lessness of being strapped in place.

His hand reached out and took hold of her hair, lifting her head and moving forwards to once more introduce his cock to her mouth. Anna accepted it, closing her eyes as she sucked, and the fingertips of his free hand ran gently over her body, touching her face, neck and tummy before moving to her breasts, tweaking each nipple back to full erection before moving between her legs and gently easing her thighs apart to gain access to her vulva. His cock rapidly expanded in her mouth. John took his time before pulling away and moving back down the bed.

Anna squirmed with pleasure, tied and helpless as he took hold of her feet and rolled her legs up, holding the ankles together. Her raised legs obscured her view of him, yet she knew that he would be able to see every detail of her sex and even between the cheeks of her bottom. The position was deliciously vulnerable, allowing him to do anything he wanted. Maybe he'd lift her legs a little and spank her, or roll her up and tie her ankles to the bed end, exposing her even more fully. Her breasts also felt deliciously prominent, her inability to touch them only heightening her pleasure. The best thing, though, was that he could do what he liked and that he obviously knew she'd just whimper in pleasure whatever he chose.

He held her legs up with one hand, the other exploring her sex with a deliciously possessive intimacy. She closed her eyes, sinking into the pleasure he was giving her, vaguely aware for a moment that he was putting a condom on and then sighing deeply as the tip of his penis touched her pussy and then slid in, filling her with its beautiful hardness. His arms wrapped around her thighs, holding them against him so that she could feel his firm body pushed against the soft flesh of her thighs.

He rode her at a slow, even pace for what seemed an eternity, her arms tensing against her bonds and her breath coming in short pants. The urge to touch herself was at once agonisingly frustrating and utterly wonderful, her pussy burning with the need for an orgasm that she knew would never come without the assistance of her fingers. His pace picked up, the strokes now pushing the breath out of her, becoming harder, his arms locked hard around her thighs, then ending in a sudden flurry as he came, groaning loudly in his ecstasy. He stayed in her for a moment and then pulled slowly away, leaving Anna empty and in desparate need of her own climax.

'Lick me, John,' she begged, thoroughly aware that the choice of whether she came or not was entirely in his hands. As soon as he had released her legs her thighs had opened, offering herself to him unreservedly.

He smiled at her, his expression slightly wry and he looked down at her body. For a moment she thought he was going to get up and walk away, but he simply altered his position on the bed so that he was more comfortable, cupped his hands underneath her bottom and moved his head down towards her pussy. Anna closed her eyes and sighed with as much relief as pleasure as his tongue touched her and began to lick.

It took very little time. Anna's pleasure mounted quickly. As he licked her mind focused on her fantasy of him spanking her. She felt her orgasm coming, then arched her back and called out as it arrived, her arms straining against the ribbon and her eyes tight shut in bliss.

After she had come she lay still while he went briefly to the bathroom and then returned to untie her and give her a chance to clean herself up. When she came back she found him lying full length on the bed, his hands folded behind his head. She lay down next to him, curling herself into a ball with her head on his shoulder.

'John?' she asked tentatively.

'Yes,' he replied.

'Nothing,' she sighed as she laid her head on to his chest. She couldn't bear to tell him that he could have made things even better than they had been. She was sure he'd just feel hurt and that it would more likely spoil what they did have than add to it.

He had begun to stroke her hair, a soothing feeling that increased her desire to snuggle into him. She gave a sigh of contentment and put an arm across him, hugging his body against her before subsiding contentedly.

For a long while they lay together without talking. Finally John got up to retrieve the wine and glasses from the kitchen. They sat and drank for a while, now in an atmosphere of relaxed intimacy. The second time they made love it was slow and easy, John taking his time to savour her pleasure, exploring each other without inhibition, mental or physical. He had coaxed Anna to orgasm twice by the time he allowed himself to reach his second climax, after which they showered together and dried each other before she collapsed on the bed in a state of rapturous exhaustion while he went to the kitchen for glasses of cold lime juice.

Anna lay on the bed, thinking to herself. She wanted him to know how he could have made their lovemaking even better, yet she felt unable to tell him directly. Maybe she could drop a heavy hint though.

John Anderson came back into the room to find Anna lying on her front on the bed, shamelessly naked, the soft curve of her back rising to her bottom, each cheek still crowned with a flush of pink where her heels had been pushed against the soft flesh. She smiled at him, her eyes half shielded by her dishevelled fringe. She still looked utterly desirable, even so soon after she had completely satiated his lust. He put the drinks down, sat beside her and began to stroke her hair and back as he might a pet. Anna purred and arched her back, pushing her bottom up for its share of caresses.

John stopped, giving her bottom a playful pat before reaching for his glass and taking a long drink of cold lime juice. He simply was not ready for another bout of love-making. Anna's mouth pursed briefly into a moue of mock sulkiness then lapsed back into a contented smile as she reached for her glass. John passed it to her so that she could drink.

'I feel so good,' she sighed as she put the glass on the floor. 'John, the bottom shelf of my book case, the little magazine. Don't say a word, just look at the cover.'

He leant forward, puzzled by her request. The bookshelf was within his reach and it was obvious which one she meant. He took it out, realising what she was trying to tell him immediately. The magazine was an old copy of an American comic, not the sort of thing he would ever have purchased, nor in keeping with the other items on her shelves. The cover showed a tweed-clad man smoking a pipe and holding a woman dressed as an American college student over his lap. Her skirt was rucked up around her waist and her white panties had been pulled down to her knees, while he was in the act of raising a ruler with the clear intention of bringing it down across her well-upholstered bottom. There was only one reason that Anna would want him to see the picture. Obviously she would like to be treated the same way herself.

Anna was facing away, obviously waiting for a response from him. He paused, unable to raise a need for a third bout of sex and unsure about his attitude to her suggestion. Not now, that was for sure, and her acquiescence to his control suggested that she would wait without protest. He closed the book, using it to trace a long line along the middle of her back and then smacking it gently down on her bottom. Anna purred and he laughed, just loud enough for her to hear, and then returned the magazine to the shelf.

He lay back, letting his feelings on the subject gel. Their sex together had been superb. In Anna he felt he had found someone who would not only let him guide and control her but who actively craved it from him. He had been able to orchestrate everything, working at his own pace and taking delight in her uninhibited response. His ex-wife Sarah, other lovers like Jan Rolfe and Catherine Marshall – none of them had been so at ease with their own sexuality as Anna. Behind his satisfaction, though, a nagging feeling of doubt lurked. The idea that she wanted her bottom spanked was harder to cope with than her acceptance of his control. Not that he wouldn't enjoy doing it. The problem rather was that he felt uneasy with the very pleasure that he knew it would give him, despite the fact that it was clearly something she would not only accept, but actively needed. He shook the disturbing thought off, deciding to resolve his feelings before doing anything about her suggestion. Tiredness was creeping up on him, even though it was still relatively early. Still, he would have to hang his suit up before going to sleep, and it wasn't a job he wanted to entrust to Anna, who took a very casual attitude to looking after her own clothes.

'John,' she said after a long silence.

'Yes,' he replied.

'Did you see the evidence we're building up for the James Draper case?'

'Not all of it,' he replied, 'only what we needed for the interview. Can't this wait until morning?'

'Please,' she continued, 'It's just a little thing.'

'Very well, carry on,' he answered.

'Did you see the chromatograph results?'

'No, but DI Krebs did. Blue-black Parker ink in both the pen and the bottle we took from Cutts's house apparently.'

'Yes,' Anna replied, 'only it wasn't.'

'How do you mean?' he queried.

'It wasn't blue-black ink in the pen,' Anna replied. 'I was playing with the chromatograph while he was at lunch last Friday, you see, and he came back early and nearly caught me. He's very strict about that sort of thing, so I put the paper in my pocket. When I emptied my pockets to put my jeans in the wash I found the piece of paper. Look, it's here.'

Anna got up and walked across to her bedside table, picking up a heavily folded piece of paper. Anderson took it, noting immediately the differential spread of ink pigments so familiar to every school child.

'On the one in the lab there's a clear band of orange,' Anna was saying. 'This is all blues and greens.'

'Are you certain?' he asked, the implications of the scrap of coloured paper racing through his mind.

'Certain,' Anna answered.

'Think carefully,' he continued, now fully alert and sitting up on the bed, 'because if you're right, this has very serious implications for the case. In fact it suggests that Dr Wells has been falsifying evidence in order to make the case stronger.'

'I know,' Anna replied. 'I swear it's genuine, you can come and look at the other chromatographs tomorrow. I –'

'One moment,' Anderson broke in. 'On the security video this afternoon we saw Cutts write a cheque at just after

2.00 p.m. He used a biro and there was no pen in his jacket pocket. That was before the murder could have taken place, when Cutts was presumably on his way to meet Charles Draper. Also, there was no ordinary blue ink in Cutts's house and he denies owning the pen. I also think that the murderer was nowhere near Hewton and the quay we searched on Monday afternoon, but at Thorn Point, which explains the lack of witnesses. In such a case, the pen must have been dropped where you found it deliberately to lead us to Cutts.'

'But,' Anna objected, 'we'd never even have found it if Charles Draper's death had been accepted as accidental, which Dr Wells was going to do until I found the bruising –'

She trailed off, looking at Anderson, her face paler than normal.

'He didn't even find the morphine traces until after that,' she began again, now speaking quietly with her lower lip trembling, 'and he wouldn't let me do any of the analysis, not even the easy bits. And he rubbished me when I said the tissue damage in the lungs was wrong for salt water.'

'So he could have falsified all the evidence? Why?'

Anna shrugged.

'Put some clothes on,' Anderson ordered. 'We had better go and speak to Robert Walsh.'

'You're wrong about Thorn Point,' Anna continued as she dressed. 'If Draper was drowned there his body would have been washed over the bar on the high tide in the middle of the night, especially as the wind would have blown it out into the channel. I think the body was dumped at Hewton quay just before dawn. I worked out the tides and explained it all to Violet. She agrees with me.'

'Maybe,' Anderson answered distractedly.

'She was going to discuss the idea with Dr Wells this evening,' Anna continued.

'Which is more or less what I'd like to do,' Anderson

replied. Then he turned to Anna, who had stopped in the act on pulling a sock on and was sitting on the bed.

'John,' she said after a moment, 'when we got to the cutting at Sparkwell there were people all over the place, but Dr Wells went straight to where the body was and then he identified James Draper straight away, even with the mess the face was in.'

'Did he know James Draper?' Anderson queried, immediately aghast at the implications of what she had said.

'I don't think so,' Anna answered, 'but, John, that means Dr Wells must have killed him, and I think his uncle as well.'

'I realise that,' Anderson answered. 'And what's more, the information I received from James Draper's friend Lindsie suggests he was working with someone local. Hurry up.'

'But John,' Anna persisted, 'Violet is with him and she's going to go over all the problems with the case. Don't you think we should go and make sure she's OK?'

'That's what we're doing,' Anderson replied, tying his second shoelace. 'He lives in some village, doesn't he?'

'Peter Tavy, near Tavistock,' Anna answered. 'It's about twenty miles.'

'Right, direct me,' Anderson ordered. 'Come on.'

Anderson took the stairs at a run, Anna following close behind him. A moment later the engine of the BMW roared to life and they pulled out onto the quiet evening roads. He drove furiously out through the suburbs, maintaining as great a speed as safety would allow and then accelerating out on to the unlit road across Roborough Down. They drove in silence, Anna only occasionally speaking to give a direction as they passed Yelverton and then Tavistock, finally turning at a sign that indicated the direction of the tiny village of Peter Tavy. After a last section of twisting lanes barely wide enough for the car to pass through they came out under the yellow street lamps of the village.

'Stop here,' Anna said. 'That's his house, the white one up the little drive where the gargoyle is.'

Anderson pressed hard on the brake, pulling the BMW to a halt in the pool of deep yellow light cast by a solitary street lamp. He leapt out and ran for the house, Anna following less certainly. Wells's car stood in the drive. The glass panels in the house's front door and windows showed only the sullen yellow gleam of the reflected street light. Anderson walked round to the side, treading stealthily in the utter silence of the night. He rounded the corner of the house, into the shadow of the street light. The moon was now the only source of light, bathing the garden in its pale glow. Wells's swimming pool, the surface as black as ink and deathly still, was in front of him, the patio to the left and beyond that the broad sliding window that opened from Wells's living room. Anderson noticed the round shape of a pool-side light switch by the window and motioned Anna towards it.

He heard a faint sound from the house. A pant? Maybe a groan. The light was dim, the interior hard to pick out. For an instant something pale glinted in the moonlight, the light dimming as quickly as it had come to leave only an amorphous shape little paler than the surround, a long bar of grey ending in a subtly bright crescent pattern. Then Anderson realised what it was. Barely discernible in the gloom, the pale shape was a bare arm, the crescent a section of a handcuff locked on to the leg of a heavy piece of furniture. Someone was lying helpless on the floor, pre-sumably Krebs, and another, blacker shadow above her could only be Wells.

Anderson acted without further thought. Next to him a massive stone urn supported a tangle of plants. He grabbed it and hurled it through the window, plate glass exploding into a thousand fragments and cascading into the room. Anderson followed a moment behind. At the same instant the patio lights came on, flooding the scene with white brilliance.

Anderson stopped, standing framed in the shattered window, staring aghast into the room.

It was not Violet Krebs who lay on the floor, but Dr Morgan Wells, his arms handcuffed above his head to the massive legs of his dining room table. He was naked, his heavily muscled body stretched out at full length, his face set in an expression of utter disbelief. Violet Krebs was straddled across his hips, naked but for a tiny corset that pulled in her waist and exaggerated her buttocks and breasts, and quite clearly riding on his penis. Her mouth was open in shock, a strand of sweat-soaked red hair plastered down one side of her face, her eyes wide in astonishment.

'I think there has been a mistake,' Anderson managed.

TWELVE
Wednesday

Joanna Blackheath was awakened by the cold. For a moment she was disorientated. She was lying on something with a markedly different texture from bed linen, completely naked and in a stream of cold sunlight. Her mouth was full of a strange taste and felt like sandpaper while her head ached with a steady, rhythmic throb. Suddenly the events of the previous evening flooded into her brain. What had she done? Had sex with Melanie on the floor of the cottage! Christ, if they ever found out about it at the station she'd never live it down! That was if she wasn't dismissed for gross misconduct or whatever charge having sex with a suspect in a sealed premises led to.

She propped herself up on one arm, looking around her with bleary eyes. At some point in the night Melanie had crawled on to the sofa and pulled a rug over herself. All that was visible of her was her feet and a tangle of brown curls. Joanna looked at her with a growing sense of embarrassment as more details of what they had done together came back to her. It wasn't her first drunken sexual encounter, but it was a definite first with another woman and a suspect at that. Would

Melanie be equally embarrassed? Amused? Annoyed? Or would she want a replay?

Jo didn't want to wait around and find out, but she knew she would have to face Melanie eventually, so she reached out and shook her awake, receiving a grunt for her trouble. She suddenly realised that she had no idea what the time was, but a glance at her watch showed that it was mercifully early. She dressed quickly as Melanie stirred and sat up, rubbing her eyes and yawning before sinking her head into her hands.

'Oh God, my head,' Melanie eventually managed. 'I need coffee.'

Jo watched in wonder as Melanie stood up, wrapped the rug around herself and shuffled into the kitchen to search for ingredients. Didn't she remember? If she did, she evidently didn't care.

'Yuck, the milk's sour,' Melanie called out as Jo finished dressing. 'I'll make black.'

Evidently Melanie had decided that the only way to handle what had happened between them was not to make a big deal out of it. That seemed sensible in fact and she was more than happy to go along with her 'just a normal morning' act. She glanced at her watch again. There would just be time to get home and shower before getting in to the station. Oh God, she'd left her car outside Mrs Herrick's! The old lady would know! No she wouldn't, well not the details anyway. So as long as Melanie stayed quiet her reputation was safe. The thought of people like Gerry Hart getting to know what she'd done was unbearable.

Melanie brought coffee in and Jo tried to drink it quickly while Melanie huddled on the sofa in her rug. They drank in silence, Jo blowing on her coffee and sipping the scalding liquid as fast as she could.

'I must go,' Jo finally said putting down her half-empty mug. 'Shut the door when you leave. I'll find some excuse to come over later and tidy up properly. Don't worry about anyone else from the station coming here, they're supposed to get my OK.'

'OK, bye then,' Melanie answered softly as Jo left the room. Her tone had been hard to read. Indifferent? Hopeful? Jo didn't want to know, her only worry being that if she and Melanie ever got drunk together again, the same thing might happen. The sunlight stung her eyes as she left the front door, pausing to glance at the statue that had been the cause of her going over to the cottage in the first place. Deciding to look at it in the bright morning light, she saw that the morning sun caught the mud at the bottom of the shallow pond, revealing a thin crescent of paler colour, a feature that would never be noticeable except when the sun struck from a low angle in the early morning. So the statue had definitely been moved, destroying her last lingering doubts about Melanie's truthfulness. In that case it seemed more likely that the rest of Melanie's story was accurate, and therefore Edith Herrick's as well. It was no good constantly dismissing everything because of the opinion of some path boy in Plymouth. She would have to get Anderson to make sure the facts were double checked.

'Honestly, John, what the hell did you think you were playing at?' Detective Superintendent Walsh stormed. 'Dr Wells is a highly respected member of his profession. Do you realise how many years he's been with us?'

'Yes,' Anderson replied, 'nevertheless the facts –'

'The facts!' Walsh broke in. 'The facts are, John, that you have become infatuated with a girl who's barely out of college and allowed her to lead you into the most stupid, ill-considered action I have ever heard of. Don't you realise what's happened?'

'I think –' Anderson began.

'No, don't think, listen to me,' Walsh continued. 'All your so-called evidence relies on observations made by Anna

Ferreira. The same Anna Ferreira who had developed a crush on Dr Wells and then determined to gain revenge because he very sensibly turned her down. Of all the "evidence" she has produced, the only thing that can be easily verified is that Dr Wells correctly identified James Draper's body, and if you'd had the sense to do some ground work before hurling an urn through his patio doors you'd have discovered that he did know what James Draper looked like. Go and ask Mallows at Devonport if you don't believe me. The rest of it she has obviously faked in a puerile effort to damage Dr Wells. For Christ's sake, John, you're a DCI, not some PC still wet behind the ears from Hendon!'

'With respect, sir,' Anderson said carefully, 'I think it would be sensible to have the forensic evidence reassessed independently. That would vindicate either Anna Ferreira or Dr Wells and avoid any accusations of prejudice or misconduct on our part should she prove to be right. I must also point out that her version of events fits the facts in every respect.'

'Yes, because she's manufactured it to!' Walsh snapped. 'One thing I won't accuse her of and that's stupidity. No, an independent assessment would just make things worse. It's embarrassing enough as it is.'

'Very well, sir,' Anderson replied, 'but I would like my request to be formally noted.'

'On your own head be it,' Walsh answered.

'I accept full responsibility, sir,' Anderson continued. 'May I also ask what the connection between Dr Wells and James Draper was?'

'Draper tried to bribe him once, years ago, I think. I was DI at Plympton at the time, so if you want the details, ask Mallows,' Walsh answered then paused and sighed, a gesture that signified weary resignation to Anderson. 'Oh, and there's a fax here from your DS in Guildford. A statue in a pond at Charles Draper's cottage was moved, apparently by the murderer. John, wouldn't it have been a simple enough matter to have called me last night before taking things into your own hands? I know you have something of a reputation for working independently but on my team such behaviour is simply not acceptable.'

Anderson mumbled something placatory, took the fax and left the office seething internally but outwardly calm. He scanned the fax as he walked down the corridor. As Walsh had said, Jo had discovered that a statue in Charles Draper's pond had been moved, and it seemed likely that it was the murderer who had moved it. It was a puzzling detail, but not one that was immediately relevant. He folded the sheet of paper neatly and slid it into the inside pocket of his suit. The story was evidently already halfway around the police station as everybody from the cleaning lady to the duty sergeant stared at him on the way out. Their attention made him even more furious than he already was, and he left the station hoping that nobody had yet troubled to pass the details on to Devonport. The only mercy was that there was no sign of DI Krebs.

Sergeant Mallows was on duty at the Devonport station and Anderson used his rank to secure a vacant interview room, although, unlike in the main station, his presence wasn't automatically a cause for strange looks and humorous remarks. Anderson set out what he wanted to know to Mallows, who didn't answer immediately but sat across the table rubbing his chin in thought.

'Oh yes, sir,' he eventually began. 'Dr Wells would recognise James Draper.'

'Why?' Anderson asked.

'Well, it's like this, sir,' Mallows continued. 'About three, four years back, Draper gets pulled in for possession of drugs, just cannabis I think, but still. Anyhow, he only tries and bribes Dr Wells. Waited outside the laboratory he did, bold as brass. Of course Wells wouldn't have any of it and it was me who took Draper in for him. He should have got a hefty sentence, but as I remember it the case didn't come off. Can't remember why.'

'Thank you, Sergeant,' Anderson continued. 'Sergeant Mallows, how long have you been serving?'

'Forty years this autumn,' Mallows replied proudly but with a trace of tiredness in his voice.

'That's very impressive,' Anderson replied. 'Now what, in your opinion, would happen to a man who tried to sell icing sugar as cocaine in this area.'

'Ah, you mean Draper, don't you,' Mallows replied. 'Well, I should say he was lucky we caught him before he sold any. There's a fair share of nasty characters around here who wouldn't take kindly to having the wool pulled over their eyes.'

'Right, thank you again, Sergeant. I think that clears up what I wanted to know.'

Anderson left Devonport station with his mind working at full throttle. Anna Ferreira was right, or at least she had damn well better be or his chances of promotion to fill Graham Parrish's shoes would be well and truly lost. No, the whole pattern made sense. James Draper must have somehow acquired a hold on Dr Wells, perhaps initially by bribing him, a supposition backed up by his interview with Lindsie. As Wells had infinitely more to lose than Draper by exposure, the situation would have escalated, Wells becoming more in Draper's power with each event. As the culmination of the process, Wells must have murdered Charles Draper, possibly in return for a share of the inheritance. Draper could then have refused to pay up, pointing out that there was nothing Wells could do about it and finally pushing the doctor over the edge. The whole plot, viewed from the ideas he had worked out with Anna, showed a careful, calm and calculating mind, with an initial set-up for Charles Draper dying an accidental death and then two levels for Wells to fall back on,

218

first murder by an unknown hand and then setting up Cutts as the killer, a much riskier third chance that had almost worked. Of course Charles Draper needed to be murdered within the area in which the forensic investigation would fall to Wells, hence the luring of Draper to Devon. Indeed, had it not been for Anna the whole plot would have worked without a hitch and it would never have been necessary to bring Cutts into it. The man who had conceived and executed such a plot needed to be strong-willed, physically powerful and utterly callous. It fitted Wells perfectly.

How Charles Draper had got to Devon eluded him, as did several other minor details. Nevertheless, the theory fitted the facts without a single discordant note and was of such complexity that the probability of it being incorrect was inconsequential. He could now go back to Walsh and demand a reassessment of the forensic evidence, if necessary going over Walsh's head. He had to be correct, and he was prepared to put his career on the line to prove it.

Anna Ferreira sat nervously sipping coffee in a café that gave her a view of the car park and Dr Wells's old Rover. Soon he would go out for lunch, following his almost invariable routine of driving down to the old harbour and eating in one of the pubs there. She knew the risk she was taking, yet felt she had no choice. If she backed down now, she could expect the sack, or worse. She and John had left Wells's house immediately after the disaster of the previous night, never voicing their suspicions. But Dr Wells had to have guessed and would now be taking steps to protect himself from accusations. He would also want to know where she was, but she would have to take the risk that he hadn't asked around for her.

She caught sight of his unmistakable figure as he left the building and her heart jumped. This was it, an action that would put the final gloss on the destruction of her career if it didn't come off. She got up and left, walking quickly to stop her common sense getting the better of her. The door loomed up in front of her, the commissionaire looking up with a friendly smile.

'I forgot my coat,' she said cheerfully, 'and Dr Wells has gone. Could I quickly borrow the spare key to the lab?'

'I'm not sure about that, Miss,' he answered doubtfully.

'Oh go on,' Anna pouted, 'you know me, and I won't be a second.'

'Very well, but be quick with you,' he replied.

Anna took the key and thanked him, hurrying away down the corridor with the certain knowledge that his eyes were glued to her bottom. She opened the lab door and slipped inside, crossing quickly to where Dr Wells kept the spare cupboard keys. The cupboard she wanted yielded to the third key she chose and she carefully removed the piece of evidence that she needed, noting thankfully that it had not been tampered with.

A thought occurred to her and she opened another cupboard. There was the pen, its small transparent chamber clearly showing blue-black ink, not the plain blue she had used on her chromatograph. Next to that were several fluid samples. Each, she had no doubt, would prove exactly what Dr Wells wanted it to, only the single item she had taken falling outside his province of knowledge.

She left the lab without arousing comment, the commissionaire not even noticing that she had no coat. The next stop was to be her flat, then the police station for a desperate attempt to argue her case.

As John Anderson drove back from Devonport he went over the facts in his mind. The case, as it would go to court to try and convict Nathan Cutts of double murder, was plausible and would in all probability convince a jury. The prosecution would be able to prove his presence at both murder sites.

Both places were remote and distant from Charmouth. He could also be linked to Charles Draper's cottage by the note on the calendar. Cutts also fulfilled the physical requirements for the murderer and the prosecution would be able to stress his taste in antique sado-masochistic pornography and his reputation as a loner and possible peeping tom.

The defence, by contrast, would only be able to try and influence the jury into delivering a not-guilty verdict on the grounds of Cutts's guilt not being beyond reasonable doubt. It would be highly unlikely to work with the weight of forensic evidence against him. Cutts wouldn't stand a chance, and his denials of guilt would only make it worse for him.

Take the forensic evidence away, though, and the prosecution had nothing but circumstance and supposition. Cutts would walk free and the investigation would be back to square one.

Without the forensic evidence there was only the accidental death of Charles Draper. Anderson pigeonholed this in his mind as result number one. Whether Cutts or Wells was the murderer they would both have been satisfied with this result.

The evidence for Draper being murdered had initially been found by Anna, a trainee with a few months' experience. Wells, a highly experienced expert, had missed the bruising in the hair, which had to be a major mark against him.

Take the remaining forensic evidence away and they would never have found Cutts and simply have been unable to prosecute. The case would have fallen flat and eventually been consigned to the bin of unsolved murders. Again, both Wells and Cutts would have considered this a good result. Again, however, it was Anna who, by discovering the pen, had pushed the case a step further.

Both Wells and Cutts would have had equal reason to murder James Draper, as whatever the motive it had clearly been created by James Draper himself. The murderer must have been faced with something that made killing James Draper a preferential choice. So he killed James Draper. Only at this stage did the benefits to Wells and Cutts not fall together. Cutts had everything to lose by his clumsy attempt to fake suicide and failure to cover his tracks. Wells, by contrast, had everything to gain by laying those same clues. Again, this had to be considered a mark against Wells.

On top of that there was the link between Wells and James Draper, tenuous perhaps, but no more so than the idea of James Draper managing to hire Cutts as a killer.

Finally, and conclusively in Anderson's view, there was the fact that Wells was the only person who had been in a position to plant and distort the forensic evidence. The remote third option, that Anna was responsible, could be eliminated by the fact that she had not had a chance to plant evidence in Cutts's house in Charmouth.

To prove his case to Robert Walsh or, if necessary, a superior, he would therefore need two things. Firstly, a solid example of false or distorted forensic evidence. Secondly, something that eliminated Cutts from the picture.

At present he had neither, although calling in an independent specialist would solve the first problem. However careful Wells had been, there would have to be something that didn't stand up to proper investigation.

One doubt remained, something that he was unable to push entirely from his mind. His chain of logic rested largely on the assumption that Anna was telling the truth. If she wasn't, if she had manipulated him from the start, then he might as well just hand Walsh his warrant card and drive off into the sunset. No, all the time he'd been with Anna he had led. Or had he? All the coy looks, the deliberate meekness, the little hints in her conversation – maybe he had been led by her.

He drew the BMW to a halt in the car park and got out. Distractedly, he pulled Blackheath's fax from his pocket and scanned it. Something about a statue being moved and Draper's car not having left the Guildford area until the middle of the night. He decided to worry about it later, neither fact apparently having a direct bearing on the immediate situation.

His adrenalin was running high, his determination to force Walsh to act absolute. He reached Walsh's door and knocked forcefully, opening it to find the Detective Superintendent talking to Violet Krebs. Ignoring the look on Krebs's face, Anderson sat down and addressed Walsh.

'I want to explain the Draper case as I now see it in full detail. My intention is to convince you that it is necessary to bring in an external forensic expert to re-examine the evidence. Furthermore, if you are not inclined to act, I intend to take this higher up the chain of command.'

Walsh's eyebrows rose a fraction. Krebs made as if to speak but was silenced with a gesture of Walsh's hand.

'Very well,' Walsh said. 'Say your piece. If you can convince both DI Krebs and myself of the need to bring in external help, then I shall have no option but to follow your advice.'

'Thank you, sir,' Anderson answered. 'It would help if I could borrow a piece of paper.'

Anderson outlined his reasoning, carefully explaining each point and frequently going back to reinforce an area of his logic. Walsh listened attentively, his expression never changing. Violet Krebs began with unconcealed antagonism, slowly changing to obstinacy and then alarm as the full implications of his reasoning became apparent. By the time he finished her throat was trembling, while Walsh sat stern and silent.

'It doesn't actually prove that Morgan killed anyone,' Krebs eventually said when Anderson sat back to listen to their response.

'I know,' Anderson agreed. 'It's entirely possible he could be shielding someone else, but who? Besides, how do you account for him going straight to the body in the Sparkwell cutting?'

'I don't know,' she answered. 'Maybe it was obvious from where other people where standing.'

'I must point out,' Walsh put in, his voice level and firm in sharp contrast to that of Krebs, 'that that information comes purely from Anna Ferreira, who cannot be regarded as reliable.'

'Why not?' Krebs asked, rather to Anderson's surprise.

'I feel that it is probable that her failure to start a relationship with Dr Wells has caused her to act against him out of spite,' Walsh replied.

'I don't know who told you that,' Krebs answered, 'but it was Anna who called off the relationship. She told me last Sunday –'

'Well, I don't think that can be relied on either,' Walsh broke in.

'Absolutely,' Anderson said, seeing a chance to achieve his aim. 'Neither of their words should be accepted. That is why I want an independent specialist called in.'

Walsh drew a deep breath before replying. 'Very well, so be it. I'll call Exeter and have them send someone over. I'm afraid they'll have to be accompanied by someone from internal affairs, and if this is wrong, John, you'll be carrying the can.'

'I've already accepted that,' Anderson replied coldly.

Walsh picked up the phone, Anderson and Krebs sitting in silence while he talked to first a Chief Superintendent and then the Chief Constable himself. Anderson glanced at Krebs. She had mastered her initial shock and no longer looked as if she was about to burst into tears, but her expression and her rigid posture still gave away the state of extreme tension inside her. For the first time he felt a pang of sympathy for her. Discovering that you have been sleeping with a killer was not a pleasant experience and it was one that he himself had been through.

The arrangements with the Exeter police were made. Walsh put the phone down with an air of finality.

'A Dr Barnes and an inspector from internal will be over in an hour or so,' he informed them. 'All we can do is wait. Violet, what does Dr Wells think about last night?'

'I can't be sure,' she replied. 'At first he was furious, and perhaps agitated, now that I think of it. Then he insisted that I go home and I came to complain to you in the morning. He can be very opaque, it's like there's always a level to him that you can't get to.'

'You'd think he'd have come over here to complain himself,' Walsh answered.

'No, he asked me to,' Krebs continued. 'I don't know why.'

A faint knock sounded at the door.

'Come in,' Walsh called out and the door opened to admit Anna Ferreira.

'I need to speak to you,' she said quietly, throwing a nervous glance at Violet Krebs and then looking at Anderson. He returned her look with what he hoped was a reassuring smile. She was holding two books and a clear plastic sample bag, sealed and labelled as police evidence.

'Sit down,' Walsh said tiredly. 'I'm glad you came over, I think you'd better stay with us. A pathologist and an external affairs man are coming over from Exeter to sort out this mess and they'll want to talk to you.'

'OK,' Anna answered meekly, 'but I want to show you something first. Please let me finish, whatever you think I've done that I shouldn't have.'

'Very well,' Walsh answered, 'say your piece.'

Anderson watched as she placed the two books on the table and held out the little plastic sample bag. In it was a tiny, coiled shell, no more than five millimetres across.

'That's evidence from the lab!' he spoke angrily. 'Anna! What have you done?'

'Please, John,' Anna answered, her voice small and scared.

225

'Let her speak,' Krebs said.

'This is the shell from Charles Draper's lungs,' Anna began. 'Do you recognise it?'

'Yes,' Walsh replied, 'and it's sealed with a reference tag we can check.'

'I recognise it too,' Krebs added.

Anderson shrugged.

'This is the standard identification key to the British mollusca,' Anna continued, holding up the top book. 'Do you want to work out which it is?'

'No,' Walsh replied. 'Didn't Dr Wells do that?'

'No, he didn't. I don't think it ever occurred to him. He's a medic, my first degree was zoology. Anyway, it's a water snail called *Anisus vortex*. Here it is in the key.'

She showed them a plate in the book. The shell was one of several similar on the same page. Anderson held the bag up to the light, nonplussed by the subtle distinctions which the book used to tell one from another. Even close inspection only narrowed it down to three possibilities.

'You can have it checked by someone else,' Anna said, 'but I know I'm right even though taxonomy wasn't my speciality.'

'Fair enough,' Walsh said. 'What is the significance of it?'

Anna opened the second book at a marker, revealing a map of the British Isles covered by a grid and black spots.

'This is its recorded distribution going right back for a hundred years,' she said.

Anderson looked at the map, immediately seeing where Anna was leading them. The black spots indicating areas from which the snail had been recorded covered south-east England almost continuously but were completely absent from the West Country.

'It needs a high calcium level in the water,' Anna was saying. 'You can see how its distribution follows the chalk and streams running off the chalk, but it's never been found in the Tamar or anywhere around here. It couldn't live there and it certainly

226

couldn't live in the estuary. I should have spotted it immediately, but I always felt so in awe of Dr Wells.'

'So you're implying that Charles Draper was drowned in fresh water in a chalky area?' Walsh asked. Anna nodded in reply.

'Such as Guildford,' Anderson put in. 'Such as a pond which is outside Draper's cottage. In her fax DS Blackheath says a statue in the middle of the pond had been moved. Blackheath now thinks the Herricks are telling the truth and also says that Draper's car didn't leave his cottage until the middle of the night on Monday. What's more, she asks us to reconsider both Charles Draper's time of death and whether he could have died in Guildford. In fact she's quite adamant about it, suggesting that our forensic team may be wrong. Surely that implies something. She's never even heard of Dr Wells.'

'And there was a bruise on the crown of Draper's head like a concrete graze,' Anna added.

'Then that's where he was drowned,' Anderson continued. 'He was rendered drunk and drugged, his face was pushed into the pond and the statue knocked over. His body was then driven to Devon and dumped. We can ring Blackheath and have her check for *Anisus vortex* in Draper's pond.'

'It'll be there,' Anna said. 'They get distributed as eggs on water plants and it'll live anywhere there's the right water.'

'Why drive to Devon?' Walsh queried.

'The shorter period the body had been in the water would have shown up,' Krebs objected.

'No,' Anderson answered, 'not if Dr Wells was doing the autopsy it wouldn't. He must have known Anna would accept anything he said or could be easily browbeaten if she didn't. As to Devon, if the autopsy was done in Guildford, then Wells wouldn't be doing the autopsy. Another thing, if Cutts was in Okehampton an hour before Charles Draper was murdered, he couldn't have drowned him in a chalk stream. Everything fits, surely you agree with me now?'

Walsh sat immobile, blowing his cheeks out before speaking. 'Yes, I hate to say it, but it does. Does anyone know where Wells is?'

'In the lab, or maybe still at lunch,' Anna answered. 'I took the sample when he went out.'

'We'll worry about that later,' Walsh answered. 'I'm going to fetch him. Violet, you and Anna wait in the incident room. John, come with me.'

Anderson rose and followed Walsh from the room, his last glimpse of the two women as he shut the door showing both white-faced and tight-lipped.

Morgan Wells walked back towards the lab, outwardly his normal self. Inwardly he was in a state of turmoil, yet it was essential not to behave in any unusual way.

'Afternoon, Dr Wells,' the commissionaire greeted him.

'And the same to you,' Wells replied cheerfully while privately cursing the man for an old fool. The lab door yielded to his key and swung back behind him. The work was done, each piece of evidence carefully balanced to suit his story. Only an expert of considerable experience would be able to tell that anything was amiss. Even the lung tissue of the unfortunate Charles Draper had been suitably treated with salt water to mimic the effects of saline water asphyxiation.

He cursed under his breath. If it hadn't been for that bloody little girl Anna the whole thing would have been a breeze. Her and John bloody Anderson, the only policeman involved in the case who had failed to be suitably awed by his personality and reputation. Well, he intended to make it anyway. With any luck when Violet complained about Anderson's behaviour Robert Walsh would send the bloody man back to Guildford with his tail between his legs.

Wells took out his keys to open the cupboards and make a final check of the evidence. The odds were that Walsh would be over soon and that Anderson might have persuaded him to have another medical man check it over. None of them would spot anything, of that he was certain. There wasn't one who would swallow the absurd idea that he had tampered with the evidence.

The first cupboard opened and he looked at each sample bag in turn, going over the contents and their real and theoretical significance in his mind. All was in order. The second cupboard proved the same, but when he came to the third it was immediately obvious that something was missing. He thought for a moment and then realised that it was the shell he had taken from Draper's lungs. But who could have taken it?

He strode out of the lab and back to the commissionaire's desk.

'Has anybody been in my lab since I left?' he asked.

'No, sir,' the commissionaire answered. 'Well, not other than young Anna. She forgot her coat, she said.'

'Thank you,' Wells replied, struggling to keep his voice even. He had assumed Anna hadn't come in because she would be too scared to face him, but obviously she had more guts than he thought. But why would she want the shell? It was just a small Ramshorn snail. No, it must be significant in some way or she'd never have taken it. One thing the girl wasn't was stupid. She must be at the station now. Would Walsh listen to her? The answer had to be yes, Walsh was a stickler for procedure. Still, any secondary investigation made by his colleagues was bound to exonerate him and he could set Anna up by making it look like she had been the one fooling with the evidence. Yes, that would teach the little bitch what was what.

Yes, he'd brazen it out. Violet would back him up and in the end it would be his word against that of Anna and John bloody Anderson, a newcomer and an outsider.

'Are you all right, sir?' the commissionaire asked.

'What? Yes, fine,' Wells snapped.

The phone rang on the commissionaire's desk as Wells turned to walk back to the lab.

'Yes, sir,' the commissionaire was saying. 'I'll give him the message as soon as he arrives. A Dr Barnes, you say, sir. Yes, sir. Goodbye, sir.'

'Did you say Barnes?' Wells asked.

'Yes, sir,' the commissionaire answered. 'That was a Dr Goodall from Exeter. Apparently a Dr Barnes is coming over to us and I'm to tell him they've covered his lecture this afternoon.'

Wells barely heard the last part of the sentence as he was halfway back to the lab by the time the commissionaire finished. If Barnes was coming over, and in a hurry by the sound of things, then he was in trouble. Barnes would go over the whole bloody lot with a toothpick. The man was a pedant, a bloody fanatic.

He felt his temper rising as he pushed open the door to the lab. He was lost – the whole bloody shambles was about to come down around his ears. Damn, and he'd been so close. His only chance now was to get the hell out of it before they came round, but his passport and everything else he'd need were at home, twenty miles away in Peter Tavy. He'd just have to chance it. Besides, he knew Barnes, the bloody man would arse around, iffing and butting until he was absolutely certain of his facts and then probably insist on writing it all up before letting anybody else see it. By that time he could be in France. Anyway, it was a risk he'd have to take.

Wells grabbed his coat and walked from the building, giving the commissionaire an excuse about feeling ill and heading for his car. He took several deep breaths in an attempt to calm himself and turned the key. The roar of the engine sent a new surge of adrenalin through his body.

His teeth were set as he pulled out into the traffic. The whole thing was now an unmitigated disaster. Of course it was his fault in the first place. If he hadn't got involved with that little shit James Draper to begin with then there would never had been a problem. He could see now that he'd been an idiot to accept a bribe from Draper, but three thousand pounds had made just changing one tiny bit of evidence too tempting to be resisted. Of course there was no way he could have known just how much of a bastard Draper was. Damn it, he should have killed the little squirt the first time he came to put pressure on him.

By the time Draper approached him to get involved with the murder of his uncle, he had been in far too deep to refuse, and besides, it should have been easy. Make the appointment to show Charles Draper a fancy clock under the name of Cutts. Arrive at Draper's cottage and kill the old fool while his nephew had a firm alibi. Take the body to Devon. Dump it in the Tamar somewhere it was bound to be found the next day; steer in a verdict of accidental death and accept a quarter of the inheritance from James Draper.

Unfortunately it hadn't worked that way. First off that little bitch Anna had had to be too bloody clever by half and notice the bruising where he had held Charles Draper's head while forcing him to drink a mixture of whisky and morphine and then drowning him. Even that wouldn't have been a problem, only she had to go and do it while Robert Detective bloody Superintendent Walsh was in the room.

That had blown his first line of defence, but he still should have been safe. The police had been asking the local morons what happened on Monday afternoon, when Charles Draper had been dumped in the early hours of Tuesday morning. That should have been that, no evidence and no case. But no, that bloody little tart Ferreira had had to go showing her knickers off to Anderson in the river and had found the pen that wasn't supposed to be discovered unless he was forced on to his third line of defence, framing Nathan Cutts. With hindsight, he realised that he shouldn't have dumped the pen until he actually needed it to be found. A fat lot of good hindsight was, though.

Actually, they would probably have tracked Cutts down in the end, but the set-up might have worked anyway even though it was much riskier. Cutts had been a good choice to set up, a loner whose shop Wells had chanced across on a visit to Charmouth some years before and who proved ideal when he came to need someone to frame. He had done it so well, it deserved to have succeeded. Having bought the cannonball on his first trip had made the choice of Cutts inevitable: it was such a good murder weapon. Then there had been the carefully planted piece of old sheet when he was called in to look over Cutts's house, a square of it for the cannonball, the rest for under Cutts's kitchen sink. Of course if he hadn't killed James Draper then he might have got away with the first murder, but probably not. Anyway, when James Draper had phoned him to demand a meeting and said that he wasn't going to pay up, it had been too much. The arrogant little shit had got what was coming to him, and whatever happened now, at least James Draper was dead.

Finally, he decided, the position he was in was the result of bad luck and the presence of Anna Ferreira and John Anderson. Christ, but if he could only get his hands on their scrawny little necks, he'd break them both like twigs. He cursed aloud, his hand going to the horn to send a blast of sound at an old Cortina that was loitering in front of him. The Cortina turned off to the left, leaving the road clear. Fifteen miles to Peter Tavy, a few minutes to throw what he needed into a suitcase and then Plymouth airport and the Continent. No, across the moors to Exeter, that would be less expected but would only lose him a few minutes. Walsh was predictable, his first priority would be to seal his own area tight, only then worrying about other options. He estimated that he probably had a lead of two to three hours, maybe more if they hadn't fully caught on yet.

John Anderson reached the door of Dr Wells's laboratory a

moment ahead of Walsh. The door swung open revealing an empty room with one of the specimen cupboards wide open.

'That's not normal,' Walsh commented. 'He always keeps everything locked when he's not there.'

The hurried back to the commissionaire's desk. The bland-looking old man with his smart uniform and row of medals looked up in surprise.

'Has Dr Wells been in?' Walsh demanded.

'Why, yes, sir, he was here not ten minutes ago,' the commissionaire answered. 'Went home, he did, said he was feeling ill, and I must say he looked it.'

'Thanks,' Walsh answered. 'Right, let's assume a worst-case scenario. He may have gone to his house, he may have made a run for the ferry or airport.'

They returned to the police station at a run. Walsh immediately ordered the desk sergeant to alert the airport and ferry terminal. The team were assembled in the incident room, Krebs explaining the situation to DS Dunning, who was clearly unwilling to accept what had happened without more concrete proof.

Walsh quietened them with a gesture. 'Right, this is the situation. We need to find Dr Wells immediately. No questions, just do as I say. DC Heath, you stay here until a Dr Barnes and an Inspector from Internal get here. When they do, take them to Dr Wells's laboratory, they'll know what to do. DS Dunning, go down to control and help coordinate the search. Ferreira, I want you involved if we get to question Dr Wells, but stick with DCI Anderson unless I tell you otherwise. DC Pentyre, fetch a pursuit car from the pool. DCI Anderson, follow us to Peter Tavy, which is his most likely destination.'

They dispersed, Anderson running for his car with Anna Ferreira in tow. They climbed into the BMW and pulled out of the car park immediately behind the pursuit car, taking advantage of the other vehicle's flashing blue light to make best time through the traffic. By the time they had reached

233

the outskirts of Plymouth, Anderson had acquired a new respect for DC Pentyre, who was driving with a speed and skill far in advance of the ordinary. Across Roborough Down it was all he could do to keep the pursuit car in view, and by the time they got to the series of hills and valleys to the south of Tavistock they had fallen well behind.

Anderson cursed softly, disliking the feeling of being out-driven, and accelerated hard down the hill they were on only to have to brake sharply at a bridge barely wide enough for two cars. Beyond that the road rose and twisted around a series of blind corners, other traffic preventing him from making the best time. Eventually he managed to overtake and in another minute they had reached Tavistock, only to have to slow to a crawl through the main street. Finally they reached Peter Tavy, to find the pursuit car pulled up at an angle across Wells's driveway, the blue lights still flashing.

Motioning Anna back, Anderson got out of the car and ran up the drive. Wells's Rover was standing in front of the house, the door open and a black carryall lying by the boot. A distant shout attracted his attention and he looked up to see four figures on the hillside above him. From Wells's garden the ground rose, becoming moorland after a single field and then slanting steeply to a tumble of black rocks that stood out against the skyline. Below the top a man was clambering over the outlying boulders of the tor. It could only be Wells, distinctive for his size even at such a distance. Behind him came a smaller figure, dark blue with a mop of flame-red hair blowing in the cold wind, evidently Krebs, who had easily outdistanced the older Walsh and the heavy-set Pentyre, both of whom were making slow going of the hill.

Anderson followed without hesitation, calling to Anna to stay where she was even as he clambered over the low stone wall that surrounded Wells's garden. A taller wall marked off the field from the open moor. Anderson caught his leg on a strand of barbed wire that lay along the top, tearing his suit and opening a long scratch in his calf. He cursed as he landed on the far side, the spongy ground cushioning his impact. Looking up he saw that Wells was lost to view. Krebs was briefly silhouetted against the skyline before she too disappeared, while the other two had just reached the boulder zone.

His lungs burned as he gasped the cold air in in great draughts, his body warming as the hill became steeper, fire building in the muscles of his legs. He passed first Pentyre and then Walsh, unable to suppress a grin of satisfaction as the two slower men fell behind him. What he had thought to be the summit proved to be a false peak, merely a spur of a larger tor. Anderson reached the ridge a hundred yards below the true peak to find that he was already higher than much of the open moorland that lay in front of him. A rocky path halfway between him and the peak led back to the village and on into the heart of the moor. Wells was on it, and with a flush of grim satisfaction Anderson saw that he was gaining. Krebs, though, was almost on her quarry and he could hear her shouting to him across the emptiness of the moor, her voice carried by the wind.

He ran on, watching Violet Krebs as she closed on the big man. He heard her call him by name, the note of pleading in her voice still apparent despite the distance and the distorting effect of the wind. The two figures danced like marionettes in the distance. Violet reached, grasping for his coat. Wells swung round, one great arm slamming into her. Violet fell back like a broken doll, her hands going to her face. Wells staggered on, leaving his erstwhile lover lying sprawled on the sodden turf.

Anderson redoubled his effort, cursing Wells for the callous bastard that he was. He glanced behind him, unable to pick out his colleagues with the sun in his eyes and the big tor throwing a long, dark shadow towards him. At least that meant that Wells would have the same trouble picking out his pursuers. A minute later, he reached Violet Krebs, finding her half sitting, half kneeling in the wet grass and moss, supported by her left arm. She was holding her face, blood trickling from between her fingers, her eyes half shut.

'You'll be all right,' Anderson gasped out, for once at a loss for what to say. Wells, he realised, was not an opponent to be taken lightly, but then she had tried to reason with him and had clearly not expected the violence of his response. Anderson had no such illusions.

He pressed on, realising that there was little he could do to help her and that backup must now be on its way. Wells had crested the low hill ahead of them and disappeared into a steep valley he had glimpsed from the ridge. He might turn either way, and would obviously know the moors so near his house, while Anderson had no idea of what lay in any direction, only that the highest, bleakest section of moor was ahead and to the left. Otherwise, the panorama of big, open hills and their crowns of rock stretched equally far in all directions.

He reached the crest to find the valley empty below him. A large hill rose on the far side of the valley, its top crowned with a grey tumble of monstrous granite blocks, glinting orange and yellow in the cold sunlight. He was tiring, and he reasoned that Wells must be at least as tired, probably more so with his great bulk. He would be somewhere down in the valley, probably concealed by the shoulder of the hill. Anderson stopped, listening but hearing only the soft whisper of water from the river below him, the sigh of wind and the distant bleat of a sheep.

Making his decision at random, Anderson turned to the left and descended the hill at a low angle. The going was heavy, streams and patches of bog forcing him to make repeated detours. Finally, soaked to the knees and with one shoe full of water and decaying peat, he reached the bottom, to be rewarded with a glimpse of Wells's brown coat disappearing behind a massive boulder no more than three hundred yards up stream.

Anderson rallied, forcing himself on despite the fatigue and pain in his muscles. For a while he was forced to leap from one granite boulder to another, then scramble along the stream bed between steep banks of crumbling peat. Finally he came into an area of flat grass in time to see Wells making heavy going of a boulder patch on the far side of the area.

'Stop!' Anderson called out, with little hope of Wells paying him any attention.

Wells turned and looked back, then jumped down from the rock he had been on to stand on the grass. Anderson slowed to a walk, watching Wells carefully, trying to judge his level of exhaustion and mental state. The big man was breathing heavily but not gasping, his tawny brown hair plastered to his forehead with sweat, the pale blue eyes narrow and glaring. Anderson stopped, measuring his breaths, hoping that he could bring the confrontation to an end without violence but privately certain that this was not possible.

'Dr Morgan Wells, I must –' he began.

'Save it,' Wells snapped. 'I'm glad it's you, because if there's one thing I want to do before it's too late, it's snap your slimy little neck, Mr bloody Detective Chief Inspector Anderson.'

'Further violence can only make matters worse,' Anderson replied, keeping his voice level but going up on to the balls of his feet in readiness for Wells's rush. He had travelled at right angles to his original course for some time, and there was every chance that Walsh or Pentyre would catch up with him if only he could stall Wells for long enough. Otherwise, he was going to have to take on the big man single-handedly, which was not a task he relished.

'Ha!' Wells barked back at him. 'Worse? Do you really suppose I'm going to fall for that crap? I've killed two people. The satisfaction of making you the third will be well worth it, it's just a shame I can't add that little slut Ferreira to my tally as well.'

Anderson backed slowly, his hands ready to catch any blow aimed at head or body and pull Wells's arm into a lock. Wells came on, as steady and massive as a bear, his face set in a derisive grin. For a moment they stood still, face to face, both waiting for the other to make the first move. Suddenly Wells's right fist shot out, aiming a ferocious blow at Anderson's chin. Anderson caught the blow and applied leverage, only to have Wells's left fist catch him hard in the stomach. He doubled up in pain, still trying to twist Wells's arm into a lock but unable to get enough purchase on the heavily muscled arm.

Wells laughed, once more slamming his fist into Anderson, this time to the solar plexus, Anderson's vision blurred with pain. Another punch followed, to Anderson's temple, blurring his vision further and sending lights dancing inside his head. He felt himself being swung round, no more able to resist Wells's enormous strength than a child. The doctor's hand clutched the back of his head, locking Anderson's skull in his grip. He tried to struggle, aware of what Wells was doing, but only receiving a numbing blow to the side of his head for his pains.

'I'm going to drown you like I drowned that ass Draper,' Wells snarled. 'Just think yourself lucky that there's no railway track near here.'

Wells laughed, a manic, deranged sound cutting through the dizzy, sick feeling in Anderson's head. Only half conscious, his muscles refusing to obey him, he could still feel a sense of absolute horror as he was dragged to the river and his face held over the water.

'Goodbye, Mr Anderson,' he heard Wells's voice as if from a great distance and then his face hit the cold of the water, shocking him back into consciousness even as it flowed over his ears. Wells's knee was in his back, the hand that held his head like an iron clamp utterly immobile. His own fingers clawed desperately at the turf, his legs kicking in futile protest.

Wells's arm was shaking with his laughter as the pressure in Anderson's head rose, quickly approaching the point where it would become unbearable and he would have to breathe in water. He felt panic rising and a desperate, impotent fury at what was being done to him, also aching sorrow. Surely he was not to die for this, the victim of a callous, pointless revenge?

Anderson's jaws burst open, the icy water filling his mouth, the precious air bubbling away to the surface. He gave a last, desperate spasm, making no difference whatever. Then the grip came off his skull and his face pulled clear of the water, coughing and gagging, gasping urgently for air. Wells's weight was still on his back, and for an instant Anderson knew the sick feeling of someone given a reprieve for life only to find it nothing more than a horrid joke. Then he realised that a voice was calling his name and Wells was no longer pushing down on him.

He forced himself to look around. Wells lay across him, his forehead a bloody mess, a great blood-stained, jagged lump of granite lying only inches from his face. His jaw was working in strange convulsive motions, his eyes slack and unfocused.

'John! John!' he heard. He looked around to see Anna Ferreira standing across the stream from him. Then his vision went, blackness engulfing everything as he slumped back to the ground.

Epilogue

'I trust you're recovering well?' Chief Superintendent Gordon Eyre addressed John Anderson as he indicated the chair opposite his desk.

Anderson took the offered seat, wondering what could have prompted the Chief Superintendent to call him in.

'Yes, thank you,' he replied.

'Nasty business,' Eyre remarked. 'I hear you're lucky to be alive.'

'That is true,' Anderson admitted, sure that whyever he was there it wasn't to give Eyre a chance to enquire after his health.

'Hmm, right, well John,' Eyre continued, 'I'm sure you know that Graham Parrish is due for retirement this autumn. Hmm? Right, well, sadly he's been feeling the strain a little lately, and the quacks say he has an ulcer, so he's been told to take it easy.'

Anderson made an appropriately sympathetic comment, suddenly more interested in the direction of his superior's remarks.

'Yes, quite,' Eyre went on. 'Anyway, I've been speaking to

Colin Farrell and one or two other senior men. Now, this is entirely informal but I think I can safely tell you that if everything goes well over the next few months, then you'll be offered the position of Acting-Superintendent until Graham actually leaves us. May I take it as read that you will accept?'

'Yes,' Anderson replied. 'I can't think of any reason to refuse.'

'Good, good,' Eyre continued. 'It had, of course, been pointed out to me that you have made several mistakes in the past, one or two quite serious. Now, my own feelings are that at worst you're a risk-taker and consider getting a result more important than any concomitant consequences. One or two others, though, feel that a more community-orientated attitude is needed for the head of our CID and would prefer to bring someone in from outside, someone with a more respectful attitude to important people. That's one trouble with this area, too many important people. Anyway, I'm giving you fair warning, play it carefully. All clear?'

'Yes, sir,' Anderson answered. 'I'll bear that in mind.'

'Good, good. Well, good luck anyway.'

'Thank you, sir,' Anderson replied. 'Was there anything else?'

'No, no, not at all,' Eyre replied.

Anderson left the office with a jaunty step, hiding the pain from the rib that was still mending until he was clear of the building. Eyre, he remembered, had come up through the ranks in Bristol before getting his current job and detested pandering to influence. Barring disasters, he could now expect Parrish's job by the end of the summer.

As he climbed into the BMW he was unable to resist a smile. He had several days' leave remaining, which he intended to make full use of, especially as for the coming weekend he would be sharing his apartment in the Mill with Anna Ferreira.

CRIME & PASSION

DEADLY AFFAIRS
by
Juliet Hastings
ISBN: 0 7535 0029 9
Publication date: 17 April 1997

Eddie Drax is a playboy businessman with a short fuse and a taste for blondes. A lot of people don't like him: ex-girlfriends, business rivals, even his colleagues. He's not an easy man to like. When Eddie is found asphyxiated at the wheel of his car, DCI John Anderson delves beneath the golf-clubbing, tree-lined respectability of suburban Surrey and uncovers the secret – and often complex – sex-lives of Drax's colleagues and associates.

He soon finds that Drax was murdered – and there are more killings to come. In the course of his investigations, Anderson becomes personally involved in Drax's circle of passionate women, jealous husbands and people who can't be trusted. He also has plenty of opportunities to find out more about his own sexual nature.

This is the first in the series of John Anderson mysteries.

CRIME & PASSION

A MOMENT OF MADNESS
by
Pan Pantziarka
ISBN: 0 7535 0024 8
Publication date: 17 April 1997

Tom Ryder is the charismatic head of the Ryder Forum – an organisation teaching slick management techniques to business people. Sarah Fairfax is investigating current management theories for a television programme called *Insight* and is attending a course at Ryder Hall. All the women on the course think Ryder is dynamic, powerful and extremely attractive. Sarah agrees, but this doesn't mean that she's won over by his evangelical spiel; in fact, she's rather cynical about the whole thing.

When one of the course attendees – a high-ranking civil servant – is found dead in his room from a drugs overdose, Detective Chief Inspector Anthony Vallance is called in to investigate. Everyone has something to hide, except for Sarah Fairfax who is also keen to find out the truth about this suspicious death. As the mystery deepens and another death occurs, Fairfax and Vallance compete to unearth the truth. They discover dark, erotic secrets, lethal dangers and, to their mutual irritation, each other.

This is the first in a series of Fairfax and Vallance mysteries.

CRIME & PASSION

INTIMATE ENEMIES
by
Juliet Hastings
ISBN: 0 7535 0034 5
Publication date: 15 May 1997

Francesca Lyons is found dead in her art gallery. The cause of death isn't obvious but her bound hands suggest foul play. The previous evening she had an argument with her husband, she had sex with someone, and two men left messages on the gallery's answering machine. Detective Chief Inspector Anderson has plenty of suspects but can't find anyone with a motive.

When Stephanie Pinkney, an art researcher, is found dead in similar circumstances, Anderson's colleagues are sure the culprit is a serial killer. But Anderson is convinced that the murders are connected with something else entirely. Unravelling the threads leads him to Andrea Maguire, a vulnerable, sensuous art dealer with a quick-tempered husband and unsatisfied desires. Anderson can prove Andrea isn't the killer and finds himself strongly attracted to her. Is he making an untypical and dangerous mistake?

Intimate Enemies **is the second in the series
of John Anderson mysteries.**

CRIME & PASSION

A TANGLED WEB
by
Pan Pantziarka
ISBN: 0 7535 0155 4
Publication date: 19 June 1997

Michael Cunliffe was ordinary. He was an accountant for a small charity. He had a pretty wife and an executive home in a leafy estate. Now he's been found dead: shot in the back of the head at close range. The murder bears the hallmark of a gangland execution.

DCI Vallance soon discovers Cunliffe wasn't ordinary at all. The police investigation lifts the veneer of suburban respectability to reveal blackmail, extortion, embezzlement, and a network of sexual intrigue. One of Cunliffe's businesses has been the subject of an investigation by the television programme, *Insight*, which means that Vallance has an excuse to get in touch again with Sarah Fairfax. Soon they're getting on each other's nerves and in each other's way, but they cannot help working well together.

A Tangled Web **is the second in the series
of Fairfax and Vallance mysteries.**

CRIME & PASSION

A WAITING GAME
by
Juliet Hastings
ISBN: 0 7535 0109 0
Publication date: 21 August 1997

A child is abducted and held to ransom. As the boy's mother is a prospective MP and his father is a friend of the Chief Constable, Detective Chief Inspector Anderson is required to wrap up the case cleanly and efficiently.

But the kidnappers, although cunning and well-organised, make up a triangle of lust and jealousy; somehow Anderson's tactics are being betrayed to the kidnappers; and after a series of mishaps and errors, and a violent death, Anderson's latest sexual conquest and his ex-wife become involved in the conspiracy. Anderson's legendary patience and willpower are stretched to the limit as he risks his own life trying to save others.

This is the third in the series of John Anderson mysteries.

CRIME & PASSION

TO DIE FOR
by
Peter Birch
ISBN: 0 7535 0034 5
Publication date: 18 September 1997

The cool and efficient Detective Chief Inspector is keen to re-establish his reputation as a skilled investigator. The body of Charles Draper has been found in the mud flats of a Devon estuary. The murdered man was a law-abiding citizen and there appears to be no motive for the killing. There are also very few clues.

When Anderson is sent to assist the Devon and Cornwall constabulary, he's led towards dubious evidence and suspects whose alibis are watertight. The investigation also brings him in contact with forensics assistant Anna Ferreira whose intellect and physical attractiveness makes her irresistible.

The only suspect is then found murdered. Local antiques dealer Nathan Cutts fits the murderer's profile but Anderson feels he's not the man they're looking for. Against the backdrop of windswept Dartmoor, the chase to catch a killer is on.

This is the fourth in the series of John Anderson novels.

CRIME & PASSION

TIME TO KILL
by
Margaret Bingley
ISBN: 0 7535 0164 3
Publication date: 16 October 1997

Lisa Allan's body is found in the corner of her kitchen by her husband, Ralph. Everyone knows Lisa was ill, suffering from a complicated heart condition, but no one expected her to die – least of all her doctor. DCI Anderson met Lisa socially only two days before her death. He found her desirable but disliked her husband on sight.

Two autopsy reports pose more questions than answers and as Anderson struggles to untangle the relationships of the dysfunctional Allan family, he becomes involved with Pippa Wright, Ralph's attractive PA and ex-mistress. When a second murder occurs, Anderson realises that getting to know Pippa was not one of his better ideas. Against a background of sexual intrigue and hidden secrets, he needs to harness all his skills and intuition if he is to ensure that justice is done.

This is the fifth in the series of John Anderson mysteries.

CRIME & PASSION

DAMAGED GOODS
by
Georgina Franks
ISBN: 0 7535 0124 4
Publication date: 20 November 1997

A high-performance car has spun out of control on a test drive. The driver has suffered multiple injuries and is suing Landor Motors for negligence. He says the airbag inflated for no reason, causing him to lose control of the car.

This is the third and most serious claim Landor Motors have had to make this year. The insurance company aren't happy, and they bring in Victoria Donovan to assist in their investigations.

Landor Motors is a high-profile car showroom situated in the stockbroker belt. But the Landor family have a history of untimely deaths and brooding resentments. Soon, Vic is up to her neck in a complex web of drug-dealing, sexual jealousy and deception involving Derek Landor's wayward and very attractive son. When Derek Landor is kidnapped, only Vic knows what's going on. Will anyone take her seriously before time runs out for Derek Landor?

This is the first Victoria Donovan mystery.

CRIME & PASSION

GAMES OF DECEIT
by
Pan Pantziarka
ISBN: 0 7535 0119 8
Publication date: 4 December 1997

Detective Chief Inspector Anthony Vallance and television journalist Sarah Fairfax team up once more when an old friend of Sarah's is caught up in the strange goings-on at the science park where she's working. Carol Davis says someone there is trying to kill her but the squeaky clean credentials of her colleagues don't tally with the dangerous and violent nature of the attacks.

When Vallance becomes sexually involved with Carol Davis, he begins to realise that she has a dark side to her nature: she's manipulative, kinky and possibly unstable. As Fairfax and Vallance peel away the layers of respectability to reveal a background of corporate coercion, deceit and neo-Nazism, they discover that Carol has not been telling the truth about the people she's working for. But who is going to reveal what's really going on when Carol winds up dead?

This is the third in the series of Fairfax and Vallance novels.